NO
LONGER
GUILTY

NO LONGER GUILTY

A STORY OF SALVATION

Norman O'Banyon

iUniverse, Inc.
Bloomington

NO LONGER GUILTY
A Story of Salvation

This is a work of fiction. All of the characters, names, incidents, organizations, and dialogue in this novel are either the products of the author's imagination or are used fictitiously.

iUniverse books may be ordered through booksellers or by contacting:

iUniverse
1663 Liberty Drive
Bloomington, IN 47403
www.iuniverse.com
1-800-Authors (1-800-288-4677)

Because of the dynamic nature of the Internet, any web addresses or links contained in this book may have changed since publication and may no longer be valid. The views expressed in this work are solely those of the author and do not necessarily reflect the views of the publisher, and the publisher hereby disclaims any responsibility for them.

Any people depicted in stock imagery provided by Thinkstock are models, and such images are being used for illustrative purposes only.
Certain stock imagery © Thinkstock.

ISBN: 978-1-4759-5676-4 (sc)
ISBN: 978-1-4759-5677-1 (ebk)

Printed in the United States of America

iUniverse rev. date: 10/17/2012

BOOK 1

NO LONGER GUILTY

A Story Of Salvation

1

THE BEGINNING

Sarah listened to the Judge's question again.

"Miss Thoms, how do you plead to these charges?" The room was silent, filled to overflowing with charged anticipation.

In a trembling voice just above a whisper, she replied, "Guilty, sir, Your Honor. I am guilty." A tear coursed down the side of her nose and dripped off her lip, and for that brief moment she reflected on all that had brought her to this.

She had only vague memories of her dad. He had been a welder, working in the shipyard in Portland, tearing down Navy ships for scrap. She was told that he had breathed a lot of asbestos. He was sick for a while and after his death there was a settlement that was supposed to keep Sarah and her mom comfortable for a long time. It probably would have, if her mom hadn't developed greedy friends and an even more demanding habit for white powder.

Sarah was in kindergarten when her mom was arrested for the third time. The Judge studied the little girl with brown eyes and short happy curls. He asked the mom, "Who was taking care of your daughter?" All Sarah's confused mom could give as an answer was a sad shrug. The judge remanded Sarah to Family Services and the long slide began. Of course her mom protested vigorously, promising to cleanup and become a model mother. Aren't words easy masks to wear?

The first foster home was very temporary, just long enough to get the paper trail started; then she was placed in three more short-term places. Sarah's fifth home was in Keizer, just north of Salem, with the Lewis family, Charlie and Barb. They had a daughter, Sydney, who was a year younger than Sarah, and Brandon, a son almost three years older. Sarah fit right in!

With each move, she had been told to be brave and not worry; she would always be cared for and protected. The faces were forever changing, but the promise was always the same: she would be cared for and protected. That seemed to finally come true with the Lewis's. They took her to Sunday school, bought her new bright purple clothes because she told them it was her favorite color, and Barb asked her to help bake sugar cookies. It was just wonderful to have a home.

She attended the first grade in an elementary school within walking distance, where she was complimented on her quiet nature, and attention. She was a quick learner and was happy to please the teacher. In so many ways this little girl seemed well adjusted. When invited to be an angel in the Christmas program at church, she squealed with delight. And when her class sang "Away in a Manger, No Crib for a Bed," there was no face quite as radiant as Sarah's.

A couple days after Christmas, Charlie and Barb had returned to work. They got a neighbor high school girl to look after the kids. Actually she just made sure they got lunch, and stayed home. The rest of the time she was either talking on the phone or texting her numerous friends. Brandon asked Sarah if she wanted to play with the new Lego set. It was in his room.

They had been quietly playing for several minutes when he asked in a hushed voice, "Do you want to see my boy-thing?" Because he was acting sneaky, Sarah assumed this might not be a nice thing. He asked again, and she shook her head. Brandon was unzipping his pants and pulling down his jeans anyway. "Look," he said, "girls don't have this, just boys do." He displayed a finger-like surprise, attached to his belly. He moved it with his fingers. "Do you want to touch it?" he asked. Again she shook her head for the same reason. "If you touch it, maybe it will grow and get stiff." She remained quite still. "If I do this," his fingers stroked gently, "sometimes it makes me tickle."

He heard the sitter coming down the hall, and quickly straightened his jeans. He stood up embarrassed, and went to the other side of his room, just as she came in. "There you two are. Your mom said we could have some chocolate milk and cookies. What do you say?" As Sarah moved through the door she couldn't understand why she felt angry at Brandon, and a snack wasn't going to make it better.

In a variety of opportunities, that scenario replayed repeatedly in the following months. Brandon exposed himself to her and asked her to touch him, stroke him, and tickle him. She refused, innately understanding what Brandon obviously didn't, that naughty behavior could compromise her continued relationship with this family. Finally one afternoon, he took her wrist and pulled her hand over his "boy-thing." It was warm and soft, and seemed like nothing special. Innocence has a quiet way of leaving. By the end of summer he had found enough of those chances that she could make him stiff, and then jump with a big tickle. Brandon always seemed happy for that.

She remembered very clearly that it was the Saturday morning after school began, that he slipped into her room before Charlie and Barb were up. He didn't say a word, but just pulled down his pajamas. Obediently, she took hold of him and began to feel it swell firm. Standing closer to her, his hand reached out to touch her leg, and then moved upward. She wanted to pull away, but just continued stroking him until he jerked with a big tickle. Unlike other times, this was different, because a runny, sticky splash got on her hand and bed. They were both shocked by it "Don't tell mom," he whispered, pulling his pajamas back up and sliding out the door.

But she did. She went directly into their bedroom and stood beside the bed until Barb looked at her, asking, "Are you alright, Sweetie?" Sarah nodded, and said "Brandon pottied on my bed." They were words that caused Barb to erupt from the covers. "He what?"

The rest of the day was a flurry of questions, and a visit to the doctor's office where Sarah was carefully examined. The sheet was also studied to determine that, in fact, it had evidence of semen, though void of any sperm cells. By mid-afternoon she was with her case-worker, who took notes of their conversation. The serious woman asked Sarah lots of questions about Brandon. It was decided that an occasional curiosity did not represent a major problem, but a repeated and escalated pattern of behavior was reason for serious reevaluation. Sarah would visit a new counselor friend, and be moved to a new foster home, where she would be safe, cared for, and protected. For the sixth time, her clothes and meager toys were boxed and amid tears and apologies, Barb said "goodbye." It was altogether sad, and so unfair. Sarah didn't say a word.

2

MISS LINN

Sarah was driven about an hour north of Keizer to a big town called Beaverton, which she would learn was next to Portland. Her new home was in a quiet neighborhood with trees and a big back yard. That was important because Barkley lived there. He was a round faced Spaniel who was always happy. Sarah liked him immediately. She would learn that he was a King Charles spaniel. She didn't understand the reference to a basketball player.

Her new home was not a typical family as before. This one had only girls in it. Kate Linn was the "mom", and there were four other girls, Sarah being the youngest. The strange thing about this home was that the girls didn't go to school. Instead, they called it "Home School". Kate taught lessons for each girl in the family room, and every day there was a counselor friend who came to talk. Everyone had a turn. The two oldest girls, Carla and Bonnie, shared a bedroom. Sarah was given a little bed in a room that also had bunk beds. Taunya and Motisha were in her bedroom, too. It was all a bit overwhelming; but she kept saying to herself, "It will be alright. They will take care of me and protect me." Carefully she slid her two boxes of treasures under her bed, and waited for more instructions.

When the girls gathered in the dining room for supper, Sarah saw that one setting was a pink plate and glass. She was told that would be her place and the special plate today was to show her how happy everyone was to have her living with them. She wondered if that was true, since she had heard the same words at the Lewis's. Macaroni and cheese with Rocky Road ice cream for dessert, however, helped her forget about the enormous events of the day.

Before bedtime, Miss Linn said she would read some more from the adventures of Sinbad the Sailor. All the girls except Carla found a place to sit near Kate. "Sarah, have you heard this story?" she asked. Brown curls shook to admit she had not. Miss Linn explained "These are stories told by a very wise Persian woman a long time ago. The king was a very jealous man and when he married a new queen, he immediately suspected her of being untrue to him," there was a dramatic pause, "before he had her killed!" She made a frightened face. "So when he married the beautiful Scheherazade," she spoke the name reverently, "she knew she had to be very smart, or she too would be killed. On their wedding night, she told the king a marvelous story about Aladdin, who had a magic carpet and a wondrous lamp. When she had finished the story, the king wanted to hear another, and his smiling wife said she would tell him another tomorrow night. He didn't harm her, because he wanted to hear another story. She told him about Ali Baba and the forty thieves, the seven journeys of Sinbad the Sailor, and riddles, and so many more stories, in fact one thousand and one. The king never did hurt her." Opening a well used book, she asked, "Now would you like to hear one?" Those curls bobbed in eager acceptance.

As she listened to the story, Sarah could see the images escape from the words, as though she were a witness to it happening. Finally, when Miss Linn announced it was time for bed, she asked, "Shall we hear more stories tomorrow night?" Sarah knew just how the Persian king had felt. "Yes, please!"

Moments later, when she came to tuck Sarah in for the first time, Miss Linn found her sitting on her bed, still clothed but crying. Motisha sat beside her comforting as much as she could.

"My goodness, Honey, what's the matter?" Kate knelt before her looking for any clue to her distress.

In a ragged voice, shredded by sobs, Sarah answered, "My nightgown's . . . gone . . . and . . . my panties . . . and my comb . . . and Archer, my stuffed . . ." her voice was no longer manageable. She just shook with sobs. The weight of the day was too much. Motisha's hand stroked her back.

Kate rose, saying, "I'll be right back." In seconds they could hear loud voices from the other bedroom. Kate's voice was the last one to speak before tense silence. Then she returned to Sarah's bed carrying her lost treasures, "I'm so sorry, Honey. You have had a very trying day and this is not how I wanted it to end. Put on your nightgown, and I'll tuck you in. Sleep was a welcome time when she no longer worried about a new house, a new family, and an unknown future.

Morning hurriedly brought two big lessons for Sarah. First, the bathroom had a sink, two toilets, and a shower. Privacy would be a rare thing from now on. Motisha was in the shower as Sarah entered, and stared.

"What's with you?" the angry voice came from the spray. "Haven't you seen a sister before?"

Sarah's voice was awed with wonder; "I wish I had beautiful brown skin like you. It's beautiful." There was no hint of anything but praise. She, of course, had recognized Motisha's dark face and curly black hair. Somehow she had not imagined the impact of an entire dark body. Leaving the room, she said over her shoulder, "Beautiful."

In the kitchen, she was confronted by a hostile Carla. Defiantly, the angry girl snarled, "You little blabber-mouth!

You tattled on me." Her hand was a blur that popped against Sarah's cheek, knocking her off balance.

The only response Sarah could think to say was, "Stealer!" Apparently Carla had helped herself to anything from the new girl's stuff that was attractive to her. Before the word was off Sarah's lips, a second slap was on its way, this time with more force, and against the head of a person already leaning off-balance against the kitchen chair.

The explosion inside her head was incredible; her head jammed over on her shoulder, and her body, hooked on the back of the chair, crashed on the table, sending bowls, glasses, and silverware clattering across the floor. Carla stood statue still. Sarah lay amidst the ruination of the breakfast table, crying. That was the first time in her life she had been struck by someone.

Kate burst in, assessing the chaos; she knelt once again before Sarah. "Oh Honey, this is not the way it should be around here." Her voice was soft with anguish. "Are you alright?" Tenderly her hand traced the red welt and hand print on her soft cheek. Satisfied there was no damage that required immediate attention, Miss Linn stood and squared up on Carla. She spoke only two words: "Pack! Now!"

Carla started to offer an excuse. "But she . . ." The words were not allowed to form. "Pack! Now! Or it all gets thrown in the trash." Before the shock of the morning could wear off, and before the kitchen table was rearranged, a blue and white patrol car parked in the driveway. Two Beaverton police officers took Carla back to juvenile detention. She had been on probation with two previous episodes of anger, and now an assault charge was added. Sarah didn't feel completely responsible for her removal. The lessons to be learned from this, however, were clear. A person does not need to be the biggest or strongest to prevail. She just needs to stand in the right, among those who are bigger or stronger. Secondly, she learned that if a person is about to be hit, it helps to be off balance and fall with a dramatic amount of evidence.

In less than twenty four hours this house had one new person arrive and one leave under duress. Sarah wondered if this was anything even close to normal, or if her world was still falling into bits and pieces.

Autumn did bring the gift of peace to their home. Warm afternoons and gentle nights gave ample opportunities for home school lessons and more stories from Miss Linn's books. Sarah actually couldn't remember a happier time. She liked spelling and reading, and when Miss Linn explained that poems were songs without a melody, Sarah had a reason to master the craft. Trips to the aquarium and zoo along with playing in the backyard with Barkley made each day bountiful.

With Carla's leaving there was a shift in the bedroom assignments. Taunya moved into the new vacancy so there were two girls in each room. Even though Miss Linn said there would probably be a new girl soon, the arrangement felt permanent. One afternoon, when Sarah and Motisha were in the backyard with Barkley, the older girl put her hand on Sarah's shoulder. Instantly there was a flash of Brandon getting too close. Her fear was put to rest when Motisha said, "I don't remember anyone ever saying that I was beautiful before." She thought about it for a bit, and then shook her head. "Nope, you are the only one who ever told me that. My true sisters used to call me "Mo" for short. You can too, if you want to."

"You've got true sisters?" Sarah asked in genuine surprise. "Where are they?"

"Well, two are married, and one is in the army, I think, and the other one is living with my grandma." A slight smile played at the corner of her mouth.

"Do you have a mom and a dad?" Sarah asked with growing interest.

"Nope," the weary answer was not what Sarah had expected. "My mom overdosed when my little brother was born and dad left us for another lady."

Sarah realized that not only her life was complicated and painful. "But you have a brother?" It was a question with some hope.

"Nope. He was adopted by some people in California before he even left the hospital. I never saw him." Suddenly the afternoon sun lost some of its warmth and the shadows seem to grow across the yard.

"I'd like to call you 'Mo.'" Sarah said, leaning against the older girl's shoulder. "I think we are special friends."

One of the other shifts that came with autumn was the regard the other girls in the house began giving to the youngest. Perhaps it was Sarah's courage in standing up to Carla. Maybe it was the fortitude she had after being knocked down. She won their respect and admiration. Even the oldest, Bonnie, seemed to like to ruffle her curly hair affectionately in the morning. Not too much, of course.

Sarah's box of school books had almost filled. The art projects were of some interest. She enjoyed spelling and trying to make rhyming poems. But most of all, she loved arithmetic, and the wonders of numbers. She loved that an answer was right or wrong, never practically right. She was becoming the math star of the house. On the rare occasion that the house watched a video, Sarah always voted for a Harry Potter one, so she could pretend to be Hermione, the brilliant, who always knew the correct answer.

One thing that disturbed Sarah a lot, and puzzled her even more, was the ease with which her sisters left the family. Taunya moved on Thanksgiving weekend, and Bonnie was gone by New Year's Day. Sarah was moved, with Mo, into the big bedroom and three new girls, Olivia, Farah, and Michelle came into her old room. She especially liked the name Farah because it rhymed with hers.

It also disturbed her to learn that the counselor friend, Dr. Tully, had information that Sarah had shared only with Miss Linn. On one of her weekly visits, she had a sheet of paper with a copy of some of Sarah's poems. "Sarah, can you tell me more about your poems?" she asked. It seemed to Sarah that they were already doing that. When she asked, "Which one?" Dr Tully read:

> "Twinkle lights and shiny wrapped packages,
> Offer gifts we long for in secret passages,
> Of peace and joy, with snow clad fields.
> What we got was rain and mud and broken
>   deals."

The doctor continued, "That is a wonderful poem, a marvelous one. It holds a complete idea, and expresses it with feeling. Can you remember if you were sad or angry when you wrote it?"

"I think I was sort of both," Sarah answered quietly. "This is my home and these are my sisters. Home is supposed to be forever, but it seems like they were only temporary. So, am I, or Mo, next to go?" Her usual perky exterior gave a quiver of dread.

"Oh no, Sarah," the counselor said, placing her hand on Sarah's. "This is your home; and that's as true as true can be. But let me try to explain something that you may now be old enough to understand. This is not like the home you shared with your mom and dad. And this is not another foster home either. It is a shelter home for abused girls." The words were like ice in Sarah's tummy. Up to now, she and Dr. Tully had only talked about Brandon and what he wanted to do, about appropriate behavior, and correct names for private parts and their functions. It was not information that Sarah deemed very important. This on the other hand was shocking!

Dr. Tully continued, "Miss Linn and I are trained in special ways to protect, and teach you. She has a very special job to live with you and keep your home safe and happy. My job is to make sure you are ready to live in a new home, either a foster home or an adoptive home. But only when you are ready." She wanted to give Sarah an opportunity to comprehend all of that, so she changed the subject.

"Now tell me about this one; it really cracked me up:

"Where does poop go when I flush,
Under the house, in a hole with a rush?
Is hell the place that's filled with stink,
Or is it just the thoughts I think?"

"First," Sarah wanted a better answer to a more important question, "tell me whose house do we live in, is it Miss Linn's?" The question came very directly and the counselor felt it should be answered as directly.

"This home is one of nine homes the state of Oregon owns and operates for the protection and development of children. Miss Linn and I are employees of the state. Rather than some large facility that would be like an institution, this is designed to be as natural as it can be in the circumstance that no parent or natural relative can offer that to you." Sarah was very still for a moment, then gently nodded her understanding. "Now, Honey, tell me more about the poop poem." A warm smile suggested that she was earnest in her delight.

Sarah opened her notebook to the back section, which held her favorite poems. "The one just before the poop poem says:

> About the toilet I don't really know enough,
> How the handle makes the watery "huff,"
> How it works and what it does.
> I need to learn all about my house because
> When I grow up I can teach my kids
> About sinks and stools and closing lids,
> So they can teach their kids.
> On and on it goes; there's a lot of learning to do,
> And if I'm lucky some teaching, too"

When she finished there were tears in Dr Tully's eyes. "That is so wonderful. Do you have more?" the counselor asked.

"Yup, lots and lots."

"Are they all about the toilet?" A very bright smile assured Sarah that the question was meant in jest.

"It's fun to write about Barkley, swinging, time, the kitchen, stories Miss Linn reads." Sarah shrugged, "there are poems just about anything."

"Will you read me some more next week?"

"Sure." Feeling that their time was over, Sarah put away her notebook and stood, but today their exchange had been less one-sided and it made her happy.

Nearly two weeks passed before she had the conversation with Miss Linn. She tried hard to comprehend the motivation for a young woman to choose to live with a houseful of squirrely girls. They were drying the dishes after supper. The kitchen was empty save for the two of them. "Miss Linn, why do you do it?"

Arched eyebrows sought more question before an answer could form. "Do what, Honey?"

"Why do you live here all the time? You don't have to, it's just a job." For such a serious subject, they were both surprised at the lack of emotion expressed.

"Do you mean why don't I have a nine to five job with weekends off?"

"No, I mean why don't you have a husband who could be here as our dad?" Now there was a hint of desperation in Sarah's question.

The kitchen was quiet except for the sound of the TV in the family room. Kate's gaze was both intense and far away. She took a deep breath and decided a whole answer was what this child deserved. "Honey, I was married. We were Quakers." When a frown captured Sarah's face, she explained, "We were members of the Friends Church. Bradley, my husband, studied Agricultural Engineering at George Fox College, and married me just before leaving for a two year federal program in Iraq. His job was to teach farmers how to increase productivity through water management and crop rotation." She smiled sadly. "He was a farmer who wanted to bring peace to the world." Before Sarah could ask what happened, Kate told her. "Some radical holy man decided that Bradley was a spy, a representative of the devil, or something like that. One morning when Bradley went to the market place, a man with a knife came up behind him." How graphic should she be? "And killed him."

Kate studied the wedding ring she still wore. "We dreamed of having a family, of serving God, of growing old together. I accepted this job, and keep it, because it allows me to do just that for both Bradley and me. This is my home and you are my family. Don't you see? I'm just one of the girls," tears began to flow down her cheeks, and her voice broke, "who needs protection and healing, like all the rest of you. I belong here."

Sarah rarely hugged. This was an exceptional moment that deserved a big one. She held on to Miss Linn until it became awkward to the house mom. Their relationship had just taken a giant step forward. Sarah went into her bedroom and started writing a poem:

> Thank you, Earth, for my surprise,
> For a beautiful sunrise with purple skies,
> That was but a dim glow behind a wall of fog.
> Thank you for a brilliant rainbow of bright hue,
> That forgot to shine, hidden as clouds often do.
> Thank you for a glorious sunset beyond my
>   sight.
> For all these gifts, I give thanks tonight,
> Even if they didn't get to me today,
> I know you gave them, anyway.
> So, I'll look for them all once more,
> When my tomorrow comes, for sure.

The following week, when Sarah was once again with Dr. Tully, she was asked, "Sarah, did you write this for Miss Linn?"

"Sort of, I guess. But I like to make things that give me hope. So it was for me too." Her brown eyes met the counselor's gaze with confidence.

"Why did you slip it under her door instead of just giving it to her?"

"If I just gave it to her, she might want to ask me about it. You know, what it means." A weak smile gave evidence of a child's timidity. "I'm just a kid, and really don't have anything I can say to her about her husband or her loss."

Smiling warmly, the counselor said, "You will be ten years old in three weeks and are wiser than most adults I know. It is a splendid poem, speaking to the power of hope in the face of disappointment. I think it was a wonderful gift for Kate." She was still for a moment then asked, "Can you tell me why you address the poem to Earth instead of God?"

Sarah pursed her lips, seeking just the right way to answer her. "I sort of know the Earth. I can smell it, hear it, feel it, but I don't know God."

"Will you believe me if I tell you that God knows you any way, and loves you?"

"Maybe, but I also believe that Hermione is smarter than Harry. I know the smell of summertime grass just freshly cut, or the first rain after a hot summer. I know that bumble bees can fly even though very smart men believe that it is impossible for them, with such small wings and round bodies. I think I'll write a poem about people with small wings who can do unbelievable things, too, and give thanks to the Earth."

Dr. Tully chuckled out loud. "Sarah, sweetheart, my job is to evaluate you and keep a record of your development. I am supposed to tell my boss when, or if, I think you are ready for another home. You are so far beyond that point in your maturity. Whenever you want to be placed elsewhere, just let me, or Miss Linn know. I am so proud of you and know that you are going to be a fascinating woman." She closed her notebook, symbolically saying she rested her case.

Mo left the following month, to live with her sister in Corvallis. It took Sarah three more years before she was confident that Miss Linn could get along without her. She loved to read, so in addition to Miss Linn's home-school assignments, more than a hundred textbooks from the bookcase were carefully explored. The math books were her favorites, but geography and biology were also fascinating, and English literature gave her great stories to recreate in her dreams. History books helped her understand the gigantic progression of civilization's development. In due course she would come to understand how carefully all that knowledge was stored within her eager brain. She fell in love with classical music, and became proficient on a computer. During that time Sarah became a de facto executive director for the new girls, establishing guidelines and settling disputes. Miss Linn was quick to admit that the house had never run more gently or efficiently. Also during that time Sarah entered puberty with budding breasts and the onset of menstruation . . . Well, you win some and you . . .

She left two poems for Dr. Tully. The first one she simply called "Watches:"

> If I had a watch, I'd surely buy another, for two
>   reasons.
> First, I could set them for different times, not
>   just seasons.
> No one is ever too late, or early, or even right on
>   time,
> But always just ARE, relaxed, at peace, sublime.
> Second, with two watches I'd have all the time I
>   need and more,
> To be the things I have only hoped, and
>   dreamed, and swore.

The second one was a prose, entitled "The Backyard Swing:"

> So high . . .
> Wind brushes my face, plays with my feet and
>   tangles my hair.
> So high . . .

Grab a leaf, close my eyes and see the edge of my
    world over there.
So high . . .
Think on being, on memories of friends and
    families and sisters,
So high . . .
Leave this world for a moment to touch heaven
    and return,
To swing back into my life to laugh and love and
    learn.
So high . . .

Stingy Michelle

I'll share your toys; I think they're funny;
I'll share your toast; I'll share your honey.
I'll share your milk and your cookies too;
The hardest part is sharing mine with you

3

THE BOWENS

Camilla Bowen, wife of the orthopedic surgeon and sports medicine specialist Dr. Dwight Bowen, came to the house for a third interview. Miss Linn was in an unaccustomed dark mood. "This isn't the way our placement procedure works," she said with a snort. "The question is not are you good enough to be in their home," she whispered confidentially to Sarah, "but are they qualified to continue your care and growth?" She shook her head in disbelief.

Actually, the Bowens had been carefully screened before the first contact. They had a very stable marriage and enviable reputation, with two daughters living at home, one fifteen and the other seventeen, a senior in high school. They had a home in prestigious Lake Oswego, and the promise of a room of Sarah's very own. That first visit still felt a little like they were sizing Sarah up to see if she was good enough for them.

The second was even more trying with Mrs. Bowen alone. She was asking questions that were borderline acceptable at best. "Do you have health issues?" "No." "Do you speak any foreign language?" "Yes" "Do you play a musical instrument?" "No." "Do you play any team sports?" "No." "Gymnastics?" "No." "Ever taken dance lessons?" "No." "Ever travel outside the United States?" "No." "Do you have a passport?" "No." "Do you have a driver's license?" In a bit of exasperation, Sarah answered, "I am only thirteen years old." For that one Mrs. Bowen smiled a weak apology.

She then directed a series of questions toward Miss Linn, her home school teacher. "Can you tell me how she is doing in English?" "Superior." "Math?" "Superior." Computer skills?" "Above average." "American history?" "Above average." "Biology?" "Above average." "World history?" "Above average." "Political Science?" With a scowl Miss Linn replied, "She is only thirteen years old." "Yes, of course." Miss Linn added, "She is currently working at a high school level in Calculus, and advanced Spanish." "Really?"

Mrs. Bowen then produced a test form and asked, "Sarah darling, would you spend a few minutes answering as many of these questions as you can?" She handed her a folder and a pencil. "I'll just set the timer for ten minutes."

When she finally left, Sarah said, "I feel like I should go take a shower. What do you think that was all about?"

They received the answer to that question when Mrs. Bowen came in the following week for the third interview. "Darling," she radiated affection. "You are brilliant. Your test scores were in the ninety ninth percentile for college applicants." The information was spoken normally, but sounded to Sarah like thunder. "With no errors, you completed twice as many in that allotted time more than we expected." She gave Sarah a large embrace.

"I know that you think our behavior is bizarre or extreme. I am sorry. Just let me explain." She straightened her dress and collected her thoughts to say it best. "We would adore another daughter in our home, but are faced with two challenges. First we have two very high achieving and motivated daughters who might be distracted by an average new student who might slow them down. Secondly, the new girl might be very frustrated if she is compared with such outstanding daughters." It sounded far too clinical. "Sarah you would be perfect. Dr. Bowen wants to join me in the invitation for you to live with us, and promises that you will be guaranteed as much education as you want, to whatever school you choose. That is the same agreement we have with our daughters. You see, it is a serious decision. Will you think about it?" She looked into the steady brown eyes that seemed unfathomably deep. There was none of the jumping and screaming she had anticipated with the offer.

"It is a very generous offer." Sarah answered, somewhat overwhelmed. "Thank you." She had always been told where she was to live, not given a choice. This was an exhilarating moment of choice. "Miss Linn will help me understand such a terrific opportunity," Sarah said shyly. "As you said, it is a very serious decision." She held Mrs. Bowen's hand warmly, to prevent another embrace.

When the woman had left, the jumping and shouting began. "Guaranteed college!" "Any school!" "My own room!" "Guaranteed!" About then the implications set in on Sarah. The decision meant that she would leave the only home she had ever loved. She would leave Miss Linn. She stopped jumping and screaming.

"I can't leave you," she said with instant tears. Perhaps the hysteria of joy magnified the possible grief of separation.

Kate embraced her as warmly as any mother could. "Honey you will be less than an hour away. I'm sure you can visit. We can talk on the phone or email every day. I need to get my job back." The laughter they shared was authentic affection. It would be difficult, but it would happen.

On the first of May she moved into the Bowen residence. A driver in an SUV came to pick up Sarah and her things. Mrs. Bowen was along to supervise the move, which was a pretty easy job. Sarah had one box of clothes and personal items, one small box of books, and her notebook of poems.

Moving into the big house was very strange. She looked at the impressive double doors both flanked by beveled glass windows, catching the afternoon sun and sprinkling a dazzling display of prism colors. Inside the door was the largest pottery vase she had ever seen. It was bright blue and subtle green and looked very old. Suddenly Sarah missed Barkley's happy face and instant welcome. There were no pets in the Bowen residence. She missed the back yard swing and flowers. The Bowen residence only had an immaculately landscaped back yard that felt inaccessible. It was strangely wonderful that her room had its own bathroom. She would enjoy privacy for the first time since she was eight. Her bedroom also had a desk, with her own computer. And then there were the sisters.

Gretchen was the older. She was obviously self-absorbed, having perfect hair, nails and makeup. Her wardrobe must have been extensive and expensive. She was most concerned, Sarah gathered, about her social network and upward mobility in it. Vassar seemed her target school, because her mom had graduated there. As the oldest daughter, she was not in the least concerned with a new resident in the house.

Jan, on the other hand, seemed much more skeptical that a total stranger from some institution could be of any interest. She was casually dressed with minimal makeup. Sarah found it unforgivable that she was frequently rude to her parents, implying their lack of understanding of the things important to her. While Gretchen might choose to ignore Sarah's presence in the home, Jan made little effort to mask her disregard for a former shelter resident. Adjusting to a new home was never easy.

Supper was later than usual for Sarah. Dr. Bowen got home a little after seven, and the cook served the meal about a half hour later. There had to be time enough for Dr. and Mrs. Bowen to share a cocktail and catch up on the news of the day, meaning Sarah. When she was directed to sit near Mrs. Bowen's end of the table, she looked for the pink plate and glass, and breathed a sigh of regret that they were not there. She waited to take her first bite until Dr. Bowen began. Jan rolled her eyes at the courtesy, but both of the parents noticed, and exchanged a smile.

Dr. Bowen asked, "Tell me, Sarah, how long were you with Miss Linn?" He realized her presence was an opportunity to have at least casual conversation at the table, a rare courtesy it seemed. Usually, only he and Mrs. Bowen spoke.

"I was there a bit over four years" she answered in a bright voice.

"Really? Isn't that longer than most girls are there before being placed in a foster home?" He seemed pretty knowledgeable about the shelter system.

"Yes sir," she answered again with cheerfulness. "Most are there six to ten months, sometimes longer if the abuse was major, or the counseling took longer to help."

"And which was your case?" He leaned forward as though freshly interested.

"Oh, neither, sir." Jan gave a snorting grunt at the continued courtesy. "I stayed to help Miss Linn get over the tragedy of her husband's murder. She needed help handling the new girls who were usually afraid and angry, which is the same thing." Even Gretchen looked at her with a bit of wonder.

Mrs. Bowen said, "I didn't know that Miss Linn was married. I thought she was gay." Sarah had to stifle the look of anger that remark caused. She had learned that she had little patience for stupidity in adults who had a choice.

"Oh yes ma'am," she said, recovering her cheerfulness. "They graduated from George Fox, were married and he was sent by the government to Iraq to help farmers there improve their productivity." Sarah recalled the very words Miss Linn had spoken. "One day he was assassinated by a religious radical in the marketplace." O.K., that word was stronger, but more dramatic as she wanted it to be.

Dr. Bowen said, "Oh my, that is tragic." He hesitated only a moment before saying, "Let's change the subject, shall we? Sarah, what sort of games did you play at Miss Linn's?"

"Well, just Miss Linn and I played Cribbage and Checkers, together, sir. Favorite games for the house were Scrabble, Dominoes, Yahtzee, and oodles of card games, like Hearts, or Russian Rummy, or Oh Well, or 31 for M and M's"

"I don't know most of those," he went on. "You mentioned Checkers. Do you happen to know how to play chess?"

"No sir, but I would love to learn." Sarah didn't understand why Jan rolled her eyes again.

"One last question for the evening," Dr. Bowen said with a smile. "Do you know what you would like to work toward becoming?"

"Yes sir . . ." She would have gone on, but Jan burst out, "Oh come on with the sir stuff. We get it; you are polite and respectful. Let it go!"

An awkward silence gripped the table for several heart beats. Then, smiling, Sarah turned to Jan and said, "Jan, I am trying to make a fair first impression with you all, and am trying to find the parameters of appropriate conversation. I could use 'Dr. Bowen,' which would become tiresome and redundant after a bit, don't you think? I could call him 'Doc,' which would be very inappropriate for a child like me. I could call him "Dwight' or 'dad,' which would probably irk you even more. It just seems to me that 'sir' is an excellent and honoring beginning." Without waiting for a reply, she turned and answered Dr. Bowen's question.

"I'm hoping to become a peacemaker, sir. It has seemed to me that if I could become very wealthy, without peace, I could lose it all. I could become very famous, but without peace, that could go away too. I could become a farmer in a far away marketplace, but without peace, I wouldn't accomplish much."

The last part of her answer was lost in the full laughter that shook three of the other four. Jan glared her disdain at losing the first encounter with this intruder.

A short while later, before the lights were turned out in Sarah's room, she was at her desk, working on another poem:

> Everyday is a fresh beginning,
> Every morning the world's made new.
> If you're weary of disappointment,
> Here's some beautiful hope for you.
> Every day is a fresh beginning;
> Listen child to this glad refrain,
> In spite of puzzles and possible pain,
> Take heart in this day, and begin again.

She was startled to look up and find Jan leaning against her door frame, smiling patiently.

"I'm sorry," Sarah apologized. "I didn't know you were there. I was writing a new poem for my book."

Jan casually stepped behind her so she could read over Sarah's shoulder. "Hmm, that's cool. Do you do that a lot?"

Sarah was surprised at the shyness she was feeling. The words seemed to stumble over her tongue. "Well, I don't have much homework . . . I mean I have lots of time . . ." Finally she said bravely, "I love to make songs with no melodies. I think that what poems are."

"Did they teach you that in the shelter?" The half smile on her face warned Sarah that there might be more to the question. "Did they also teach you table manners, how to impress your foster folks?"

"Courtesy was important to Miss Linn," Sarah answered with growing pride. "She said it was a good way to show respect to the other girls who lived there. It was a free gift we could give each other."

Jan turned toward the door with aloof, saying, "Whatever. I can warn you that dad will try to teach you to play chess with him. He tried on Gretch and me. We refused because it so irritated him." She turned down the hall leaving a tangible wake of ugly distain. Sarah wondered how someone who had so much could be so impoverished.

The next morning Sarah opened her eyes, wondering for a moment where she might be. There were no familiar smells, or sounds. Her big bed seemed out of proportion. She convinced herself that it really was happening, but she missed Miss Linn. She made her bed, showered and dressed in the same clothes she had worn yesterday. Mrs. Bowen was waiting for her in the kitchen.

"Good morning Sarah. I hope you rested well."

"Good morning ma'am. I did. You look beautiful this morning."

Sarah couldn't be sure if the smile she received was genuine or merely indulgent. "Sweetheart, we usually look after ourselves in the morning. There is always cereal in the pantry. There are English muffins or bagels in the refrigerator with cream cheese or yogurt, or frozen waffles for the toaster. Any of that sound good to you?" She explained that the girls had left for school over an hour ago.

When Sarah had rinsed her cereal bowl and placed it in the dishwasher, Mrs. Bowen had that pleasant half smile that

Sarah was beginning to understand meant that she was pleased with her behavior. She also noticed her slide a cell phone across the counter.

"Yes, it's for you," she said seeing the light in Sarah's eyes. "I've put Dr. Bowen's number on speed dial one and I'm on two. Miss Linn is on three, and you can call her whenever you want." She also pushed a debit card across to Sarah. "This, Honey, is your allowance. Just like the other girls, you will have a hundred dollars deposited each month. Do you think that will be enough for incidentals?" Sarah's mouth moved but no sound came out. She just nodded vigorously. Finally, Mrs. Bowen said, "My plans for the day are to take you shopping for some new clothes, and we have an appointment with Marjorie Milton at Waluga Junior High School. Your records are being sent to her for evaluation so you can join your class in the fall." It was all happening too fast.

Sarah replied, "Do you suppose Jan might have some hand-me-downs from last year, or maybe the year before? I know I'm lots smaller than her, but I would love to be as pretty." That was blatant politics, but she was sure that Mrs. Bowen would pass it along anyway, and part of it was true. She was smaller than Jan.

Mrs. Milton's office was spacious, with a conference table on the other end of the room from her neat desk. On the table was a thick file containing Sarah's history. As they discussed the possibilities, she found Sarah attentive and quick to answer well. There was even occasional humor, which was unique for a frightened child. It was decided that if Sarah could be taken to the District office, they could test her and determine whether she should repeat the sixth grade, or be ready for the seventh. Mrs. Milton said in farewell that she looked forward to getting to know Sarah better, that she would be ever so welcome here.

It turned out to be a lengthy afternoon. When Sarah was finally back in her own room, the first thing she did was call Miss Linn. She was refreshed just to hear that familiar voice, and assured her that everything was going well. Oh, there was the thing with Jan, but it was made up by Mr. Bowen's laughter and interest. She told Miss Linn that she might be in the sixth or seventh grade. When Sarah heard Miss Linn say, "I doubt that," her feelings tumbled for a moment. Then her friend said, "I'm thinking eighth at least. You are way ahead of where anyone expects you to be. Mark my word."

So when the District office called the next day and asked if Sarah could come back in for more testing, Sarah thought it was a good thing. Mrs. Bowen didn't. She was sure Sarah would be placed in an elementary class, forgetting completely her success on the test she had taken a couple weeks before.

That same scenario was repeated the following day. The mood in the Bowen residence was doubtful. They were pretty convinced that Sarah would be placed in a remedial or special needs class. Even Jan showed signs of concern. Maybe she just didn't want to live with a retard! Sarah kept remembering Miss Linn's faith: "Mark my word." Thursday passed with no word from the school, as did Friday. There was a bright spot when the mail came with two forwarded notes from Mo and a card from Miss Linn.

On Saturday, Jan searched through her old clothes to find anything small enough to fit Sarah. When she found a shirt, Sarah greeted it as a prized gift. Jan found some tan Capri's, and smiled at Sarah's same response. "Do you usually get your clothes at Goodwill?" she asked in a voice that was somewhere between a tease and an insult.

Sarah was so focused on the wonderful clothes that she took it as a tease. "Your throw-away things are more wonderful than anything I could ever buy."

Jan started looking more carefully and, of course finding. Some shorts and tops, a pair of jeans that hardly showed any wear, a matching skirt and sweater caused Sarah to giggle, then weep with gratitude. "I've never had so many nice clothes," she said to Jan, suppressing the need to give her a hug. The grand prize was a bib overall that was tan with a light blue stripe. Sarah waddled down the hall to her room with an armful of treasures.

On Sunday the Bowens were supposed to go to church together, but Gretchen said she had a graduation planning brunch, and Jan said she also had a school project, so Sarah asked if she could stay home and answer her mail. Dr. and Mrs. Bowen enjoyed sitting in church together.

On Monday the District called, asking if Sarah could be at a 10 o'clock meeting with the superintendent and two school principals. It sounded pretty serious. When they arrived, Sarah was happy to see Mrs. Milton, the Junior High principal. Also present were Superintendent Long, the two women who had administered Sarah's tests, and a tall man named George Hanoska. The superintendent started the meeting by thanking everyone for promptness, and turning to Sarah, he said, "We have a serious situation this morning. Miss Linn would have been here but she has two new girls that she can't leave."

"Sarah, how much time would you say Miss Linn spent in school work with you each day?" His gaze was serious, but not threatening.

Trying to answer as honestly as she could, Sarah replied, "Mmm . . . maybe three or four hours."

"And how much time did you spend in homework each night?'

"Mmm Maybe an hour most nights, some none at all." She was beginning to think Miss Linn or she was in trouble.

"But we had a big bookcase with textbooks that I was allowed to read as much as I wanted."

"Here's the problem we face today, ladies and," looking at Mr. Hanoska, "gentleman; using dated textbooks, minimal time and effort, with no support supervision, this young woman has exceeded the quals for our high school juniors, and has placed in the top twenty percentile of college freshmen." A huge relief made Sarah feel that she could soar. "And her proficiency in all disciplines exceeds, right now, what we are hoping to achieve in our high school graduates. My question is, how did Miss Kate Linn accomplish this while being the director of a women's shelter?"

"Our immediate task is to place Sarah Thoms in an appropriate class situation." He looked at her smiling face with admiration. "But appropriate to what? Her age suggests that she be placed here at Waluga in the seventh grade. But she has already read all the text books you use, George, through your junior year at Lakeridge high school, and then some. She would merely be reviewing for four years." He spread his hands in exasperation. "For all I know, she could teach the darned class, and she's 13 years old!"

He lowered his voice to share this further information with them, "The State Superintendent of Education has given us a green light to negotiate a placement that is satisfactory with us all, including you Mrs. Bowen, as foster parent and designated guardian." Sarah had not heard that complete designation for the Bowens, nor thought about its impact on her.

"Let me ask you first, Mrs. Bowen, what do you think an ideal situation for Sarah would look like."

"I haven't given it much thought," she lied. "Our first concern has been to establish Sarah in a normal home, and let her adjust to being out of the shelter." She said the final word like it was something on the bottom of her shoe. "We did have some independent testing done before her placement with us, and were very pleased with her aptitude." She smiled broadly, using an academic word.

"Marjorie, where are you in this placement?"

The Junior High principal answered, "I am so proud that a girl with all these challenges can rise above them all." Looking fondly at Sarah, Mrs. Milton said, "She would be a very welcome part of our ninth grade class. I'm only afraid she would lack the challenge to grow that she deserves, and might find less productive ways to spend her time."

"George, that sort of puts her in your court. How do you suppose this should work?"

"Golly, wouldn't it be great if more of our problems had this sort of potential?" Mr. Hanoska also smiled encouragingly at Sarah. "My only concern is the social minefield a high school can be for an immature person. I am convinced that she has, and will continue, the aptitude to function academically. But asking a 13 year old to mingle, at this point in their lives, with women and men five years older than she is would be a big stretch, potentially devastating. If she could voluntarily exclude herself from many, maybe all, of the heavier social activities it might be a plus." He paused as if weighing the value of his next remark.

"I have been sitting here wondering about an even bigger step for Sarah. How would it work if she could have regular class assignments at Lakeridge that would amount to a part-time involvement and at the same time plug into the Multnomah Community College advancement program on-line? I know we might simply be shifting the problem to a higher level, but then she might be more able to handle it."

The superintendent chuckled loudly, "She might have her Bachelor's degree before she's eighteen!"

Mr. Hanoska nodded, "But with more maturity she might be more equipped to deal with it."

Finally, the superintendent turned to Sarah, asking, "Well young lady, you've heard a lot of good things. How do you feel about our meeting?"

Smiling broadly, she asked back, "Do you know how it feels to go into Baskin and Robins? There are so many great flavors to choose, and they are all good. I wish Miss Linn could help make the decision for me." Then with a big breath, she went on, "But since she is not here, I will trust you, like I trusted her. That always seemed to work. Anyway, I wasn't in the second grade or fourth or sixth, so it is just a number. I will try to be the best student I can be wherever you place me." She won the heart of each teacher there. On the other hand, Mrs. Bowen was wondering how Jan would receive this news. They would conceivably be in the same class.

Mr. Long said to the others, "It feels like we are in agreement with George's suggestion that Sarah attend Lakeridge mornings," he looked at them for confirmation, "and Multnomah Community for on-line work." Do you agree?" It only took a moment for all to show their positive support.

"Friends," the superintendent concluded, "I think we have an amazing opportunity here. Usually we only realize our good fortune after it has passed us by. Sarah may be the most brilliant student we will see in our lifetime. That is an incredible statement, and may be grossly overstated. We just don't know right now, so let's do everything possible to help her. I'm going to see if Grace Tully can be assigned as her school counselor, at least for the first year of this trial." Speaking then to Mrs. Bowen, who was trying to grasp the depths of this conversation, he asked, "Can we have Sarah for some summer tests to set her class schedule, and help our teachers prepare for next September? We are bringing the hen into the fox-house." He chuckled at his own humor, while Sarah smiled. She was a hen; no longer a chick!

On the way home, Mrs. Bowen suggested they keep the decision of the meeting confidential for a bit. She would tell Dr. Bowen the good news. But it would be good to wait until they knew where Sarah would be placed before telling the girls. Gretchen may well be at school before then anyway.

Learning the functions of the house was the next thing on Sarah's agenda. She learned that Paula was the cook's name. She did most of the grocery shopping, and planned the meals. She was also the housekeeper part time. So basically, she was there all the time, and went home only to sleep. Jonnie was the clinic driver, available to Dr. Bowen whenever he needed him. It was he who had driven the SUV from Beaverton in the first place. So Sarah got to know him pretty well. He drove her to all of the district tests, and twice back over to Beaverton to see Miss Linn.

One evening when Sarah came to the dinner table, she was surprised to see only three places set. Apparently Gretchen and Jan were elsewhere. She was also delighted to see a chess board waiting for her first lesson, and remembered Jan's forecast. Patiently, Dr. Bowen carefully explained the function of each piece, and the aim of the game. "You win the game not by how many pieces you have captured, but when your opponent's king is in check and can't get out by either moving, blocking or capturing the attacker."

"So," Sarah said in review, "these little guys, called 'pawns,' all get one or two steps to start, but then only move one step at a time."

Dr. Bowen nodded and added, "And they capture how?"

Sarah was happy to know the answer; "On the angle forward." He thought she was going to continue the inventory of pieces when she added, "But they also capture 'en pasant' I believe you called it, in passing." The Dr. nodded delightedly.

She touched the castle. "And this is the rook." She looked into his eyes for concurrence. "It goes parallel to the edges of the board as far in a straight line as he wants as long as he is not blocked." Again she received a nod of approval. "The bishops are the same except they run on an angle. There is a light and a dark one."

"The knights," she hesitated trying to remember the complete pattern, "move in an "L" shape, one step up, and two over, or two steps up, and one over." When she didn't add any more, he reminded her that they can move backwards in the same patterns. Sarah nodded her understanding.

"The queen is the best," Sarah said emphatically. "She can go in one straight line like either a castle, or a bishop." Without waiting for affirmation, she concluded, "The king can move one step in any direction, but not into check, and I have sort of forgotten about the castling thing."

Their first couple of games didn't last very long before Sarah's king was trapped, but she seemed to understand the idea. The last game on their first night was much longer and she demonstrated a strong defense. Dr. Bowen only won because he queened a pawn and trapped her under-protected king.

"But you didn't tell me there were more queens," she lamented. To which he confessed that it was a complicated game, and that she had done quite well for a first venture. He offered a chocolate sundae for her effort. All in all, the evening was a success.

That summer was the most challenging Sarah had ever known. The atmosphere around the Bowen house was anything but pleasant. Gretchen was not accepted at Vassar, because of her poor final semester grades. She had to be satisfied with her second choice, Brown, in New York City. She pouted for days. Jan's presence was no more pleasant. After their initial experience of the hand-me-downs, she seemed to avoid Sarah as much as possible. Jan's two favorite slurs to her foster sister were, "Brainiac," and "Chess mate." When she used the latter, it was in the company of, "Daddy's little chess mate." After Gretchen left for school, Jan found more and more reasons to be absent from the dinner table in protest. Her boyfriend, Kent, however, enjoyed the situation immensely, because when she had nowhere else to go, Jan was in his arms, sharing her woes, and quite a bit more.

Sarah had her own challenge to address. Most weekday mornings she arrived at the district office at nine and was tested until noon. She always left with a list of subjects she would be tested on tomorrow, but of course, she didn't have the textbooks to study. Most of her answers therefore, were from the stuff she had read at Miss Linn's. Little did she know that she was working through the student learning list from each quarter of the school year, beginning with the seventh grade. By late July her test results finally began to fall below the honor list level; she was answering questions from her second quarter of her senior year. She only broke into tears twice, well twice from frustration, and a third time with joy when she got to meet with Dr. Tully.

"Look at you," her counselor and friend had said in greeting. "I think you will be the poster girl for home-schools this fall. Have you talked with Miss Linn recently?"

"Not since before the tests started. There hasn't been any time," Sarah answered a bit concerned.

"Well young lady, you have caused such a stir that both she and I have received new job offers." When Sarah raised her eyebrows in question, her counselor continued. "I, as you know, am going to be working with you and two other gifted students, to maximize test results in the high schools." She nodded her head in emphasis. "And I only heard about this last week. Miss Linn is going to be asked to supervise home-schools for the entire state. I don't know if she's going to do it."

By the first of August, Sarah was meeting with her planned teachers: Mr. Burrell would teach second year chemistry; Mrs. Edith Sather would teach second year biology; Miss Ada Ross would teach English Appreciation; Mr. Jay Scholtus would teach business law, bookkeeping, and business principles, and finally Hank Jordan would teach yoga and karate. All of them were morning classes which allowed the afternoons for on-line time. Since she had already satisfied enough graduation requirements, except for physical education, she would be officially enrolled as a junior but a footnote indicated that she could receive her diploma at any time she requested it.

She met with each of her teachers and received textbooks for the fall quarter. She thought the reading assignments were very manageable so when the first day of school arrived, she dressed in her favorite outfit, Jan's hand-me-down bib overalls and a bright purple rayon blouse. Lakeridge colors are purple and white, so she thought she could show some school spirit.

She hadn't even made it to her English class when a hurrying shoulder caught her squarely and banged her into the wall, her papers and books fluttering all over the hallway. A couple girls helped her gather them up, but since she was at least a head shorter than anyone else, they dismissed her quickly. After English it happened again. In the press of hurrying students there was another collision that knocked her on her rump, amid some snickering. An hour later, heading for the gym and her yoga class it would have happened yet again but for the intervention of a very large arm and hand that reached over her and deflected the on-coming frame. Larry Scott, All

State right defensive guard, shoved the intended prankster so forcibly that he slid across the hall and folded in a heap at the base of the wall. "Knock it off Todd, you jerk," his soft voice filled the hallway. "This is Jan's little sister."

Sarah looked up, way up, and thanked him for saving her. "You are my hero this morning. You saved me," was all she said with an incredible smile, but she remembered her old lesson: "A person does not need to be the biggest or strongest to prevail. She just needs to stand in the right, among those who are bigger or stronger." There were no more hallway contact sports.

That evening, she was eager to tell Jan about her first day at Lakeridge, but Jan's chair was empty. She probably had some other pressing engagement. Sarah happily chattered about the day to her interested listeners. She was especially happy to get started with the Community College. Her two classes were computers and accounting. She believed that the latter would dovetail with her bookkeeping class in the morning, getting two birds as it were. She was, at least for the moment, caught up with all studies, so Sarah settled for two more chess games with Dr. Bowen. She lost both by attrition. She spent so much of her time thinking about defense, that she failed to attack his king.

Tuesday was pretty much a duplication of her first day at school. She followed the superintendent's suggestion that she always sit in the front row, farthest from the door to minimize the possibility of an incident. She made sure she didn't drink much for breakfast and went to the bathroom just before she left home so there was no use of a school bathroom. Defense was her intention. So when she got to gym class she was glad to hear Mr. Jordan say "Karate is the art of self-defense. It means literally, the empty hand. If you have been confused by Hollywood's notion of a little howling super hero, we will find out that it is much different." He explained how a person can use the force of an attacker by going with the attack, but deflecting it away. He asked one of the boys to help him demonstrate, but promised not to hurt him.

He instructed the student to push him in the chest, and try to knock him over. As the boy lunged forward the teacher merely grasped the front of his shirt and rolled away, pulling his assailant with him. Rolling away, the boy found himself unable to do anything but collapse under the teacher, who agilely rolled free and stood up. They repeated the demonstration; even though the student knew it was coming, he couldn't avoid the takedown.

"Now pick a partner and practice that basic move yourselves," the teacher instructed. Sarah looked for a girl to partner with, but was immediately confronted with a young man. "Hi, I'm Kent. Let's do this." He tapped himself on the chest, inviting her to attack, and said, "Go for it."

Furtively Sarah looked for any other alternative, but saw only students rolling on the floor. So she gave a push at him. To her surprise, there was no resistance, in fact, she was jerked forward. Her body was twisted as she found herself headed facedown for the mat. Unlike the demonstration however, her partner did not roll away, but flopped down on her back, pushing her more firmly into the spongy mat. His face was right behind her head when she heard him whisper, "You're my hero. You saved me." A chill ran through Sarah and she struggled to get out from under his dead weight.

"Mr. Scott," Hank Jordan's voice thundered, "get off that child!" The words were still echoing in the gym when Mr. Jordan realized that this endeavor with Sarah, regardless of its righteous intent, was destined to fail. Sarah had realized it one heartbeat sooner. She grabbed her yoga mat, books and jacket and hurried to the front entrance to wait for Jonnie.

As soon as she got home she changed into some sweats and called Dr. Tully. Sarah told her about the collisions in the hall and the guy lying on top of her and whispering her words back to her. "It was creepy!"

Grace listened and offered words of concern, but pointed out that some high schoolers can be pretty insensitive and crude. Perhaps it wasn't meant to be a threat, just a poor joke. She advised Sarah to take a couple days off before trying again. Perhaps that would give folks time to adjust to the idea of her presence. She promised to have her absence excused. They chatted for quite a while, and then Sarah sent emails to Miss Linn and Mo.

The remainder of the afternoon slipped by with her on-line studies. It was amazing to have real time conversations with instructors. She asked questions first about her computer, and learned some great aids to increasing her security. She then surprised her bookkeeping instructor with her math knowledge and its application to a fresh discipline. Twice he asked her why she wasn't at Reed College. When it was time for dinner, she couldn't find her overalls, so she wore her sweats. Somehow she felt under-dressed, but nothing was mentioned, and again only three of them sat at the big table.

"Check!" she said with a victorious flair. Dr. Bowen smiled as he blocked her queen with his knight. She answered by moving up her other knight, just one more move from the action. Her opponent smiled slyly, and castled his king out of danger. Sarah lost the game in a half dozen more moves.

"Honey, why didn't you capture my knight with your queen?" The doctor was replaying the moves to demonstrate for her.

"Because you would have taken my queen with the pawn," she answered correctly

"If that had happened," he agreed, "your bishop would have captured the pawn and I would have been checkmated." He moved the appropriate pieces through the exchange. "See? That would have been a sacrifice of your queen, but a sure victory. I have no place to escape, no way to block, and I can't take your bishop. Checkmate!"

"I didn't look far enough ahead, did I?" She had an understanding expression.

"That was too close for another game, how about a chocolate sundae?" He made it sound like they had never had one before. Sarah was suspicious that he really had one every night. She was just a convenient excuse. No mention of Jan's absence was brought up.

The next morning, Sarah still couldn't find her overalls. When Paula came in to begin her chores, Sarah asked her about them immediately." "Yeah, I remember. I tot they were Chan's. I put in her homper." Sarah had not realized what a strong accent she had. She thought about it as she made her way upstairs.

Jan's door was open, but Sarah had the strong sensation of being in forbidden territory. She tiptoed across the room. Sure enough; her favorite overalls were there in Jan's clothes hamper. As Sarah lifted them out, she started to close the lid, and paused. Something seemed strange about the hamper. She looked again inside it, and then at the outside. The bottom was wrong. She looked again. The inside bottom was about eight or ten inches higher than the outside bottom. She reached in and tested the hard thin bottom. It moved slightly. She managed to hook her thumb nail on the edge and lifted.

She knew at first glance that she was in trouble. She could see three or four containers of pills, most of them white but one light purple. There were three or four bags of leafy stuff, and two square packages taped tight. Trembling, she carefully closed the false bottom, rearranging the few articles of dirty clothes, and closed the lid. Back in her room she didn't know what to do. Should she call Dr. Tully, or Miss Linn? No! Should she call the police? Oh, no! She should keep her mouth shut and pray that no one finds out that she is aware of, not a user's stash, but a dealer's!

She stayed in her room for four days, except for meals. She actually had everything she needed. She managed to get further ahead on the Community College study schedule. She wrote poems in her notebook, streamed Classic FM during the day, and watched the Discovery Channel at night. Several times she was asked if she might be feeling poorly. Always she assured them that she was feeling fine. She did see Jan twice during that time, and wondered why she had a grim grin on her face.

For the next two weeks Sarah attended Lakeridge classes in the morning, doing only yoga for Mr. Jordan's class. No more contact karate. Her afternoons were more productive than the other on-line students. Friday September 21st was Homecoming for Lakeridge. It was a day that, even in her worst nightmares, Sarah could not imagine. Supper was a pot pie alone because Dr. and Mrs. Bowen were attending the philharmonic, and Jan was at the football game. She went upstairs and sent emails to Mo and Miss Linn.

4

TROUBLE

The party started a little after ten, and got louder until eleven. Sarah was trying to finish a poem:

"No matter how hard we strive for peace,
The chaos and conflict never cease.
But it need not be so, if just you and I agree
To help each other, work together we'll clearly
    see,
Day after night after day like sister, and brother.
We can achieve a great . . ."

Suddenly her door burst open and a furious Jan entered, shouting, "Why did you fuck with my stuff?"

Sarah's mouth tried to say something but she was too terrified.

"You used my computer you little puke!" Jan shouted as she charged across the room and grabbed Sarah's arm. She jerked the smaller girl out of the desk chair.

"No I didn't! Honest!" was all the now hysterical girl could answer in defense.

Jan grabbed Sarah's notebook and began to drag her from the room. Several other girls were in the hallway witnessing the spectacle. Down the stairway she stumbled. There must have been forty kids in the family room. Jan towed her through them like the bow of an ice breaker. Nothing stood in her way. Sarah recognized Kent Scott from school and by his reaction realized that he was with Jan. When she got to the fireplace she spun and said, "I'm sick and damned tired of your lies. I always close my computer and you left it open. Did you go through all my shit?" She gave another jerk on Sarah's arm for emphasis.

Now sobs were the main sound that came out. "I didn't I swear!"

"You lying little punk. I'm going to teach you a lesson! Here's what happens when you fuck with my shit!" She threw Sarah's notebook into the gas flame. It landed open and the pages began to burn immediately. They all watched, fascinated, as the paper curled into charred ashes.

The piercing scream was more than anyone expected. Sarah wrenched her arm free and dove into the fireplace to retrieve her ruined treasure. She felt the searing pain, but pulled the notebook out anyway. Flaming sheets of paper scattered over the crowd of youth, settling on the carpet, then on the sofa and pillows. Smoke and sparks filled the air as the crowd tried to run for the doors. The kitchen smoke alarms went off and a drape began to burn.

"Kent, get her out of here," Jan screamed, as others tried to stamp out the fires, "and teach her a lesson."

He grabbed a fistful of Sarah's hair and headed for the front door. Someone else had her arm and tried to steer her through the frantic crowd. As their feet reached the tile at the entryway, Sarah's foot slipped and she staggered. Immediately Kent released her hair so he could slap her face. "If you know you are going to get hit," she reminded herself, "go with it." Sarah saw the blue vase on its big stand. Kent's hand slapped against the side of her head, sending an explosion of pain through her; she was accelerated along an already deadly path toward the blue target. It was more solid than she expected, unlike a tilting chair and a fragile kitchen table, but just like that earlier incident, her collision was horrific. Her shoulder slammed into the base of the wooden stand and the vase folded over with growing momentum. When it hit the crystal window it shattered along with the glass. She felt the edge of the stand tear into her scalp, and a large shard of pottery cut the top of her head.

The person holding her arm let out a shout and said, "Jesus Christ, Kent, you're out of control. Chill, man!" They drug her through the door to a nearby shiny black car. She only caught a flash of the license number. Sarah was thrown into the trunk like a bag of refuse headed for the dump. As the car sped into the night she repeated to herself, "You will be safe; we will take care of you!" Minutes passed with turns and stops. Finally the trunk lid came up and Sarah once more was at the whim of her attackers. They ripped off her overalls and shirt. She begged. They tore off her bra and Kent hit her again. She tasted her own blood.

"You little bag of crap have been a nuisance from day one," Kent growled. "Robb grab her arm and hold her down!"

She was kneeling down trying to hide her nude body. She sobbed, "Please don't. Please!" Her attackers rolled her onto her back. "Jesus, help me!" was all she could utter. "Help me, please!"

Kent grabbed her hair again and punching her in the face, said, "If you bite him I'm going to knock out all your teeth."

She felt the hideous weight of a body pressing down on her. "NO!" she screamed. Then a searing pain stabbed through her body. She screamed again. Sarah finally fainted, unaware of Kent rolling her over, and completing the insult to her unresisting body.

Merciful minutes of oblivion later she opened her eyes to total darkness. There was no one near her. She tried to move but cried out in pain; her head felt wet and sticky from her own blood. She sobbed uncontrollably, and then started to think. Her clothes were lying nearby; painfully, she crawled to her shirt, then her overalls. In the bib pocket, she found her phone, and speed dialed 3! Miss Linn's sleepy voice answered almost immediately. "Sarah, what's wrong?"

Sarah tried to talk but her voice could hardly make a sound. Gravelly, she croaked, "I've been raped. I think I'm in a park."

Now on full alert, Kate asked, "Can you see anything to tell me where you are, buildings, streets, anything?"

"There's a sign," she rasped. Trying to get a better look at it, she twisted about, screamed and vomited. Frantic words from Kate promised to find her, help her. "Just stay strong, Sarah!"

"I think the sign says, Try Creek." Her weary voice faded, and she dropped her phone.

"Sarah, Sweetie, help is on the way. I'm coming to you right now. I know where you are." Kate hung up and called 911. She reported that a rape had occurred in Tryon Creek Park, and the young victim was barely alive.

From a great distance and through a dense fog, Sarah heard the sirens. She hoped they could find her in time. She lost consciousness again. Before she opened her eyes, emergency vehicles made an island of light in a sea of darkness, with her in the center.

Two patrol cars arrived before the first ambulance. Eventually there were three ambulances, a battalion fire commander's vehicle, and four police cars, including Lieutenant Kay Lynch's, who was in charge of the investigation. While the emergency technicians were assessing Sarah's injuries and covering her with a thermal blanket, Lynch was trying to get initial information from Sarah, her name, the address of the Bowens, her age.

"You are only thirteen?" the incredulous officer asked. "What's a thirteen year old doing out with a bunch of men?" Her question implied a bias brought on by too many inner city police files.

"No," Sarah whimpered. "I was in my room when Jan dragged me out and burned my notebook." Her body writhed as another dry heave shook her. "Jan . . . Jan started it." There were more sobs. The EMT said they were ready to transport.

Sarah's blistered hand grabbed for the Lieutenant's sleeve. "Wait," she said desperately, "Jan's got drugs . . . lots of drugs in her hamper. If she knows I found them, that's why she . . ." Her raspy voice trailed away as once more she fainted.

Miss Linn ran to the pool of light and offered her assistance. "I'll follow to the hospital," she finally said, realizing there was nothing here to do. "Which one?" she shouted.

"Legacy Good Sam," came the answer.

Officer Lynch was on her radio. "This is 418, requesting a patrol to meet me at 16610 Laurelhurst South, with a probable cause search warrant. It might be a good idea if narcotics can come along too."

Within minutes the pool of light was reduced to two patrol cars whose personnel were gathering and tagging any evidence. There really was not much to find.

Officer Lynch pulled into the sweeping driveway, noting that most of the lights were on in the Bowen residence. As she stepped to the door, she was aware of the shattered glass and pottery. No effort had yet been made to clean it up. The door opened and an excited man bid her "Come in! Thank you for such quick response. We have been so vandalized!" His arm swept toward the glass, and also toward the family room. "She did quite a number on us."

"Who is that, sir?" Lynch asked.

"Sarah Thoms," he answered. She crashed our daughter's homecoming party. She was so mad to be uninvited that she threw her notebook in the fireplace. Burning paper did considerable damage to the furniture and carpeting. We won't be able to get an insurance adjuster here before Monday."

Lynch took out her notebook and began to write. "Excuse me, could I have your names?" Finally, turning to Jan, she asked, "And you are?

Mrs. Bowen immediately offered, "This is Janice Jane, our daughter." Lynch couldn't read the expression on the girl's face. It was something between smug fear and indifferent distain. "Jan, tell me what you saw."

"Well, we had just got home from the football game. It was about 11:00 o'clock. We were just having a good time when Sarah came down the stairs shouting for us to be quiet. I was right over there by the fireplace. When she got to me she sort of tried to hit me with her notebook, but it slipped out of her hand and bounced into the fireplace. She was so out of control. Someone raked it out of the fireplace because the burning pages were getting all over. I think they threw it out on the driveway. I didn't see. But then, she did try to run out the door, and kicked the base holding the vase, and that crashed into the window and broke all to hell." Three more police officers arrived.

"These officers are going to see if they can find any evidence about this crime scene." Dr. Bowen nodded with satisfaction, which soon disappeared when Officer Lynch added, "and this search warrant allows us to collect whatever we feel might shed some light on the incident. Please stay in this room for a few minutes. We will try to hurry."

"By the way, Jan, where is Sarah now: do you know?"

The teenager shrugged her lack of knowledge. "The last time I saw her, she was beating feet out the door." An officer came in from the driveway holding a charred notebook in a plastic bag.

The family listened as the officers went from room to room, quiet voices exchanging information. The only evidence they found in Sarah's room was the overturned chair. Jan suddenly had an ominous realization that they might discover her hidden cache. Those fears became full blown when the police officers came down from the upstairs; they were carrying two laptop computers, and Jan's clothes hamper.

"What the hell is the meaning of this?" Dr. Bowen roared. "I'll call the m . . ."

"I'll tell you who to call," Officer Lynch cut him off. "You'd better have a serious legal team." She opened the hamper to reveal a sizable cache of drugs and three handguns." Jan was suddenly pale, and her dad was silent. "Doctor, did you know that it is a felony in the State of Oregon to have a loaded handgun unsecured in the residence of a minor? We have three here. I suppose you have the registrations for them."

Dr. Bowen nearly shouted, "You can't take our property." He didn't know how to protest more.

"Oh that's not all we are going to take." Nodding to one of the uniformed officers, she said, "Jan Bowen, you are under arrest for the possession of, and intent to traffic narcotics." The officer pulled the girl's hands behind her back and snapped on handcuffs. "We estimate the value of this stash at somewhere north of a hundred thousand dollars and a street value of five times that. With that kind of large, you will be tried as an adult." Leveling a glare at Dr. Bowen, she added, "Daddy, you better bring a real good lawyer." Her Miranda rights were read to Jan on the way to the patrol car. She was crying too loudly to hear them.

Dr. Bowen mumbled incoherently, "Jan, what have you done to us?"

In the emergency section of Good Samaritan Hospital, Sarah was the attention of a team of nurses. Forensic nurses were gathering as much information as they could, collecting swabs and wiping biological samples. She was trying to be brave, moaning on occasion, and when the rape kit pelvic exam began she flinched and stifled a scream. Her rectum was so torn and bloody she cried out in pain and violently pulled away from the nurses' attempts to assess the damage.

Miss Linn had to go home and be with her girls, she told Sarah. The tears in her eyes told her so much more. She promised to be back as soon as she could.

One of the nurses got a camera to record the bite marks on Sarah's back and shoulders, and the bruises around her neck. "It looks to me like someone tried to strangle her from behind," she mused. "Maybe because she was unconscious, they thought she was dead." After collecting all the biological evidence they needed, Sarah was given a long cool shower. Even though there were wounds that still needed attention, and so much of her was sensitive to the water, it felt wonderful to wash all the filth away.

Just before six o'clock, Lieutenant Lynch came into her room. "Sweetie, you look so much better already. I know the doctors haven't seen you yet, but I'm about to go off shift; do you feel strong enough to tell me what happened?"

Sarah nodded, and began telling how Jan had pulled her from her room.

Officer Lynch asked for clarity, "She came to your room and forcibly dragged you downstairs?" Sarah nodded again, "That's where these came from." She showed her scratched and bruised right arm. "Her fingernails scratched me." As she continued with her account, the officer wrote, "Scrape left hand fingernails for biologics."

"She called you names and threw your notebook in the fireplace?" Sarah nodded. "And you burned your hand getting it out?" Sarah showed the angry red blisters. "It was Jan who told Kent to take you outside?" Again Sarah nodded. "And you think Robb pulled you to the door?" Sarah displayed the bruises on her left arm. She also showed the bruise and deep gouge on her back from the wooden stand. "You say that Kent hit you and you fell against it?" Sarah nodded. "You didn't kick it?" Lynch asked for clarity. "I was facing away from the stand toward the door, when I slipped on the tiles." She showed the wound on the back of her head. "And you think it was Robb who tried to get Kent to stop?" "Uhhuh" she concurred. "But you were thrown in the car trunk anyway?" Again Sarah nodded, "I think some of the numbers are B 761." Officer Lynch was amazed at the fortitude of this young girl who could now speak about her nightmare ordeal. "I hit my head on the roof and side of the trunk when they slammed the lid." There wasn't much more to tell. "Kent hit me when they tore my clothes off, and then held me down for Todd. He punched me in the face and said he would knock out my teeth if I fought back." She didn't want to go any further.

Lieutenant Lynch sat beside her bed for several quiet minutes. She wished there was a hand she could hold or back she could stroke, but there wasn't any place without a wound. This young woman had been beaten all over.

In the basement of the jail, Jan sat in an interrogation room. She had been so tired that for a while she laid her head on the table and tried to sleep. Pictures of how terribly wrong her evening had gone flashed before her, however. She had only wanted to humiliate the girl in front of her friends. She had only wanted to demonstrate that she was still the main girl in the house. She had finally cried all the tears she could. How had everything gone so wrong?

The door opened and a frazzled looking man came in. "Hi, Jan Bowen?" When she nodded, he sighed, "Good I'm not lost." She thought, "What a loser!" He turned to invite another man into the room. She recognized the emblems and shirt of an EMT. He came around to her side of the table and asked her if he could scrape the fingernails of her left hand. At first Jan wanted to resist, but finally said defiantly, "Knock yourself out."

While that simple task was being done, and tiny samples were placed in plastic containers, the frazzled man said, "Miss Bowen, I'm from the DA's office. Until your representation is present, I cannot ask you any questions about the incidents in your home last night except to determine the identity of witnesses that might confirm your testimony." He gave her a pad of paper and a pencil. "Would you jot down the names of as many folks who were there as you remember?" The EMT left the room and the man began leafing through the file that he had brought with him. After a few minutes he looked up. "Looks like a couple dozen. Good, but is that about all you can remember? I think there were more there than that." He turned the pad toward him so he could read it. "Let's see, Kent Scott is your boyfriend, right? Yup, there he is," underlining the name. "And his buddy is Robb . . . . ?" He left the question hanging for her to finish. "Gerrod," she finally said with a scowl. "Yup, there he is," underling the name. "And wasn't Todd there? I don't see Todd . . ." Again he left the question hanging for her. "Todd Wallace. They are all football players." Her tone became sharp, impatient, as he wrote the name and underlined it.

"You know, I'd be pretty tense too if I was looking at these charges. We've got you cold on the drugs. We are just trying to figure out where they came from. The Oxi, Vicodin and Marijuana are Mexican for sure. The Meth came from Canada, and we are still working on the Cocaine. We can hold you for 24 hours without charging you. Then it will be another 24 before you can be arraigned and make bail. By Monday morning we will be testing the classes at Lakeridge to see how many kids have bought stuff from you. You won't be able to warn your friends. But as I said, that's a slam dunk. You're lookin' at twenty to thirty, minimum." His manner was sloppy to the point of irritation.

"The big one is whether you were involved with Sarah's abduction. Charges are being filed right now for the arrest of these three men." His finger pointed to the underlined names. "Let's see, kidnapping, assault, sexual assault, rape and attempted murder of a thirteen year old child. That has got to be life without parole. I sure hope you didn't have anything to do with it. Their lives as they know it are over. Sad, they could have had bright futures" He wearily rose and, tapping his papers together, turned and left without another word. Jan would have screamed, except her throat was constricted with fear.

In Sarah's hospital room, an IV drip had been attached to her arm giving her hydration and sucrose. It also delivered sedation, which her weary body gladly received. She was drifting in and out of slumber when a young doctor came in asking if he could fix some of those wounds on her head. He needed to shave the hair from the injury sites, and since there were three, back, top, and side, he asked, "Would you like me to take all your hair off?"

"No," her drowsy voice answered. "I like my hair." There was a pause as she struggled to explain. "But you're the doctor, so it will grow back." She didn't seem to feel the clippers, or the sutures.

Dr. Tully came into her room in the late afternoon, after the doctors had finished the last of the repair, giving Sarah an anti-pregnancy drug, and another to remove her memory of the attack. She would remember that it happened, but vivid details were dulled, as was her pain. Grace sat quietly while Sarah slept. The next afternoon, Sarah was awake when Miss Linn came in, and brought Mo with her! The two friends looked at one another for a long moment before Mo said, "I love what you've done with your hair." If Sarah didn't laugh, she at least tried to smile bravely.

She took the plastic mouth-guard out saying, "To keep my teeth straight after they were knocked loose." She put the wet device on the table. "Mo, you are beautiful. I can't believe it. You've grown up!" It had been nearly four years since they were together, although they exchanged emails constantly.

Her friend gazed at the gauze pads on her hands, the compresses on her head, and the blue-green bruises on her face. "You would probably say I'm stretching the truth if I said that you look wonderful, too," She leaned against the bed awkwardly. "But I mean it with all my heart!" It was probably the best healing potion Sarah could have received.

Mo had been advised not to ask about the attack, so she told them about her sister's house, her new friends, and being a big high school sophomore. Sarah said with a bit of a twinkle, "I was in high school for twelve days."

Miss Linn asked, "Do you know where you'd like to go in a couple days? I think they want to keep you until all the tests are over." Sarah hadn't given it any thought. Kate continued, "Well Honey, your old room is vacant right now, and I would love to have your company."

A tear traced down Sarah's cheek. "And I fit the requirements for placement." All three of them had a moment of silence. "I'll think about it," she said wearily.

An hour later Dr. Tully knocked on the door and came in with a smile. "You are looking tons better than yesterday." Looking at her shaved head, she added, "and you've got the new fad sports look." She handed Sarah a stuffed toy tiger. "I know it's been a long time since you had Archer, but here he is all grown up, too." Sarah shifted a bit to cradle the toy. "He will keep you company." She then chatted with Sarah about the next step. "Honey, I think you are going to need an attorney." When Sarah started to object, saying she hadn't done anything wrong, Dr. Tully assured her that everyone knew that. There was about to be a lot of trouble for many folks and it would be good if Sarah could stay out of it. An attorney would speak for her. Understanding, Sarah nodded her head. "I have a friend who will be just perfect," the counselor offered.

"One last thing," Dr. Tully said, "When you are ready to leave the hospital, I don't think you will want to go back to the Bowen's. You can go back to Miss Linn's, or you can come live with me for a while. I have a spare bedroom and would love the company." Sarah seemed to be running low on energy, so her counselor said, as she got up to leave, "We'll talk about it tomorrow. Get some rest, Sweetie."

Monday was a traumatic day for Lakeridge High School. At 9:00 o'clock sharp a squadron of technicians from Drug Enforcement and several Portland and Lake Oswego police cars arrived. The announcement was made that all classes would participate in a drug screening test. Each door was blocked by officers preventing early dismissal. Robb Gerrod, Kent Scott and Todd Wallace were arrested and taken by a police van for booking, and thirty seven students were suspended for failing the drug tests. At the same time police officers entered the dental office of J. William Scott, DDS. Presenting a search warrant, they asked to see his black Lexus, license number GBQ 761. He agreed immediately, but said he had just had the car detailed Saturday.

"You wanted to get rid of any evidence?" one of the officers asked aggressively.

"What evidence? I do it all the time. I like a clean car." They found it in the parking garage. He unlocked the doors and stepped back. One officer looked in the driver side, another looked in the trunk, and a third stood just behind Dr. Scott.

"I told you I like a clean car, show-room clean." His voice had a defensive edge. The officer looking in the trunk was not looking at the freshly shampooed floor carpeting, but at the ceiling and side. He took a swab and gathered a sample, then another. "Yeah," he reported, "it's blood."

The officer behind him grasped his wrist and pulled it behind his back, snapping on a handcuff. "J. William Scott, you are under arrest for obstruction of justice by destroying evidence, and as an accomplice to kidnapping, assault, sexual assault, rape, and attempted murder of a minor" The dentist's knees went weak. He tried lamely to prevent his other wrist from being restrained, but felt the bracelet tighten like the restriction in his chest. Sometimes the sins of the son wreak havoc on the father as well.

While Sarah was oblivious to that drama, she was surprised to have some of her own. Mrs. Bowen came to see her. At first she just stood inside the door, trying to grasp the scope of Sarah's injuries. "Oh my," she finally whispered. "Those boys hurt you so much." She shook her head as though erasing the painful thoughts. There was a long pause, as though she were waiting for Sarah to say something. When she didn't, Mrs. Bowen finally said, "And our Jan has been arrested for drug possession. It's just dreadful." She finally stepped beside the bed, but made no attempt to touch Sarah. "The doctor says you may be ready to come home Wednesday. I'll have Jonnie pick you up."

Sarah was slowly shaking her head. "No, that's not going to happen. Dr. Tully will come by for my clothes, and I would appreciate the use of my computer until I can get another. It has all my school stuff."

Mrs. Bowen was obviously confused. "Of course Darling; but where would you go?"

Sarah pursed her lips. "Somewhere they will keep me safe and care for me." She closed her eyes. As far as she was concerned this conversation was complete. She didn't hear Mrs. Bowen leave.

On Wednesday the rectal stitches came out, and Sarah was finally released from the hospital. When Dr. Tully picked her up, she had four boxes of clothes from the Bowens, and her laptop computer. Sarah didn't remember that many clothes.

That evening, she also had her first meeting with Gail Gilbert, her new attorney. Their meeting wasn't very long, but tremendously important, for it set the tone for the conference meeting on Saturday morning. The attorney explained to Sarah that justice meant more than punishing the young men who had hurt her. It meant establishing a condition of security for Sarah and her future. "I do believe those young men are about to experience the shock and unbelievable consequences for their violation upon you, Sarah. Things are about to go surprisingly bad for them." She gave Sarah a tender hug of assurance before saying "good night."

On Saturday morning, the clarion trumpet call of justice sounded in the conference room of the Multnomah Juvenile Detention Center. Gail's Gilbert's voice immediately took control of the gathering. Robb Gerrod and his mother sat at one table, with their representation. Todd Wallace and his dad, along with their lawyer sat on the other side. Kent Scott, his father and two attorneys filled a table, as did Dr. Bowen and his legal team. Jan was still in Multnomah County jail for her drug charge. The boys were wearing white coveralls with MCJD in orange letters on the back.

"Folks, we have with us the Prosecuting Attorney's office, the Director of Multnomah County Juvenile Detention, and an attorney from Family Services. We have before us a multimillion dollar crime, with liabilities beyond each family represented, to the School District, and the State Family Services. This is not a negotiation meeting, but a proposal. I am aware that attorneys are present with each family. That should make it easier. Not all perpetrators are equally guilty, but since you all contributed to the crime, you will all be offered the same opportunity. Robb, you tried to stop Kent's destructive behavior." One of the Scott's attorneys started to stand in protest. "Sit down!" she said commandingly, "I said this is not a negotiation. There is ample evidence that can be paraded out if you want to seek proof. We know every moment from the time that girl was dragged out of her room until we came to her aid in Tryon Creek Park. So knock off any legal bullshit until you hear the proposal." Her eyes stabbed at the other attorneys.

"These three young men will be tried as adults; with the evidence collected they will be found guilty of all charges and spend most, if not all, of their adult life in prison. Dr. Scott, you will face the same charges as an accomplice. Dr. Bowen you face three felony gun charges, and Jan, as instigator of the assault, is also charged with a major drug possession as a dealer. She will be paroled in forty years, if she's lucky. On top of these legal charges there is a waiting line of attorneys that want to bring personal injury law suits against you all, the school, and the state. As I said, this is a multi-million dollar crime." She took a deep breath. Todd sat silently, his head cradled in his hands. Kent's stony expression showed no feelings at all.

"The prosecuting attorneys' office is willing to mediate the charges in consideration for assistance to Sarah. She is our primary concern, and so our offer is a simple one. Each family will pay a settlement of one hundred thousand dollars to Sarah." A silence deeper than night held the room. "Plus," she went on, "an equal portion for your complicity Dr. Scott, and another for yours, Dr. Bowen, for three weapons charges. You will each share her hospital expenses, of approximately sixteen thousand dollars, and my billable fees of about the same. This settlement is for Sarah. Do you understand?" The parents could only look blank, but the attorneys nodded.

"Now for your compliance, the prosecutor will treat your sons' cases as minors, which means two years confinement maximum, and early release with good behavior. Dr.s Scott and Bowen, your charges will be dropped. Even Jan's drug charge will be treated as a minor, and she will have no adult record. Let me be clear about this, we are not interested in nickel and diming with you. It is everyone in, or the charge dates for all will be issued Monday morning. If you feel this is too inflexible, fine. Get ready for a lengthy public, expensive legal battle, and more prison time than you can imagine." She didn't want to overdo the point, but just to be sure they understood, she added, "by Monday morning nine o'clock I must have your answers, and payment will be received by the end of the month." A profound silence held the room. "Gentlemen, do you understand?" The attorneys all nodded reluctantly.

Before they got up to leave, Gail made one last point to the three young men in white. "Gentlemen, you are correct in thinking that it is not fair that the money that might have taken you through a prestigious college into some wonderful career is going to a thirteen year old foster child. It is definitely not fair to your family who saved it for you. And it is not fair that you so callously wasted it." She quietly folded her papers; they were finished. Robb was looking at the floor, quietly weeping.

5

Dr Tully

The settlement marked an entirely new era for Sarah. She had a room in Grace Tully's condo, which overlooked the Willamette River and on clear days had a marvelous vista of shining Mt. Hood. With Gail Gilbert's guidance they had placed her money in a certificate account that deposited interest every six months into her bank. It would accumulate more money than she could imagine. The Lake Oswego School District had delivered her High School diploma, along with a very tender letter from Superintendent Long, expressing his admiration for her scholastic talent, and apologizing for missing a great opportunity to share more of her learning journey. Her injuries were all healed and her hair was growing back, perhaps even more curly than before the attack. She was free from any obligation, and able to choose her own study path, which she did with enthusiasm.

Their initial living agreement was that Sarah would be a temporary guest with Dr. Tully. But since she was still officially a ward of Family Services and on their support account, a monthly check was paid for her care and keeping, including her school tuition.

"Sarah, I can't make money on this arrangement," Grace protested. "I can apply part of it to our food, and you can have a part for clothes and personal expenses, but that still leaves too much for rent." The counselor was obviously perplexed.

"Let's send some of it to Miss Linn," Sarah suggested. "I'll bet she could use some help." She thought it was a pure solution.

"Honey, the state wants that money to go for your support, to help you." She thought for just a minute and concluded. "I'll open another investment account for your education use. It will take a signature from both of us to get to the money, but it will have accountability." Over the next two years, that account could receive over $30,000.

They were seated at the breakfast table one morning, still trying to find their way through the new arrangement. Grace had said there were no rules, merely guidelines. "If you continue with the schedule you had with Miss Linn, I think you will get a lot accomplished every day. The alarm wakes us at 7:00 o'clock. O.K.?" It was a place to begin the covenant. When Sarah nodded, since she was always awake before that time, Grace continued. "I can usually make my bed, get ready for work and have a protein drink with fruit for breakfast, and be in my office by 8:30." Again she looked at Sarah for her understanding.

"I usually stop at the gym on Tuesday and Thursday for a while, and on Friday evening Eric likes to have supper with me and watch a video."

"Who's Eric?' Sarah asked with surprise.

"Eric is my . . ." Grace hesitated. "Eric French is my boyfriend. He's on church staff at Moreland Presbyterian."

With a bit of confusion, Sarah declared, "Your boyfriend is a minister? I didn't even know you had a boyfriend!" A playful smile lit her face. "Really? You have a boyfriend?" It was a testament to the professional nature of the relationship that had never given Sarah reason to consider her counselor's private life.

Grace nodded, enjoying the innocence of the moment. "I do, and some Sundays I like to join them for worship. Would you like to attend with us?"

The smile did not fade, but Sarah's head shook with a negative response.

"But you might really like it," she persisted. "There are lots of youth and the music is really great."

Again Sarah's head shook a quiet decline, but now the smile faded.

"Honey," Grace asked with tenderness, "have you ever been to a church?" Her eyes were warm, but searching this young woman's face.

"I did when I was little, but I really don't have any interest in religion. It's the cause of so much war and violence, especially when it is the source of so much stupid cursing and profanity. Radical people do mindless and terrible things because of it." She got up from the table and started toward her room. "I need to spend a lot of time today getting more classes at Multnomah." Grace would come to understand that this pattern of retreat to a safe refuge was Sarah's first line of defense.

In her room, Sarah created a new file:

My Book of Poems That Can't Be Burned!

I wrote such a beautiful poem for you,
'Bout rainbows and sunshine,
And dreams that come true.
But the hate ate it, oh what a mess!
That's not true, I must confess,
It was thrown in the fire, to my distress.

So, I wrote you another one, nearly as fair,
With humor and hope because I care.
If it can never be quite as great,
Blame the hate, for the one she ate!

Across the yard from yesterday
She sometimes comes to me,
A little girl just back from play
The child I used to be.
And still she smiles so wistfully
Once she has looked inside of me.
I wonder if she hopes to see
The great success I'm going to be.

Sarah couldn't understand her excitement. Yes, it was Friday evening, and Grace had said that Eric usually joined her for supper and a video. Sarah had chosen her tan Capri's and a pink blouse to wear. She looked into her dresser mirror again and decided to change into her bibs instead. Nervously, she sat down at her computer to play another game of chess, which she lost due to distraction. She kept wondering how she should talk with a minister. In fact, except for Dr. Bowen, she had little experience talking with men at all. Maybe she should change into her Capri's.

Her anxiety was put to rest when he arrived, wearing jeans and a Garfield Cat sweatshirt. He had blue eyes that she liked to look at, and brown curly hair about the same length as hers. Maybe the evening wouldn't be all bad. Sarah wondered how much coaching he had received about things not to talk about.

Grace had brought a big pizza home with a two liter bottle of root beer. It would take something pretty bad to mess up this dinner. At first they talked about their day, what they had accomplished, and the challenges they had handled. Sarah listened more than contributed. She was going to enjoy a bit more pizza.

He mentioned that his dad would celebrate his birthday soon, which invited Sarah to ask, "Is he still working? I mean, is he retired?" Inwardly she blanched at such an awkward attempt at adult conversation.

Eric smiled, happy for a chance to chat with her. "He works for the Shell Oil Company in Houston. He is a geologist." He wondered if another question might follow.

"What does a geologist do for the oil company?" Sarah's question was sincere, for her interest was genuine.

"Well," Eric wanted to keep the answer brief. "He graduated from USC with a degree in chemical engineering. But the geology world was just beginning to talk about plate tectonics and he was fascinated by it, so he studied for three more years and combined the degrees. Now, as a geologist, he helps the company know where to find new oil deposits, and as a chemical engineer, how to retrieve the most oil possible."

Sarah squinted a question, "What are plate tec . . . ."

"Plate tectonics is a theory that the earth's crust is divided into eight big parts that are moving very slowly." Eric wondered, "How had they gotten to this sort of discussion?" Since Sarah gave a slight understanding nod, he quickly changed the subject, asking about her on-line classes. All in all, each of them was pleased with the conversation.

The video was, "Blind Side," which Sarah thoroughly enjoyed, about a homeless guy who became a famous football player. She was especially impressed to see that Eric had tears in his eyes as well as she and Grace. They chatted about the meaning of the film and the message they took from it.

Finally, Sarah asked the question she had been mulling for a couple hours. "How do they know there are eight big plates that are moving, and where are they going?" Both Grace and Eric enjoyed the sudden return to their previous conversation.

"Isn't that a hard thing to understand?' he answered. "I believe it is because the scientists had a lot of bits and pieces of information that could only be explained in that theory."

"So they really don't know?" she said firmly.

"It is the only explanation that works in light of all the evidence," he replied. "And it solves some other mysteries about fossils and volcanoes. It is a pretty comprehensive theory."

Sarah had followed much of his answer until the word "comprehensive" gave her a whole new question. "So they really don't know?"

Grace asked, "Do you think there should be a clearer way to know something?"

"Well yes," came the response from Sarah. "We know that today's sunrise was at 6:40, and tomorrow it will be 6:42. We can see it on the clock."

"I completely agree," Eric said. "Because knowledge is the accumulated evidence or information we have collected and wisdom is the application of the information. But what happens if the power is off, or we set the clocks ahead an hour? Does that change the sunrise?" Eric had a playful smile, suggesting that he knew where the conversation was heading. "I think the only way we can know something is to have faith that our information is correct and will remain correct. We must have some faith in our clocks, or the electricity, or other people who tell us important things." He certainly had Sarah's attention.

Grace asked, "Is that why we call ignoring the evidence 'ignorance?'"

Eric nodded. "Of course, there is too much information for us to know, so the words of Socrates apply to any of us. He said, 'The beginning of knowledge is knowing that we don't know.'"

Sarah's frown was obvious as she asked, "Did you go to a lot of school?"

"Yes I did. My major at the University of Oregon was in psychology. That's where I met this fine lady. I received my Master's degree from Princeton where I studied the theology of faith development."

Grace nodded and added, "I studied psychology and personality disorders, and completed my doctorate in adolescent therapy."

"So you guys are both really smart and know a lot?" Sarah's question was meant to be a compliment.

"Yes we are," Eric said with a growing grin. "And I know that all calico cats are female."

Both listeners were quite still, trying to grasp the significance of his claim.

Grace joined in the smile, for she had known the subject would come up, just not when or how.

"What?" Sarah asked in confusion. "How can that be? If they were all mama cats, how could there ever be more kitties born?" Grace nodded in agreement.

"I'll tell you what," he bargained, "tomorrow morning let's go to the Paw's Shelter and ask them if they have any calico kitties. If they have any boys, I'll buy lunch at Red Robin. If they don't I'll buy a kitty for Sarah."

Sarah gasped at the proposal. They hadn't even talked about a kitty. She hadn't even imagined having her own. Suddenly she was very fond of this boyfriend of Grace, and wanted to know how he could make such a happy bet.

Grace reached over and patted her arm reassuringly. "It's O.K. He asked me first, and I said it would be a good idea, since you spend so much time alone. It would be fun to have someone to talk with. But you're going to be in charge of feeding her and cleaning the litter box every day." Her eyebrows arched in a question. Sarah's huge smile was all the affirmation needed. It was a great plan.

> Could it be, in this moonless night,
> Amid the sounds of fear and fright,
> There is a heart beating just for me,
> To take my love and set me free?
> Could there be someone brave and tall,
> To open my cage, once and for all?

Sarah opened her eyes before the dawn gave her room any light at all. Quietly, she made her bed and showered, pondered the proper wardrobe for their appointed activities, and still had enough time to finish two bookkeeping assignments before she heard Grace in the kitchen. With such an early start, they would surely accomplish wonderful things today.

Grace was lifting a pan of cinnamon rolls out of the oven as Sarah came into the kitchen. Instead of putting the pan down first and giving her a hug, Grace simply bumped first hips and then shoulders as a way of saying, "good morning." Sarah thought it was a perfect way to greet the day.

Before the sticky treats were cold, Eric arrived announcing that he had acquired a pet crate, soft towels for kitty blankets, a litter box, and dishes for food and water. Obviously, he was taking seriously the priority of the morning. "They open at 9:00 o'clock, and have several kitty offerings for us to see." Then adding as though he might be closing the sale, "and two of them are calico." Sarah wondered if it might not be obvious to Eric that she was already too wound up by the prospects of seeing cute kitties.

The lady at the Paws Shelter led them down a long aisle of cages holding eager cats. Some rubbed against the wire doors, and some reached their paws through, as though they could capture more attention. Sarah thought each was adorable. Grace was quiet, hoping to allow Sarah the choice; but Eric seemed to have something fun to say about every possibility.

He pointed to a fluffy white one saying, "She could be called 'Snowball' and do rich cat commercials." Sarah actually rolled her eyes in disbelief. He pointed to the next one that was light grey. "She could be called 'Smokey' and be a poster girl for home safety." Sarah stopped in the aisle and stared at him.

Grace asked, "Eric, are you going to try to name every kitty in here?" He got the hint, and offered no more names, but was still enjoying each new resident. Finally they found a calico. "I'll bet she's a female," he said proudly. When the attendant nodded, he went on as though he were the docent, "All calicos are female."

The lady corrected him, saying, "That is nearly right. There is very rarely a male calico, and he is always sterile." When Sarah asked for clarification, she went on to say, "Calico is not a breed of cat, but a color. It has to do with the chromosomes. Every female mammal has two X chromosomes, and the males have an X and a Y. Color is controlled by the X, so a male can only have one color with white highlights. The rare male calico has an extra X chromosome, but that only happens once in several thousand. In Dutch the calicos are called 'lapjeskat' or 'Patches Cat,' and the whole world over they are considered good luck." They walked on looking for the right kitty.

In the next to last cage, Sarah found her. She had a predominantly white face with orange ears and neck. Small black markings were on her front shoulders and tail. "I think this is the cutest kitty here, maybe in the whole world." It pressed up against the wire door, begging attention.

"What will you name her?" Eric asked, assuming the deal was already closed.

Sarah looked at Grace, who had been pretty quiet during the whole episode. Her warm smile was all the encouragement Sarah needed. They told the lady they would like to adopt this affectionate kitty, and were informed that half of the fee would be refunded to them if the kitty was spayed within six months. Sarah didn't understand completely what that meant. Her heart only told her that at any price this small carrier of affection was worth it. She thanked Eric for arranging this meeting, and Grace for agreeing to take in another shelter girl into her home.

As they were making their way back out to the car, Grace eased up beside Sarah and bumped her tenderly first on the hip, and then on the shoulder. It was pure affirmation as far as Sarah was concerned. All the way home they speculated on available names. Eric had most suggestions: "Lady Antebellum," "Guinevere," "Gloria" which was briefly considered, "Abigail," which was not, "Edie, which means happy," "Bella," "Kate," which had more favor than most, "Sadie, which is diminutive for Sarah." Finally they were home and the naming game could be postponed. After profusely thanking Eric and Grace again, Sarah took the kitten into her room and closed the door. They would work it out themselves.

When Grace knocked on Sarah's door sometime later, and asked if she was hungry for supper. Sarah eased the door open and asked, "Is Eric still here?"

"No he left quite a while ago. Are you hungry?" Grace knew that Sarah had not eaten since breakfast and must be ravenous. "Did you choose a name for your kitty?" Her question was light and hopeful.

"What do you think about the name 'Trixy?" Sarah asked. Before Grace could tell her it was a cute name, Sarah continued, "'Cause she is tri-colored and has two X chromosomes. It is not only what she is, but a playful name, don't you think?" Now she waited for an answer.

"It shows me that you have given it some serious thought, and if you two agree on it, I love it too." As Sarah came out of her room, Grace placed her arm across her shoulders and gave that bump "hug."

"Can you tell me how you feel about Eric, Sarah." The question was asked in the manner Sarah so appreciated. It was merely an invitation for information.

"I know he's trying to get me to like him," she answered. "Maybe he is trying too hard. And he really is funny." She was still for a bit before finishing her answer, "You know, he's a religious guy. I don't think he would be a radical, but some of them are, and that's who killed Miss Linn's husband. Religion sucks." Grace was a bit surprised with the intensity of Sarah's feelings.

Grace said softly, "He does want you to like him, because we will spend time together. I do know he is a very gentle person, and could not be a radical." The smile on her face was only affectionate.

When Sarah returned to her room, Trixy came out of her crate with a big stretch; she rubbed against her leg and crawled up on her lap as soon as Sarah sat down at the computer. It was a situation the new friends would come to accept as the normal place for each.

> Here's a comforting thought at the close of the
>   day,
> When I'm weary and lonely and dismayed,
> What grips my fragile young heart,

And bids it be more happy and glad?
What gets in my head and drives out the blues,
And finally thrills me through and through.
It's just a sweet memory that chants this tune:
"I'm glad I bumped shoulders with you!"

To me you are brave; to me you are strong.
Did you know there was one leaning long?
Did you know I listened and would gladly have
    heard,
And been cheered, by your simplest word?
Did you know that I longed for that smile on
    your face,
That you welcome me into your personal space?
Did you know that stronger and better I grew,
For I had merely bumped shoulders with you?

I'm glad that I struggle, I battle and strive,
For a place where I can more than survive;
I'm grateful for sorrows I meet with a grin,
What destiny sends, whether thick or thin.
I may not have wealth, nor ever be great,
But I know I shall always be true,
For I have in my life the courage you do,
When once I bumped shoulders with you.

The fall quarter came to an end; Sarah's GPA was a surprise to no one. She had a 4.0 across the board in the four classes she finished. The holidays crept by slowly. The only thing she could do was prepare lessons to be sent in after the winter quarter began,

In about the sixth lesson, she found a mistake in the textbook. Her addendum to the worksheet noted: "There seems to be a printing error on line 22 of page 83. The sub total of the first section should be $84,478,341. Instead of the printed $81,478,341. That $3 million error skews the answers on the following page line 18, 11% instead of the correct 19% increase, and page 86, line 11, the conclusion shown as a minimal increase (.03) to stockholders should be corrected to reasonable gain (.28). Is this an extra credit additional problem?" Submitted ST.

She sent in all her work as soon as the winter quarter began

Along with her previous classes, she added a fifth, Development Investments and Risk Management. It required her to have an ETRADE account, which meant she must have a social security number. Gail Gilbert assured her she had received one when she was a baby. Together they made the necessary application and Sarah bought her first stock with a required $100 initial purchase. She wanted to be conservative so she chose shares of Chevron Oil.

She set herself a daily schedule of breakfast with Grace, emails to Mo, Miss Linn and occasionally Gail Gilbert, then two lessons in each subject. She anticipated a greater accomplishment than other students who might need to be employed as well as give their attention to school. She would check the stock market, noting changes in her favorite stocks, and also played at least two chess games with other on-line opponents. Her win column began to out-distant her losses by double.

It was typical for her to receive copies of her lessons with errors noted and suggested correction, although that rarely happened. So when she received an email from the TA addressed to Sarah Thoms, ST, she had no idea of its content. "Way to go ST! Dr Morton applauds your discovery. We have used this lesson from University of Phoenix for the past year, and no other student has caught the error. You should be in our accounting program. It is superior to book-keeping for sure. There is no such thing as a gold star for a 4.0 student, so know that you are on the fast-track for Dr Morton's next phase, and UP will print a correction to their lesson series. Way to Go! Submitted MW"

Sarah printed the email and placed it in her memory book.

Time seemed irrelevant save for the accumulation of lessons submitted. The only way Sarah was aware of time passing was that Trixy was no longer a little kitty. She was becoming a long-legged teenager. Grace carried her, in her crate, to the vet. When Trixy came home her tummy was shaved, and she had stitches. Sarah remembered how unpleasant those can be, so Trixy had special care until they came out. Her fourteenth birthday was not a big celebration, but Sarah was grateful that Grace had brought a DQ cake home, and invited Eric to share it with them. As usual, when he brought up the conversation of the church, Sarah excused herself early to retire to her bedroom and studies. She just didn't trust a minister, or thoughts of God.

Winter rain changed to spring rain, although no one could tell the difference. Leaves were greening on the trees and the Rhododendrons were in glorious bloom when she received another email from MW: "Way to go ST! Usually you must contact the Admin Office to get your grades, but they are so outstanding I feel obliged to tell you that I have never seen any student match your scores. Your promptness and dependability are also far above expectations. I would like to share a cup of coffee with you, to have a face to go along with this marvelous academic work. Submitted MW"

She printed this email also for her memory book. First, she showed it to Grace asking, "Is he inviting me on a date?"

Grace grinned and said, "I think he is praising the lessons you have turned in." Then bumping her shoulder, she added, "But he does sound like he'd like to meet you, doesn't he?" They both giggled. The year she had shared with Grace had made them feel like family. But when Sarah thought about it she wasn't sure if it was mother to daughter, or as sisters that had grown so close.

With the end of the winter quarter Sarah was pleased to see that her stock investment had done well. With Grace's agreement, she took a thousand dollars out of her investment account and purchased eleven shares of beef futures. She had read that China was increasing its consumption of beef as their economy flourished. It seemed like an appropriate venture. As her class on business law came to an end she signed up for tax law, and added the H and R Block tax preparation class.

She hadn't expected it, but when another email arrived from MW, she opened it immediately: "Hi ST. I was glad to see you signed up for another heavy load of classes. When am I going to get that cup of coffee? I'll be watching for your reply. Have a great day. MW"

Sarah thought he was pretty bold, and the more she thought about it, the less likely she was to reply. She did print it and add it to her book, however.

A month later, she received another email: "Hi ST. You are doing remarkably well, far ahead of everyone else on-line. I don't know how you are managing such a strong load. Well done! I am finishing as Teacher Assistant here at Multnomah, and will enroll at Reed to complete my computer science degree. Since MCC closes for the summer, you might want to use my personal email if you want to continue these conversations: mwall@comcast.net. And look into the University of Phoenix program to keep going. By transferring your credits from here, your degree could be finished in less than two years. Wow! You are terrific. I'm only sorry we didn't share that coffee."

"One last thing, we get requests regularly from folks who need a bookkeeper at less than industry prices. If you think you might be interested in about four hours a week, contact Jon Dalton in Salem at 503-555-2793. He has a small cherry orchard west of town. Good luck in all your endeavors. Your admirer MW" There was much to consider in that email, not the least being the signature, "Your admirer." It contained a host of possibilities, and was, of course, copied and added to the memory book.

When she called Mr. Dalton, she learned that he was in poor health but wanted to keep the orchard operating. Before her death, his wife, Dot, had taken care of "the paperwork." He needed someone to keep track of orchard expenses, write paychecks for the seasonal help, and pretty much run his personal checkbook too. Even though Sarah had never written a check, she said she could take care of all that, but when invited to come to Salem for the application, she informed him that she lived in Portland and would get back to him after speaking with her attorney. It sounded very impressive. Actually Mrs. Gilbert would need to give her approval before Sarah could become involved with any job, especially one she was not sure she could legally do.

> Why fear the future, tender heart?
> Why dread the future's way?
> We only need to do our part
> Today, dear child, today.

> The past is written! Close the book
> On pages weary with dismay;
> Within the future don't look,

Sweet child, but live today, today.

In this grand hour, destiny is traced;
Now we must obey;
To make our world a better place,
So live today, today!

By the time she had an employment agreement the cherry picking season was complete. Sarah was certain Mr. Dalton had broken several laws by paying his laborers in cash at the end of each day. She wondered how many of them had green cards, or social security numbers. She was determined to do it correctly next year. Mrs. Gilbert had asked for a one year contract for Sarah. It was reviewable and new figures would be established by her performance. In the large box of information he had sent her, Sarah found receipts for pruning, spraying pesticide, and ground grooming. She started a calendar of contacts. Daily email exchange also guaranteed she would not get behind in the few payments that she had to make. It was a fun first job.

The summer brought three very major developments. First, Sarah surprised herself by sending an email to MW. The following series of printed copies were added to her Memory book:

"Hi MW, remember me? I took your advice and was able to get a summer set of classes at University of Phoenix. The change was easy, just as you predicted. How are you doing with Reed College? Did you get the classes you wanted? I'd be happy to hear from you. ST Sarah."

"Great to hear from you, ST Sarah. I'm glad you are in with UP. Yes, I am all set for September at Reed. A couple of my classes did not make it in the transition, so I either have two really hard years ahead, or maybe I'll plan on an extra year and finish my Master's while I'm at it. Maybe you can tell me how you manage to do so much. Let's stay in touch, MW"

"Hi MW. Hey, am I talking to a Mary or a Mike? I don't know a thing about you. In answer to your question, I have a plan. You know, 'Plan your work and work your plan.' I just plan to never get behind. I know I can do two lessons per class per day, so at the end of the week, I have done ten times as much as the average student will do. I watch no TV. In fact, I don't have much else to do except chess, so it's all school, all day. But I did get the job with Mr. Dalton. So far that's only about an hour a week, however. Pretty easy stuff. Thanks for answering. It's nice to have someone to chat at. ST, Sarah."

"You know, when I read your email I thought I might be talking with a nun, St. Sarah. Are you? My name is Max Wall. If I say it too fast, it sounds like Maxwell. I have an older brother and sister. Dad is a Civil Engineer with the city, and mom teaches cello, and is in the Portland Symphony. Do you have a sig other? Are you married? I know you are a very special person. Have a very special day. MW"

"I don't like 'buzz-bonics' so I refuse to write LOL, but you did make me laugh out loud! I'm fourteen years old, a charge of Family Services, living with my counselor. It has been real complicated. What sports or hobbies do you like?" Your friend, Sarah."

"Now, I am speechless. You seem much more mature and confident than the women I usually chat with, although there aren't that many. I have been a real game-head. For a time I thought I would try to develop computer games. Now I see that programming is the future, and design the challenge, so I am trying to be more serious about the computer. How about you? What hobbies or sports do you like? Do you attend a church? YF2 (Oops, I meant to say, 'your friend too!') ☺ Max"

Sarah was unsure why she was less than enthused to send another email to Max. Had she given it a bit more thought she would have understood that the subject of religion had raised its irritating head again.

The second major development to take place that summer was Eric proposed to Grace! He did it quite romantically, Grace reported. They were at dinner at the Chart House, with a lovely patio table overlooking the valley. Eric had asked the manager before-hand if the ring box could be delivered with dessert. When it was time, Eric got down on one knee and asked her if she would "grace" the rest of his life, as his wife. "Wasn't that tender?" The wait-staff all applauded, as did the other guests on the patio. Grace said she felt like it was right out of a storybook. She was thrilled, and of course, said, "Yes!"

Sarah realized that the announcement also signaled the end of their living arrangement. When she and Grace talked about it a while later, Sarah said cheerily that their agreement had been for a temporary visit. It would be time for both of them to have a new situation. Interestingly, it was also Sarah who suggested that they compile a list of options. They had lots of time. The wedding was set for August of next summer.

The third major thing that summer happened on the Saturday after the 4th of July. Sarah was with Grace in the food pavilion at the mall when an angry voice said right behind them, "Look at this, rotten lambs, out where the wolves can get them, again." Sarah looked around and recognized Dr. Scott, Kent's dad.

"Why don't you stay under a rock, where you belong?" His voice was slurred and his motion unsteady. Grace recognized intoxication when she saw it. She started to stand to address him. But suddenly he lurched, or staggered at her, his hands groping threateningly. "Sit down, you brainy bitch." It was the only words he would utter.

As Grace fell backwards over her chair into the folks that were seated next to them, there was a groan, or a cry, or perhaps a growl from Sarah, who had launched herself at the attacker. "Not again, ever!" was all she said. Her hands grasped the shoulder of his shirt, and pushed him away in a violent spiral that ended when he crashed into the cart of trays and dirty dishes. His head bounced off the cart and thudded on the floor where he lay still in the chaos. A mall security guard burst on the scene as the dentist began to shout obscenities. Accusations and threats were flying fast and very furiously. Grace rose up on her elbows to look incredulously at Sarah, who had learned self-defense in her yoga class after all.

City police finally arrived, took statements, but because of the dentist's insistence, backed up by his obvious injuries, Sarah was charged with assault and given a court date to tell it to the judge.

Eleven days later, accompanied by Gail Gilbert they appeared before District Court Judge, Wesley Jenson, who had been a partner in the law firm where Gail worked. There was a side-bar to fill in some of the history that would affect this complaint. The Judge finally said, "Let's do this correctly."

"Sarah Thoms, you have been charged with aggravated assault with the intent to do bodily harm, how do you plead?" She was still so he asked a second time. Sarah listened to the Judge's question again.

"Miss Thoms, how do you plead to these charges?" The room was silent, filled to overflowing with charged anticipation.

In a trembling voice just above a whisper, she replied, "Guilty, sir, Your Honor. I am guilty, of trying to protect Dr. Tully and myself from his attack. I'm guilty of defending myself." She thought for a heartbeat, then added one more word, "finally."

After two witnesses verified the defense account, the judge dismissed the case. They later learned that Dr. Scott had a high enough blood alcohol level to receive a citation for public intoxication, which only added to the misery of his failed marriage and bankruptcy. Sarah felt something had changed between her and Dr. Tully, however. She was afraid that her violent reaction was not what the counselor would have chosen, but there was a quiet respect for what she did. As they walked out of the court house, there was no conversation, just a bump, followed by another.

The day after Labor Day a knock on the door startled Sarah. She was still thinking about the encounter at the mall. Since there were very few people who visited this condo, she was on her guard. When she opened the door she met a representative of the University of Phoenix who asked if he could have a few minutes to verify her application.

"I've already completed a summer quarter," Sarah replied defensively. "What needs to be verified?"

"May I have your date of birth?" he asked, smiling to forgo any further offense.

"I was born March 3rd, 1995," Sarah answered, but she still barred the doorway, preventing him from coming in.

"Do you have some documentation to confirm that, Miss Thoms?" His features remained friendly, but Sarah was seriously offended by him.

"Yes, I do," she answered softly. "If you will just wait out here for a minute," she began closing the door. "I will contact my attorney who will be here in about fifteen minutes." The door closed and she locked it quickly.

She heard him say, "Wait, couldn't we . . ." Sarah called her legal counsel, again.

When Gail Gilbert arrived she found a frustrated man waiting outside the condo door. He tried to explain that he was merely verifying the application information, which Gail saw as a complete subterfuge. "You have one more chance to tell me who you are, and what you are doing here, or we call the police." Her tone, and the cell phone in her hand, made it clear that she meant business.

"I'm Taylor Pierce from the Oregon City office of the University of Phoenix," he handed her his card. "I'm here to verify," the man said with a twinge of panic, "that Miss Thoms has done the work submitted herself, she alone with no assistance from others. I would like to be able to examine her computer, and see her workspace."

Mrs. Gilbert asked, "And you were going to pull off this sneak inspection under the guise of verifying her date of birth?" She shook her head in disbelief. "You have set back the University's credibility by more than you will ever know. "I'll tell you what, Mr. Weasel, I will attend your 'verification,' protecting my client's interest, and billing the University for my time; that's $500 an hour, and we have already used 36 minutes. Behind her frown Gail was smiling with joy. Sarah was as good as everyone believed she could be. Her first round work with the University was so good, they had to send an investigator to make sure she was doing it herself. "Way to go Sarah!"

Summer gave way to a warm Autumn as the leaves began to turn golden. For Sarah it was just another series of subjects, plowing through the assignments. The only break she permitted herself was the training sessions with Trixy. Sarah had obtained a clicker, which became the command for the calico cat. With one click, Trixy learned to go into her crate for a treat. Two clicks meant to jump onto Sarah's lap, for a treat, of course, and three clicks meant, "Find the treats." There were always three treats hidden in the bedroom. "Who said cats are dumb?"

6

THE PLOT

One drizzly Sunday afternoon in October, Sarah was playing a chess game with Max, each with a chess board in front of them, texting the moves back and forth. She smiled as he brought out his queen in a power move. She blocked with her bishop and when he moved his queen back two spaces, Sarah knew that she had her trapped. "You lose her in three moves," she challenged. "No way," he responded, swinging his knight into the battle. Regrettably for him, Sarah moved her own knight, forking his king and queen. "Check." Max was frustrated to be so constricted, he had to move the king instead of capturing the knight. Sarah captured the queen, saying, "in three moves it will be checkmate." As Max studied the board he was sure she was right, but hoped he could find a way out. He couldn't. "Can you call me?" Sarah texted. "It's important."

When Max called her cell phone, Sarah told him she had a question that might not be a safe thing to do. Of course she had his interest.

"Max, do you think you can get information from the Department of Corrections?" The question caught him completely by surprise.

"I'm assuming you mean more information than is publicly available to anyone." What in the world could she possible want with that sort of information, he wondered.

"I would really like to know the status of three young men who were sentenced to Juvenile Detention about a year and a half ago. They must be about ready to parole." Her heart beat more quickly; it had been a long while since she even thought about them.

"It sounds like this is something you think might be clandestine, on the down low, huh?" He was already thinking of ways this might be done. "Are you going to tell me why we are interested in them?"

Sarah grinned at his use of the word "we." "I can't tell you a little without telling it all, and that is uncomfortable for me. The minimum I can tell you is that they hurt me, and I am afraid of them being released," she said crafting the truth. "They are why I am living with Dr. Tully, my counselor." That was true.

"Well, let me see if I can find a small police station that leaves its computers on at night. If I can get in, I might be able to then access Corrections without raising suspicions." It was almost like a computer game, and he loved to play. "I'll get back to you. Thanks for the chess lesson."

When they hung up, Sarah thought about how nice it was to have a male friend. Not a boyfriend, mind you." She smiled at the thought.

On Wednesday evening she was startled when her cell phone rang. It was after nine o'clock, and she was ready for bed. "Hi," Max said. "It's late but the only time I can use the lab computers without prying eyes. I think I found a portal. The Sandy PD leaves their computers on at night. Unless there is someone there looking at the screen, I can hack us into Corrections. Who do you want to know about?"

Her voice was small and hesitant as she told him, "Todd Wallace," she said the names slowly, "Robb Gerrod, and Kent Scott." Then she added, "And if you can find anything about Janice Bowen, I would welcome that information too."

Max said it was like a Mission Impossible. "Can you tell me any more about these folks, like driver's license numbers?"

"No, I don't have any of that. Maybe next time I can fill in some blanks, if you get some good intel." She tried to go with terminology of the game, to make it less frightening, She wasn't sure why she was asking about another connection with these people.

It wasn't until the following Saturday night that Max called again. He reported a circuitous route, but one, he was sure, was undetected. "I read their files. Are you ready to write?" he asked. "Janice Bowen was released after serving only three months, it looks like. There is no evidence of education. If I understand their references, she turned over on her supplier, but I don't think she's in witness protection. Nasty lady. Todd Wallace got out last June. He got a GED while incarcerated, and is now in the Marine Corps, Camp Lejeune. Robb Gerrod also got a GED, and is now at Boise State University. He must have had some kind of help, because he is a walk-on football player. Kent Scott was set to be released on his eighteenth birthday in June. But he was a bad boy twice and got an additional nine months tacked on, so he is in the general population penitentiary in Salem. I guess that means he will get out in March or April. Is that what you wanted to know?"

There was silence for several seconds before Sarah sighed, "Yes, that's what I wanted. Thank you for doing that for me." Then she told him about her journey from Salem to Miss Linn's, to the Bowens, and finally here to Dr. Tully's. She stopped to weep a couple times along the way, and Max knew that his heart was completely hers. He had never been allowed to walk such a painful path with such a brave woman, let alone a fourteen year old one.

"Now what are we going to do with this," Max asked.

"Nothing," she sighed. "I just wanted to know the rest of the story, as they say."

"May I look a little deeper?" Then he quickly added, "If I don't get caught that is."

"I don't want to take their place behind bars," Sarah said. "Please be careful. I want to play chess with you again." Her tone had returned to happy and playful.

> Please don't tell the Bee she can't fly
> Her body's too round, not fit for the sky.
> Please don't tell her she can't fly;
> No Use flappin' no good to try.
> Her tiny little wings would just ruin it,
> 'Cause she's so busy, just doin' it.
>
> Success is failure turned inside out,
> The silver tint of the clouds of doubt,
> And you never can tell how close you are,
> It may be near when it seems so far;
> So stick to the fight when you're hardest hit,
> It's when things seem worst that you mustn't
>   quit.

Sarah realized that the University of Phoenix was not bound to the traditional school quarter program. She had completed a full term in less than six weeks. It affirmed her progress and if anything, caused her to kick it up a notch. She could send in twelve assignments a week instead of the ten she had been doing.

Two important things happened before the month of November began: Gail Gilbert paid another surprise inspection on Sarah's computer. She came unannounced with an IT person to check her history data.

With arched eyebrows, she said, "It seems someone has been investigating our friend Miss Bowen. Her name popped up on the DEA watch list, and I was contacted as the opposing counsel." She put her hand on Sarah's shoulder. "Honey, I don't think you had anything to do with that, but I'm keeping a record to make sure we stay squeaky clean." Sarah had an unfamiliar twinge in the pit of her stomach, a guilty conscience that hinted a different conclusion.

It only took a moment to view the record pages of school assignments, and the only emails on the hard drive were to Miss Linn, Mo, MW, Gail, and Mr. Dalton in Salem. When Gail asked about the emails to MW, Sarah explained he was the Teacher Assistant from Multnomah Community College. They had played a lot of chess together. A couple random looks verified her claim, but Gail had a sweet smile. Even in this restricted living situation, Sarah had managed to make contact with a fellow. Sweet! At any rate there were no unexplainable computer contacts. She thanked Sarah and they left. Sarah didn't know if she should weep, or contact Max. Finally, she did neither, she had done nothing wrong.

The second important thing began with a phone call from Mr. Dalton. His weak voice reported that he had fainted in church and was in the hospital for some tests. "Sarah, could I get you to drive out to the house and make sure that Winnie, my pooch, and Brandy the Donkey are in the barn. If you can do that I will be glad to pay for gas, and our usual hourly rate. I don't have anyone I can ask, but you." There was a weariness that Sarah hadn't heard in his voice before. "It would be great if you can feed Winnie with a can of food from the pantry. And toss some fresh hay in the manger for Brandy, and she would love you forever if you give her a scoop of oats from the bin. Do you think you could do that for me?" When Sarah said she would get someone to drive her, he added, "There is a key to the kitchen door under a fake rock by the steps. You have taken a load off my mind." In fact, his voice sounded stronger. She got his room number at Salem General so she could report back when the task was finished.

She asked Grace, who thought it would be a fun adventure on a blustery day, if Eric drove them. With his GPS, there was no challenge in finding the place in the Eola Hills. As they drove in the long driveway, Eric pointed out the faded paint on the white board fence. "I'll bet in its time, this was a marvelous farm," he said.

A grey and white dog jumped off the porch, barking at their arrival. As soon as they stopped, however, it returned to the shelter of the porch, where it could survey these strangers. A donkey was braying from the side of the barn. It too was protesting the arrival of newcomers, or being left in the rain. Sarah gazed at the unlit house with a big porch, and said, "I feel like I have been here before." They looked at the rows of cherry trees with bare branches. "It seems spooky familiar."

The two chores were finished in a few minutes. They found a blanket on the floor of the barn. Winnie seemed to be comfortable there, after her supper. Brandy the donkey was happily chewing the last of the oats. They left the doors slightly ajar so the two critters could come and go as they needed. "I love this place," Sarah said as they were leaving. "Wouldn't it be fun to fix it all up?" She had no idea what a huge task that would be.

They stopped at Salem General Hospital to meet Mr. Dalton, and report that the chores had been cared for. The thin man on the bed had a broad smile. "If I had known this is all it would take to get to meet you folks, I would have passed out months ago." He was holding Sarah's hand like a family member. "I'll try not to abuse the privilege, but if this could be an occasional visit, I would be glad to pick up the tab."

On the way back to Portland the idea was framed to take a Thanksgiving meal to his house in the orchard. It almost made Sarah giddy in anticipation. As soon as they got back to Grace's, Sarah thanked Eric for driving, and wrote him a check from Mr. Dalton's account; then she went into her room to try to get ready for tomorrow's assignments. But the memory of the old barn smell, and feel of stability, was such a pleasant recollection she couldn't think of anything else. Being Sunday night, she also anticipated a chess game with Max. She texted, "Who gets white? Oh, yes, you lost the last game, your move."

On Thanksgiving morning, it had taken three boxes to carry the feast to the farm. All the traditional elements were included: turkey, of course, with cranberry preserves, potatoes, mashed with crispy bacon, sweet yams with marshmallows, cranberry salad, a Waldorf salad, rolls, and both pumpkin and pecan pie. The table had been adorned with linen cloth, and lovely china, with crystal glasses and candlestick holders. The scene could have easily been from a Norman Rockwell painting.

They sat in the glow of gluttony in the dining room. "Dotty would have loved that dinner. I'm glad we used her good dishes, and especially glad for having new friends at our table." Jon's words were thick with emotion. "I can't tell you how thankful I am to have you all here. You are far more than gracious." He gazed into each face, lingering on Sarah's.

Mr. Dalton had asked several interested questions about Eric's work at the church and Grace's special counseling activities. It wasn't until later that they all realized he had been working his way toward Sarah.

Finally he said, "The doctors tell me my old heart is getting much weaker. They don't want me living alone way out here in the hills. They think I should sell the place and move into town, maybe a retirement place. At least they want me to hire a home health care nurse who will look in on me a couple times a week." He looked at Sarah, and then at Grace.

"I have a proposal to make that you will have to decide is in or out of line." Looking at Grace he said, "I'd like to hire Sarah to be a housekeeper as well as my bookkeeper." He shifted his gaze toward Sarah. "I'd like it to be part time to full time, whatever she can do legally, or with her school." Having said it, he sort of relaxed, showing how difficult it had been for him to mount the courage to ask the question.

Before Sarah could say anything, Grace responded, "What a kind offer, Jon. There are several things we would need to explore before she can answer. As you say, I'm not sure if a minor can be employed more than twenty hours a week, and transportation would be a challenge. Let me chat with her attorney to explore the possibilities before we answer. Would that be a satisfactory next step? Her smile was radiant for she could see the joyous expression on Sarah's face as well.

"It would be an answer to prayer for me," Jon said nodding in agreement. "I know it would be a reach, but I'm praying real hard that it can happen." Sarah's smile faded a bit with the notion of prayer. Why do people always want to throw that in?

Grace and Sarah washed and dried the dishes, with little conversation. There was suddenly a large agenda to consider. They loaded the leftovers in Jon's refrigerator, confident they would feed him for three or four days. After a final visit to the barn to feed Winnie and Brandy, who relished an apple treat, they were on their way back to Portland. Even though the subject was not mentioned again, it was the main thing on their minds, all the way home. Sarah had so much to share with Max!

It was nearly two weeks before Gail Gilbert set an appointment with Grace and Sarah. When they arrived at her office, Sarah was surprised to see the attorney for Family Services as well. Something was up! She had a foreboding that this meeting might not go as well as she hoped.

As expected, Gail began by saying that some of the time things don't work out the way we expect. She said that her office had been in negotiation for ten days with Sarah's mother. The words were like ice on her skin. "We played a mean trick on her," Gail admitted. "She has had a rough decade of drug treatment and incarceration. We sent her a letter saying that you have incurred significant school expenses, and wondered if she could accept responsibility for them." She allowed the improbability of that request to sink in. "Since you are already a ward of the court, would she rather pay the balance of your tuition expenses, which are sizable," a wicked smile turned up the corners of her mouth, "or would she sign a relinquishment document, allowing you to be adopted." That last word exploded inside Sarah's mind! "Adopted?" "By whom?"

"It's only a piece of paper that allows the state to investigate the possibility of establishing a permanent living condition for you." She looked at Sarah for several seconds, giving them all time to catch their breath. "You have had a very tumultuous decade as well, Honey. This may be a wonderful final chapter of your journey with the State of Oregon."

"We have had several conversations with Mr. Dalton, on your behalf," she continued, "and conducted extensive background checks. We have no reservation as to his integrity or dependability. I explained to him the problems of hiring you as his housekeeper. At age fourteen we do not put anything beyond your capabilities. But your priority is school, not house-keeping, besides it wouldn't be legal. The challenge of transportation is going to be in front of us for another year. Regardless of your brilliance, you can't have a driver's license until you are sixteen. And he will not qualify as a foster home prospect." She took a deep breath,

"But he could adopt you, taking full legal responsibility for your care and protection. There is certainly no law against that, and in light of your current situation, it is the most realistic option for your protection and continued educational opportunities." There, it was said. All eyes were on Sarah, who didn't lose her smile.

Gail added, "Our proposal is that you have a ninety day trial period to see if living so far from city facilities and conveniences, in relative isolation with a senior citizen," her smile widened, "all be it a very sweet one, would work. The state will continue to support you by direct deposit into your account, but at the end of that period, if you are both supportive of the adoption, all financial support will end. What questions do you have?"

Sarah's was the first. "Does he agree to the proposal?"

"Sarah, he was ecstatic! He has no heirs, so you would become his daughter in the truest sense. He has a lot of love to give. But, let's be clear," the cheeriness left her voice; "he is in poor health and might be a financial liability with no medical insurance other than Medicare, that could consume everything."

There were several questions about the mechanics of transporting Sarah to the farm, providing adequate furnishings and connectivity, establishing a program of accountability for her to check in with both Grace and Gail daily. Finally Sarah asked, "When can we start?"

"How about two weeks, on January first? That's the day Mr. Dalton is hoping for. He said it would be the best New Year ever." Sarah gave both Grace and Gail an uncharacteristic hug, thanking them for all their work. In one respect this would be a massive change, but on the other hand, everything in her life had felt temporary. This felt solid and permanent, and a simple thing to do.

7

An Understanding

On Friday night, when Eric brought calzones and spumoni ice cream for supper, Grace was explaining the events of the week. She said she would miss Sarah's wonderful presence, but applauded the decision, knowing it was the very best thing for her. Eric chimed in brightly that if Sarah would attend the Christmas Eve Candle Light Service, he would drive her to the farm. Grace tensed at the offer, but Sarah became like ice.

"No thank you, Eric," she said holding in her emotions that wanted to erupt. "I'll get someone else to drive." She started to get up.

"Wait, Sarah. I didn't mean to offend you. I just think you would enjoy the service so much." Eric realized he was on a very slippery slope.

Sarah sat back down, with a tight smile that represented no joy. "I believe you meant well, Eric, and I'm not angry at you. I'm just sick of the sound of how good religion is." She took in a deep breath, and began to release pent-up emotions that had been smoldering for too long. "The night of my assault," her voice trembled, "I prayed." Her chin quivered and tears began to run down her cheek. "I screamed for God's help!" As she replayed that awful scene, her voice rose in pitch and volume, and her hands curled into tense fists. "I pleaded for God's mercy as hard as anyone can beg." She struggled to regain control. After several aching moments of silence, she asked, "Where was that loving Savior?" She rose and headed for her room. "No thanks, I'll pass on the candles."

Max had texted her earlier asking if she wanted to play chess, and yes, he would play white again. "Pawn to king four."

They were both surprised at the brevity of the game. She trapped his king in a rook barrage. "Check mate!" Then she asked him to call her.

They talked for over an hour while she told him the details she remembered from the assault, especially her panicked prayer. She had finally, tonight, realized the shift from her childish views of religion to this near pathologic resentment of feeling abandoned by God. There had been no response to her passionate cries for help, just pain and fury.

"What did you expect, Kiddo?" Max asked. "Did you think Captain America would sweep in with his powerful holy shield, and knock them on their ass?" Max had never been this blunt.

"I don't know what I thought, I just . . . . I just know that it didn't happen. There was no help." Once again Sarah was struggling with her tears.

"I really, really like you, so I don't want to say anything to make you angry or sound like we are having a dispute, O.K.?" He was quiet until she said, "O.K."

"O.K., if God couldn't stop the assault because these three or four arch villains had decided to wreck their lives and yours, it seems to me that the prayer started to be answered by the cell phone that stayed in your bibs, and Miss Linn answered, and knew where you were and called for help. It continued when that lady police officer talked to you and went to the Bowen's house, believing in your story. It got even stronger when the doctors and nurses made you comfortable and patched your wounds. Then it was answered more by Dr. Tully pitching in for you, willing to share, her home for your safety. Wow, it got massively serious when your attorney faced off against those guys. She is one bad-ass angel, kind of a Michael-sized sword wielder." Sarah was smiling too much at Max's description of diminutive Gail Gilbert to take any offense in the conversation. "I think I might even have been part of the come-to-the-assistance-of-Sarah plan. I don't know why I wanted to have a cup of coffee with you, but I sure did, and still do, by the way. I don't even drink coffee. And then there is Mr. Dalton; he's like a saintly prophet of God, offering you love, and sanctuary. The argument could be made that all of us are part of a picture, a mosaic, of God's mercy, answering your prayer."

Sarah realized somewhere in the conversation that they were talking about God in a way that made sense, yet didn't make her angry. "Thank you Max, for listening, and giving me a picture I hadn't even thought about." She was quiet for several seconds. "That may be the most helpful lesson I've ever . . . ." Her voice trailed away leaving the thought unfinished. "That is a wonderful gift."

"Hey Max," her voice brightened as she quickly changed the subject. "Do you have time later in the week to drive me to the orchard?" Sarah had been thinking it wasn't a farm, but an orchard. "I'd love to get some Arby sandwiches to take lunch to Mr. Dalton, and introduce you to him. He's old enough to be my grandfather, but he will be my dad! I'll pay for gas."

"Do you think you can find it again?" Max was teasing only a little bit.

"Hey, this is going to be my home," she replied boldly. "I could find it in the dark." But she still printed the Map Quest turn by turn directions for security. Turn right onto SR 221, 2.3 miles. Turn left on Orchard Heights Rd, 4.3 miles to Doakes Ferry Rd. proceed straight 1.3 miles. Turn left on Morningside Rd 1.6 miles. 13773 Morningside Rd on the right hand side. It would be the first of very many trips Max was to make in the future.

Sarah's heart skipped a beat when she heard the knock on the door. "What would he look like?" she asked herself. When the door swung open, she was delighted. Max was just a bit taller than her, with dark brown eyes and a dazzling smile that was playfully crooked. His well-trimmed curly blonde hair had an athletic look. The fact that he had finished high school a year early added to his youthful appearance; he had just turned eighteen. They awkwardly shook hands at the meeting, which made Sarah like him even more. He offered her a bright pink Gerber Daisy. It was a perfect meeting!

"My car is mom's old Honda Accord, but it is really dependable."

Sarah smiled happily, they were beginning an adventure.

8

THE ORCHARD

By moving day, Grace had convinced Sarah to accept Eric's offer to move her boxes in his Subaru, which had enough room for her three boxes of clothes, another of books and computer, and Trixy's crate. Her worldly possessions were sparse by any measure. It was a chilly overcast day, but dry.

"I wasn't sure what the food supply was here," Grace said, with a bit of tears in her eyes. This parting was more painful than she had expected, even though it was the right thing to do. "So I picked up some groceries, bread and peanut butter, some instant oatmeal, some snack crackers, fruit and . . ." her voice trembled, "and some of your favorite pasta dinners."

Sarah found herself in the unaccustomed position of encouraging her counselor. "Thank you, that was super thoughtful. Jon can drive us to the store. It's about fifteen minutes down the hill." Then leaning close to Grace's ear she whispered, "I'm more concerned about the one bathroom." She arched her eyebrows. "But I am sure we will work it out. This is going to be great; different, but great!" A delightful chapter of her life was closing.

There were hugs around as Grace and Eric got ready to leave.

As they stood in the driveway, watching the Subaru leaving, Sarah looked at Jon and asked, "Is this weird for you?"

Before he could answer she said, "Yeah, it is for me too. But I think we can work it out, don't you?" She remembered the times at Miss Linn's; when she had to help new girls adjust to the new house.

"I think I should ask you, what would you like me to call you?"

When he grinned and raised his eyebrows, he answered, "What feels less weird?"

"Well, I don't want to keep calling you 'Mr. Dalton', and 'Jon' feels like we are less than family." Her smile was contagious. "It is still hard for me to grasp that you will be my father. Would it be alright with you if I call you 'Dad'?"

"I think that would be spectacular," he nearly giggled. Then becoming a bit more serious, he added, "And if I accidently call you Dotty, please forgive me. She was the only woman in my life for over fifty years, and I love her a lot."

Sarah hooked her arm inside his, giving him an "invisible" hip bump. "We'll work it out just fine, Dad. Can we walk through the orchard? I would love to see it."

He called Winnie to come along with them, and wondered how long it had been since his heart was this happy. They followed a faint path along the north property line. When they came to a brush line, Sarah could make out what was left of an old wooden fence. They turned west, looking out over the distant valley. "This property", he said, pointing into the brush, "was for sale about ten years ago. A winery wanted to buy it, and my place, but I refused, and the deal died, so did the owner of this. I think his kids live in Texas."

Sarah asked, "How much land is it?"

"About the same as mine . . . ." he paused to correct himself, "as ours, a little over fifty acres. But there's no road into it, no well or utilities." They walked to the last row of cherry trees. There was no western fence. "I like not seeing the end of our place," he explained.

Sarah had never imagined the beauty and symmetry of rows of trees, even winter bare ones. "How many trees do we have?"

He loved the question, especially the "we" part.

"Over four thousand," he answered with pride. "Some of the time I think that's too many, but today it seems just right." They strolled on as he explained how pruning was necessary before the bud break. It should happen before the last frost, the same time winter damage is repaired. He explained how the ground should be groomed to keep weeds down, and rodents under control. With a frown, he explained that spraying for flies was a huge springtime chore. When they reached the neighbor's wire fence, they turned back toward the house. They strolled through almost a full hour of introduction of the trees to Sarah, and she loved it.

Back in the cozy kitchen, Sarah said, "I remember in Miss Linn's shelter home, I would ask a new girl to help fix the lunch, because it gave her a sense of belonging." Jon was again aware of how rough this young woman's past had been. "So, Dad, could I fix you some soup, and a grilled cheese sandwich?"

As they were finishing lunch, Jon could not conceal his joy. "I can't tell you how good it seems to have someone else in this old house."

"Well, do you have a cribbage board? I'm pretty good at that and checkers, but don't get me started on chess. I am wicked good at chess." They were working it out. Trixy came out of the bedroom to check on the dog. Since Winnie was in the barn, Trixy found a warm place to doze on a furnace vent. They were working it out, for sure.

Sarah changed her study schedule to include an orchard routine. A new high speed internet connection had been added to her bedroom, so she did school assignments from about 6:00 o'clock until a quick breakfast, then back to studies until 10:00 o'clock. Then it was orchard time! A crew of workers arrived early. Watching the pruners, Sarah found a deep respect for the care given the trees, and an understanding that they were the foundation of success for this property. She learned to start the tractor and run the mower. There was also a forklift, but that remained a puzzle. She thought driving was a blast, but controlled the temptation to expand the thought. She explored the barn and found a treasure chest of possibilities, especially in the garage, which was out of sight in the back. After a 1:00 lunch, she was back on the books until suppertime. She could still get her ten assignments in, but thought it wouldn't hurt for a while to cut back a bit. Evenings were either spent reading or in conversation with Jon. The winter was passed before they knew it.

One March afternoon, Jon said he was going to run into town; would she be O.K. for a few minutes? Sarah grinned, wondering if he hadn't been aware of the hours she was alone in study. "I'll be fine."

When he returned she was surprised to see a large bag from Kentucky Fried Chicken. He also had a birthday cake and a large gift wrapped box. He smiled broadly. "Happy Birthday, Honey." Sarah had forgotten her birthday, but he had not.

After blowing out her candles, Sarah said honestly, "I think all my wishes have come true. Thank you for taking me in." She carefully unwrapped the box. Inside she found a tan wool car coat with green and black plaid collar and cuffs. It was gorgeous, and she was speechless.

"I think," Jon said with pride, "that the plaid is the Dalton clan tartan colors, which are yours now. It will keep you warm."

She slipped it on and was delighted that the fit was perfect, which meant it had just the tiniest room for a girl to keep growing. "It is wonderful, the most beautiful coat I have ever seen," she said honestly. She turned and gave him a first, and large, embrace. "Thank you, Dad. Thank you!"

Twelve days later she returned the surprise. She fixed a spaghetti dinner, and had a yellow cake with chocolate frosting, his favorite, with only a few candles. "It's the ides of March," she said boldly, "a day to celebrate your birthday, too." She had ordered a framed poster of an orchard in bloom. Tucked in the corner of the picture, Sarah had printed: *"What is love and kindness? Love is the power to forgive, to heal, to create joy, to build communities and families. Kindness is a contribution that we can each make to those around us through the power of our compassion, our courage, and our honoring each other's differences and similarities. These two powerful qualities can assist us in transforming our families, community, nation, and world."*

A birthday card to "Dad" had words of appreciation concluding with "You have given me love and kindness in abundance. I love you!" Sarah

"Dotty would have been so proud of you," he said softly. "You are truly the daughter she always wanted, and could never have." Jon's voice faded off the end of the sentence as he remembered again his precious wife.

The 1st of April fell on a Sunday, so at 9:00 o'clock the next morning Sarah and Jon were in Gail Gilbert's office, joined by Kate Linn, Grace and Eric, and Max was there too. There was no ceremony, just the signing of documents by Jon, and then Gail as legal counsel for the state. She said, finally, "Friends, it is my pleasure to be the first to introduce Sarah Grace Dalton, daughter of Jon Brian Dalton." There were, of course, tears, and applause perhaps none more vigorous than that of Grace Tully who realized Sarah had blessed her by choosing her middle name. Before they left the office, Jon signed his new will, making Sarah his sole beneficiary.

As soon as Sarah could, she emailed Mo, telling her the wonderful news. Almost immediately Mo called. She wanted to hear the details, slowly. Finally she concluded their conversation, by reminiscing, "Who would have ever guessed that the little girls in Miss Linn's place would turn out to be a farmer and a chef?" She explained that she was entering the culinary school at the vocational college. "I'll make you something real good," she promised, "something from the farm." They laughed at the improbability of their journeys.

Later that night, in the living room, dad and daughter were musing the events of the day. "It was purely wonderful," Jon said with a sigh. "I still have to pinch myself to make sure I'm not dreaming. How could something this wonderful happen?"

Sarah was sipping the last of a cup of peppermint tea. "Dad, what would you do if you had the property next door?" It was the sort of question she would ask to begin a conversation.

"Oh, I don't know," he speculated. "I'd surely want to clear the brush off, and probably plant more cherry trees, although there is good money in plums, too."

"Would you ever want to have a vineyard?" The question was only idle curiosity.

"There was a time when lots of folks thought that would be the real deal. Today, I think there are too many into it; you have to put a lot of money in to get some money out. The odds are against a small grower." He thought for a minute before saying, "Of course, if you only grew the grapes and sold them to whoever wanted to crush and process them, there might be more to be made. I don't know." He was quiet for a bit. "Shall we buy it?"

"Miss Linn used to tell me if I wanted to talk about something big, I should start by asking about something bigger. Then the something I wanted to talk about wouldn't be so big." She smiled a quirky expression, reflecting on how that must have sounded.

"I know just what you mean," he answered with glee. "I once got a new shotgun by first telling Dotty I wanted to buy a new car." He chuckled, "Is that what you mean?"

"Yes, it's exactly what I mean. You are fun to talk with." She cleared her throat. "Now that we have the stage set, and as long as we both know I'm going to stay here, can I ask you something?"

"Ask anything," he grinned.

"Well, if I paid for it, do you think we could add a room onto the back of the house for another bedroom, with a bath in it?" She took a piece of paper and crudely showed how an extension off the kitchen could pick up the water and sewer lines without much trouble.

Her dad looked at it a bit then took the pencil and squared off the lines to make an attractive wing addition with a large family room. "Don't you think that would make more sense?"

"No, I don't want to change your house that much." She hadn't meant to say "your house." "I would just like to have a bathroom."

"Sarah, Sweetheart, it's our house, and believe me, you have already changed it for the much better. Besides, I'd like you to have a bathroom too." He smiled warmly. "It is the dickens trying to worry about who's doing what when." After a pause he asked, "But what do you mean, you'll pay for it? I've got plenty saved that could do the job."

Sarah explained the events of her journey with the Family Services, excluding the grim details of the assault. "There was a big settlement that pays about $2000 of interest a month into my account; it has a balance right now of over forty eight thousand, and I have another account from the state support for my living and education that has about twenty seven thousand dollars right now, and I have . . . ." She would have continued had he not raised his hand.

"Lord, Sarah, you are a rich girl! I don't know what to say."

"Then say 'yes' and we will find someone to draw plans, and get going on permits, and get a carpenter out here. I want that bathroom yesterday. We can decide who pays for it later." Her teasing jubilance was more than contagious. It had been the most extraordinary day Sarah could recall.

Before the lights were turned out, Max called to ask if he could bring Arby sandwiches and milk shakes for lunch tomorrow. He wanted to see the orchard again. Sarah smiled as she switched off her light. She hoped is was more than the orchard he wanted to see.

"How did you get out of classes this afternoon?" Sarah asked after lunch.

"Reed is closed for Holy Week," Max answered. "Next Sunday is Easter. It is like our spring break." They were in the loft of the barn. "Wow, this is as big as a gym. We could throw Frisbees in here." His admiration scanned the rafters. "I wonder if there could be owls up there. They could help with the rodent problem." It was information that Sarah would file away for a conversation with Jon. They had roamed through the orchard, and made their way into the barn to see Brandy.

"Why do they call it 'Holy Week'?" she asked

Before he answered, he wondered aloud, "If I tell you, you're not going to get mad at me are you?"

She promised that those days were over. She promised not to get mad at him unless he deserved it.

"In that case," he turned as though he would walk away.

"Come on," Sarah giggled, "I'm not going to get mad, I promise."

Max turned and said, "The Church made up a calendar to tell the story about the last days of Jesus' life. Last Sunday was Palm Sunday, when Jesus entered the city of Jerusalem on a humble donkey. Thursday, they remember the Last supper, and Holy Communion. Friday is called 'Good Friday', which might be hard to understand because that was the day of his arrest and crucifixion, and next Sunday is Easter, when the disciples realized that the tomb was empty and Jesus had risen."

Sarah was shaking her head. "That is way hard to understand, crazy hard." But she wasn't angry.

Max said, "It might make more sense if you were to watch an Easter worship service to hear the music and sense the beauty of it. I think I told you that our church webcasts its service. Just go to Mountaintop.org at 9:00 o'clock. Should I email you that address to remind you?"

"If you get any more pushy, I might get mad," she smiled. "I can remember Mountaintop.org."

9

EASTER!

On Sunday morning, Jon came into Sarah's room wearing a white shirt and his suit. He was dressed for church. When her monitor flashed from the church's home page to the live cast, and they saw the cross surrounded by several hundred Easter lilies, he said, "Oh my, that is so beautiful."

Sarah smiled; the program hadn't even started and he was already enjoying it. She listened to the familiar stains of Beethoven's Ode to Joy.

A man in a pale grey suit with white shirt and yellow tie, stood, and welcomed the folks with a joyous "Happy Easter! This is a great day!" He welcomed those seated in the narthex and community center, and those watching around the world on line. Suddenly Sarah realized he had included them in his gracious welcome.

The camera panned to the left to reveal an orchestra, which began with a drum passage then horns and then the congregation began to sing! She was swept up by the beauty of the sound:

"I serve a risen Savior; he's in the world today"

Sarah was amazed that Jon was singing along with them.

"I know that he is living, whatever foes may say"
"I see his hand of mercy; I hear his voice of
      cheer,"
"and just the time I need him, he's always near."
"He lives, he lives, Christ Jesus lives today."
He walks with me and talks with me along life's
      narrow way."
He lives, He lives, salvation to impart!"
"You ask me how I know he lives? He lives
      within my heart."

Sarah was amazed there were happy tears in her eyes. She listened enthralled as they sang another verse, and then the choir filed in and they all sang the last verse.

"Rejoice, rejoice, O Christian, lift up your voice
      and sing,"
"Eternal halleluiahs to Jesus Christ the King."
"The hope of all who seek him, the help of all
      who find;"
"None other is so loving, so good and kind."
"He lives, He lives, Christ Jesus Lives today."
"He walks with me, and talks with me along
      life's narrow way."
"He lives, he lives, salvation to impart."
"You ask me how I know he lives? He lives
      within my heart."

A lady stepped to the microphone and said that the Easter lesson text was from the Gospel of Mark, chapter 16, the first 8 verses. "When the Sabbath was over, Mary Magdalene, Mary mother of Jesus, and Salome bought spices so that they might go to anoint Jesus' body. Very early on the first day of the week, just after sunrise, they were on their way to the tomb and they asked each other, 'Who will roll the stone away from the entrance of the tomb?'"

"But when they looked up, they saw that the stone, which was very large, had been rolled away. As they entered the tomb, they saw a young man dressed in a white robe, sitting on the right side, and they were alarmed."

"Don't be alarmed," he said. "You are looking for Jesus the Nazarene, who was crucified. He has risen! He is not here! See the place where they laid him. But go; tell his disciples and Peter, 'He is going ahead of you into Galilee. There you will see him, just as he told you."

"Trembling and bewildered the women went out and fled from the tomb. They said nothing to anyone, because they were afraid."

"Amen." The lady said, and she returned to her seat.

The choir stood and began to sing another song.

> "In the bulb there is a flower, in the seed and
>   apple tree'
> In cocoons, a hidden promise: butterflies will
>   soon be free!
> In the cold and snow of winter there's a spring
>   that waits to be,
> Unrevealed until its season, something God
>   alone can see."

Jon reached over and held Sarah's hand. She turned to look into his eyes, and found his gaze endearing. He gave her an encouraging squeeze. Together they listened to the choir continue.

"There's a song in every silence, seeking word
and melody;
There's a dawn in every darkness, bringing hope
to you and me.
From the past will come the future; what it
holds is mystery
Unrevealed until its season, something God
alone can see."

Sarah whispered to no one in particular, "This is so beautiful. It's like nothing I've ever heard." The choir concluded their anthem.

"In our end is our beginning; in our time
infinity;
In our doubt there is believing; in our life,
eternity.
In our death, a resurrection; at the last, a victory,
Unrevealed until its season, something God
alone can see."

Sarah looked at Jon to see great tears on his face, and joy in his smile.

The man in the grey suit stepped back to the microphone, asking folks to pray with him. It was a brief request: "In the beauty of this morning, Mighty God, help us put aside the distractions and hurtful habits that have kept us from letting Easter finally happen to us. Open the miracle of this morning in Jesus' precious name. Amen."

With a smile of assurance, he began his sermon: "In Mark's account of Easter, it began in darkness. Look with me as we see a sad and solemn procession on a lonely journey. Three women are moving quietly through the streets of Jerusalem toward a tomb in the garden. The first rays of the morning sun were just beginning to lighten the sky. Look closely at those women. Notice their eyes. Pay attention to their faces. There was a look of sadness, of deep grief. Their slow somber steps suggest a weariness and heaviness of heart and spirit. They were carrying spices to anoint the body of Jesus. This was part of the preparation for final burial that was cut short by sundown on the day of crucifixion, by the Jewish Sabbath. All work was prohibited at the beginning of Sabbath. Now, as they trudged slowly, they asked a single question: 'Who will roll away the stone for us from the door of the tomb?' Their focus was upon a massive, immovable impossible problem."

"The stone was a tragic reminder of the death of Jesus. The women were still in a state of shock as they recalled the events of Friday. They had seen their leader and Lord strapped to a post and beaten with 39 lashes of a leather whip that left him bleeding and weak. They had shuddered when a cruel crown of thorns was pressed down on his head as a mockery. He had been sneered at and spit upon. On Friday they heard the crowd yell for the release of Barabbas, a criminal, and scream for the crucifixion of Jesus. On Friday they saw him carry his heavy cross until he collapsed under it, and Simon of Cyrene was compelled to carry it to Golgotha. On Friday they heard the ring of the hammer against spikes driven through his wrist and feet. They saw the cross lifted up, and they watched Jesus struggle for every breath of air until he whispered, 'Father, into thy hands, I commit my spirit'. On Friday they watched as the dead body was taken down, and was wrapped in a linen shroud and placed in a borrowed tomb. All those terrible sights and sounds rang in their ears as the women asked the question, 'who will roll away the stone?' It was the grim reminder of his death. They had no thought or hope of resurrection. The purpose of the anointing with spices was not even to preserve the body, but to simply cover the stench of decay.

Woody Allen speaks for most of us when he said, 'I don't mind talking about death, I just don't want to be there when it happens.' That stone at the door of the tomb is too heavy for us. We, like the mourning women, can't solve the dilemma of death."

"The stone also represents the unfairness of life. The women will tell you that it was completely unfair. They will tell you that Jesus had done only good in his ministry. He had healed the sick, and reached out to the hopeless. He had compassion on the grieving and outcast, still he died an agonizing death between two criminals. It wasn't fair. Heart attacks, strokes, cancer—all sorts of illness come along. Tragic accidents or distant wars leave bodies twisted and broken. It doesn't make any sense, and life isn't fair. The stone is the reminder of the tragedy and adversity that can come to the people we love, just as it had come to the person loved by Mary and Salome."

"The stone is a reminder that many things happen to us over which we have absolutely no control. There is one thing, however, you can do this morning. You can keep headed forward, and Let Easter Happen to you! You can refuse to let another Easter pass you by with a casual nod and a few colored eggs. You can open your life to the wonder and mystery of the day of days."

"Part of the tragedy that we see in the first part of the story is that the women didn't know that it was Easter. They were living with a Friday mentality. Their focus was still on the discouragement of defeat and despair. The real turning point in the text comes in verse 4. 'And looking up, they saw that the stone was rolled back; for it was very large.' Mark doesn't say, 'and looking back'; because lots of us are good at that—looking back at discouragements or disappointments. Some of us go through life looking at past failures and magnifying our inadequacies. Some of us spend every minute looking down at the negatives and problems. We refuse to lift our eyes. Others of us are always looking around—simply distracted by all the shiny things around us, a cuter wife, or an exciting new husband."

"Letting Easter Happen means that we look up, in a new fresh and powerful direction and see that God is ushering in not just a new life, but a new way of living, a more powerful way of living. Here's what Easter is about: God is making all things new, and the project is unstoppable! A stone won't stop it, a tomb won't stop it; it is the most powerful force in the world! Then God is inviting us to join in that unstoppable rescue mission of new creation. Paul tells us, 'If anyone is in Christ, they are a new creation. The old is gone, the new has come.' Easter is about so much more than getting our rumps into heaven. Well, that too, but what it really means is that the God, who created everything in the beginning, is now recreating everything through Jesus, and we are a part of that unstoppable force, which means we can be bold."

"For instance, fear can't stop it. It is not that fear doesn't exist, it does, of course. The disciple's lives did not get easier after Jesus was raised from the dead. In fact, they got harder. All but John were martyred in horrible ways for their faith. Fear still exists, but Jesus' resurrection shows us that there is something stronger than fear, stronger than death. We sing: '*Death in vain forbids him rise, Christ has opened paradise.*' And if God's making new of all things cannot be stopped by death or fear, what chance do you suppose, guilt or shame have. Nothing can stop it."

No Longer Guilty

"But Jesus' resurrection gave his disciples crazy amounts of courage, even in the face of persecution or death, because they knew that beyond this life, they would share a new life with him, just as he was. Not some disembodied soul floating around on clouds playing harps. No, that's cartoon stuff. You in a new resurrected, eternal body. Here's the deal: if you know Jesus, you are in for a serious upgrade, you 2.0!"

"Now I know that for many of you that is too great a stretch from reality; you don't buy into this discussion of Jesus rising from the dead. I get that. I used to be an atheist. That's why in the bulletin there is an insert that lists just some of the reasons that convinced me, a former atheist, that this really actually happened. If you doubt, I encourage you to have the intellectual integrity to read some of these reasons. The books are listed there, because there is a lot of evidence that Jesus was raised from the dead. And we don't ever need to fear death, or shame, or guilt again. We can live bold new-creation lives. We can let Easter happen to us, this morning!"

"C.S. Lewis said, 'If the resurrection is false it is of no importance. If it is true, it's of infinite importance. The only thing it can't be is moderately important.'" Indeed! Jesus is risen, and that means we can live big, non-ordinary, bold, non-moderate lives where all of life becomes an adventure as we partner with him to make all things new, and see him working in amazing ways. We can join his rescue mission to the world."

"As many of you know our church has purchased some homes adjacent to the upper parking lot to be used to house teens that don't have adequate safe housing of their own. Some of those homes needed repair and improvements. Volunteers from our congregation rolled up their sleeves and accomplished a lot of the improvements, but there was just a lot more to do.

So one of our members called his brother-in-law in Seattle who is a Christian and who happens to run a construction company. Once a year the company chooses a worthy charity to do a project pro bono. They even pay for the materials. They close their doors for a week, and they go serve someone in need."

"So the member called his brother-in-law to tell him about these houses, and the big need, but the brother-in-law didn't answer. The member called again, no answer. He tried a third time and the brother-in-law finally answered, but sounded irritated, or frustrated. 'What is it?' he asked sharply. 'I'm in a meeting with our board, but you keep calling. What's so important?' The member told him about these houses and the young men and women whose lives would be changed. The brother-in-law laughed and said, 'Oh well, the reason I wouldn't answer your call is because we are praying right now. We are asking God to show us what our next project should be, where he needs us to serve.'"

"Don't you love that? Here is one group praying 'Lord, just show us what you want us to do. What's our next project,' while the phone is ringing with an answer to their question, and they are not picking up!"

"How fun is it to have your prayers answered like that, and know that the God of the Universe is interacting with you, talking with you, showing you his unfailing resources! That has to be a rush, and it makes life feel big, and anything but moderate."

"So what things in your life need to be made new? Is it a marriage, a relationship, a career? Maybe it's a sense of boredom and you need purpose and challenge. Maybe it's a financial issue, or a health issue. Jesus can make those things new, too. Either by some miraculous event, and I have seen that happen, or by giving you an unbelievable supernatural sense of joy and courage that will fight on, even in the hard times. There are many people in this room who have faced illness, loss, financial problems and have felt Jesus right there beside them. And that has given them an eerie, crazy sense of indestructibility, courage and joy, even in those hard times."

"Let me tell you something about life, dear friends. You were not created to be intimidated by the immovable stones. You were created to live victoriously; to share the victory of Jesus Christ. God wants you to know this morning that your life really matters. It matters ultimately and finally. Every moment of your life is important because the things that you do are making all things new. Your labor is not in vain. At times I wonder if it is worth it all, and then comes Easter singing: 'Christ the Lord is risen today, Alleluia! Earth and heaven in chorus say, Alleluia! Raise your joys and triumphs high, Alleluia! Sing ye heavens, and earth reply, Alleluia!'"

"Because as Pastor John Ortberg puts it, 'that first Easter, death lost its sting, the grave lost its victory. Hell was defeated, darkness derailed, the devil demoted. Hope got vindicated, the prophet validated, the soldiers aggravated, the disciples animated. Sin lost, shame died, joy soared, and love won!"

"It's the greatest victory over the darkest enemy by the noblest hero for the loftiest cause in all human history. We can be brave, we can be bold, we can be sure that God's making new of all things is an unstoppable force against which there can be no immovable object. Earths sorrows do not have the last word. The stories of tragedies and grief are not the final verdict. There is a power that rolls away stones. Through Him, we are more than conquerors, and through Him no weapon formed against us can remain, for one reason and one reason alone: Jesus Christ is risen; He is risen indeed! Let's pray!"

"So Jesus, You are an unstoppable force for good. We ask that you would release all that power as we go from here in our lives and in our world, and we will give you all the glory. We pray this in your powerful name, Jesus. Amen."

As the choir stood, the congregation joined them to begin singing:

> Christ the Lord is risen today, Alleluia!
> Earth and heaven in chorus say, Alleluia!
> Raise your joys, and triumphs high, Alleluia!
> Sing ye heavens, and earth reply, Alleluia!"

The words were printed on a large screen on the wall so Sarah could sing along. They sang with full voices, joining the congregation and choir.

> "Love's redeeming work is done, Alleluia!
> Fought the fight, the battle won, Alleluia!
> Death in vain forbids him rise, Alleluia
> Christ has opened paradise, Alleluia"

Sarah looked at Jon, his face wet with tears and his eyes closed. "Are you feeling alright?" she asked.

"Oh yes," came his happy response. "I was just telling Dotty what a splendid Easter service that was." They listened as the choir sang on.

> "Lives again our glorious King, Alleluia!
> Where, O death is now thy sting? Alleluia!
> Once he died our souls to save, Alleluia!
> Where's thy victory, boasting grave? Alleluia!"

Sarah felt a brightness inside of her that wanted to giggle.

> "Soar we now where Christ has led, Alleluia
> Following our exalted Head, Alleluia!
> Made like him, like him we rise, Alleluia!
> Ours the cross, the grave, the skies, Alleluia!"

The service continued as an offering was taken and a lady sang another beautiful song. Sarah said, "I feel like he was speaking just to me."

Jon nodded, "I feel just the same. He is a strong speaker." In light of previous conversations, he wasn't sure how far this one should go.

The camera was panning from the choir to the cross, when Sarah pointed saying, "Hey, there's Max." Sure enough near the front was a familiar face, looking back toward the camera.

"I think he's hoping that you are watching," Jon said with a chuckle, "Looks to me like the lad is sweet on you. What do you think?"

"I think I'll call him in a while and tell him we watched the church service," she answered, hoping they might talk about seeing each other again.

10

REVELATION

At lunch over soup and grilled cheese sandwiches, which were becoming his favorite, Sarah said that she was feeling strange. When Jon asked if she was ill, she said, "No, not at all! But since the worship, I've been feeling sort of light-headed, or extra happy, or like some nagging problem has been solved. It seems really wonderful."

He smiled warmly, "Honey, it sounds to me like you've been made new, like the minister said. It's a good thing, isn't it?" His eyes searched hers.

"Yes, it is, but what should I do about it?" she wondered. "What do I do now?"

"Just love Him back, and do what your heart leads you to do. It seems to me that you might want to study the Word, praise Him in prayer, and let His peace flood your life." Not wanting to say more, he suggested, "Maybe you could talk with Max."

Sarah felt like the subject was going to change, so she said she would call him as soon as they were finished. They talked about the work schedule approaching. Jon explained that things in the orchard were going to get busier.

Sarah said she had watched the pruners. "Who are they?"

"You must know that agriculture today is dependent upon transient labor." Sarah nodded. She partially understood.

"There is a good size group of workers who have made a home in Buena Vista, a little town just southwest of here. Their number swells in the summer glut of work. Then we can't find enough help. The rest of the year I can count on getting whatever orchard work I want done pretty promptly."

"How many will we need when the picking starts? Can I help?" It was a sweet offer, and her dad doubted that she had ever picked a cherry.

"We always want a hundred or more," Sarah's eyes were wide with surprise. "but we usually only get seventy, maybe seventy five. When it is busy, all the orchards need them. On top of that, the pickers don't all stick around to the end of the harvest. It is hard work moving those big ladders and frames."

As though he just thought of another subject, Jon said, "Tomorrow you will want to stay inside most of the day, I think. We're going to get five and a half tons of fertilizer. They will be spreading it and the dust is really bad."

Sarah tried to remember seeing any receipt from last year for fertilizer. When she asked him how much that would cost, he guessed at about three thousand dollars, which was the first of three applications during the bearing season. Jon said that he usually tried to pay for these early expenses out of last year's profit. It felt like he was helping this year's crop.

Sarah said, "This year you have a bookkeeper who can write checks. That is something I can do." He nodded in agreement. "I can get a list of green cards and social security numbers too, and collect employment tax," she asserted. He nodded with a growing grin. It was like talking with Dotty.

"I have so many questions about the orchard. I hope you don't get fed up with them." He assured her that nothing could make him happier than her interest in the orchard. "Max asked me if there were owls in the barn. I said I didn't think I had heard anything about them." Jon confessed that he hadn't seen any owls around for years, but knew that they were good hunters for rodents.

Sarah went to call Max, but she had a new subject to explore. "Where would a girl go to get owls?"

While the fertilizing was happening Sarah interrupted her school assignments to look in the county tax records for the property next door. It was listed as "No access easement", and had and assessed value of only $87,700. She wrote a letter to the listed owner asking if he might be interested in selling. Remember, she told herself, "information is always neutral."

On Tuesday, eight port-a-potties were moved into place. And later in the week there were two days when it was dry enough for her to run the mower up and down the long rows between the trees. It gave her enough time to seriously ponder what it would mean to join in God's rescue mission of making all things new. Could she really believe in that? She realized she missed talking to Max. How could she let all this new stuff get in the way? When she finally did call again, it was Saturday afternoon. She was delighted that he was so eager to hear her voice.

"Yeah, I'm turning into a real orchardist. Is that even a word?" He said if it wasn't at least he understood exactly what she meant. "And I'm driving the mower!" He wondered how happy the trees might be about that. It was a fun conversation. She asked about Reed, and the folks he had met.

"Max, I would like to watch the church service in the morning. Do you think you could drive down and join us for a country breakfast at about 8:30? There's lots of stuff I want to ask you, and show you, too.

She was awake early, showered and in the kitchen before Jon was up. A fresh cup of coffee greeted him. "I'm not sure how that will taste," she apologized. "I've only tried to brew a pot once before." When he sipped the steaming brew, he declared it just right, strong enough to stand a spoon in. He told her he was teasing. If she could make it like this all the time it would be marvelous. By the time Max arrived, the eggs were scrambled, bacon crispy fried, and the French toast was ready for the griddle. It really did feel like a country breakfast.

When the webcast flashed on, the three were seated in front of Sarah's monitor. She was in the middle. There was no orchestra this week, but the choir was ready to begin a gentle call to worship. Sarah was aware that her hands were trembling in anticipation.

The pastor once again welcomed the congregation and those joining on the webcast. Once again, Sarah felt included. He said, "God had invited us all to hear words of life-giving love. You are here because God has something He wants to say to you." As the first hymn began, she felt like it was in stereo, for she heard the words being sung from both sides of her:

> "Thine be the glory, risen, conquering Son;
> Endless is the victory thou o'er death hast won."

Sarah recognized the music as that written by Handel. The men sang on.

> "Angels in bright raiment rolled the stone away,
> Kept the folded grave clothes where thy body
>   lay.
> Thine be the glory, risen, conquering Son;
> Endless is the victory thou o'er death hast won."

There followed some announcements, and prayer. Then a young man stood at the microphone to read. "That's my buddy Sean." Max whispered, as though he might interrupt the service.

"From Paul to the church at Corinth, the young man announced, "When the perishable has been clothed with the imperishable and the mortal with immortality, then the saying that is written will come true: 'Death has been swallowed up into victory.' Where, O death is your victory? Where, O death is your sting? But thanks be to God, who gives us the victory through our Lord Jesus Christ."

The choir sang another wonderful song, and prayers were spoken. Sarah had the impulse to bow her head while those words were being shared. Finally, the pastor stepped to the front, and with a warm smile began his sermon.

"This morning I want to listen with you to the lesson of Easter again. I want to experience with you the power and potential of this season. I want to see the expression of joy in the faces of Peter and James and John and Mary, and all the others who came to know the reality of Jesus' resurrection. I want to feel with you the tremendous power of this day, because in this congregation this morning there is pain that will be relieved. There is sorrow that will be comforted. There is guilt that will be lifted; there is brokenness that will be mended. There is sin that will be confronted and challenged and revealed for what it really is. This morning, because of this wonderful Easter message, there is despair that is going to be banished. Dull boring living will be put aside as we experience the reality of energized new life. The new beginning is available to each of us."

"The New Testament makes it clear that the alternative to Easter is not pleasant. Without Easter life is like a land caught in the grip of unending winter. Think what it would be like if spring never came. Do you recall the cold of the second week of January? Snow and ice covered our homes and roads. Schools were cancelled, businesses closed, homes were without power; no one was able to get around in the brief hours of daylight. What if warmth never returned to the earth? What if trees never budded, flowers never bloomed, or birds never sang? How discouraging and depressing that would be! It is either Easter and resurrection victory and hope, or it is oblivion and darkness. At a very profound level of our existence, we know that life is not what we hoped it would be; and that we are not what we could be. Most of us have gathered today with a receptive attitude, open to some good news and some new possibilities."

"In our text this morning, I see Paul standing on a cliff, shouting into the threatening abyss—shouting into the darkness with the swirling mist, 'O death, where is thy victory? O death, where is thy sting?' Paul is speaking to death—by name. It is almost like Paul is saying, 'Hey you down there, are you asleep? Are you there?' I want to warn him, 'Paul don't disturb the dragon, don't wake him up! Let him rest, there's no defense. One blast from his breath and you'll be toast. We'll all be done for! Paul, come down from there."

"Here's this little man shouting from the edge of the darkness, 'Hey, death are you there?' And you and I can hear the stirring in the void; we can hear the rumbling and growling of the stirring beast. We can hear about fatalities and divorces, and abuse, and empty desperation. Death is stirring, Paul. Watch out! Paul stands there and shouts out his defiant challenge to sin, to death, to the devil. He is confident that these ancient enemies no longer have the power to oppress and destroy. What is Paul's secret? He turns toward us and cries out, 'But thanks be to God, who gives us the victory through our Lord Jesus Christ.' He is saying, 'Jesus has won the victory! Hell, you've had it! Death, your days are numbered! Sin, there is a greater positive power than you at work in this day.' The message I hear this morning from the word of God is a cosmic message, one of incredible importance. It is the ultimate news concerning the result of conflict. The message I hear, and that encouraged me is this: 'God gives us the victory through our Lord Jesus Christ.' Let's focus on just that one verse from Corinthians 15. I hope you will read for yourself the Easter gospel at the conclusion of Matthew, Mark, Luke, and John. Look at the great truths in just one verse."

"God gives,—think of it—God gives! We expect to hear that God requires, or God demands, or God expects.' As I listen with you, my life is touched by the gracious generosity of God. He gave us the world, we didn't create it. He gave us life; it isn't something we formed. He gave us friends and family—and he gave us himself. Christmas is not so long ago that we have forgotten that Emanuel means, 'God with us.' I'll bet that if you ask the person next to you what her favorite verse of scripture might be, she would answer, 'God so loved the world . . . . Notice that the focus is upon the world imperfect and flawed as it is, not on the church, nor the good people as we might expect to hear . . . that he gave . . . not a new ritual nor a fresh set of laws, not a philosophy . . . . His only son, that whoever believes in him should not perish but have eternal life.' The verse that follows surprises many of us: 'For God sent his Son into the world, not to condemn the world (isn't that what many of us expect?) but that the world might be saved through him.' The word saved (soteria) means healed, made whole, put together, fulfilled, restored. God gives that! It sort of takes your breath away. Our hope is grounded not on our accomplishments but in God's generosity. What I hear today as I hear the good news of Easter is an amazing announcement. It is not just that God gave, but even more wonderful, God gives! His action continues."

"Notice the next little two letter word, a tiny word: us. God gives us! We might expect to hear that God gives them. We must understand the power of this tiny word. Just as I am included in the tiny word 'all, as in 'all have sinned and fallen short of the glory of God', so now I am addressed and included by the word us. It's not us without a you. I'm indebted to that profundity by my daughter. All of us" His arm swept the entire gathering.

"Do you remember seeing the news not long ago of a man going through mountains of garbage at the land fill? Do you remember that he was searching for his lost lottery ticket? By mistake, he had thrown a winning ticket in the trash. It was worth $20,000. For hours he struggled in vain to find that ticket. Can you imagine the look on his face had he found it? He would have jumped in the air with glee, shouted and praised. Instead he found a lot of garbage, a lot of trash, and no victory."

"God gives us 'the victory.' It is not just a victory, it is the victory, the ultimate victory. In the ancient world, when an invading army approached a city, the defenders would go out to face the conflict. The fate of the city was determined by their success. If there was defeat, it meant total devastation, death or slavery for them all. The city would anxiously await news from the battle, brought by a runner, If his clothes were torn and he was covered by ashes, his words would be 'woe, woe, woe,' and the people would try to flee. If, however, as he ran he carried a palm branch, his cry would be 'Nikos, victory!' His announcement was called, 'gospel' because it was good news, and is the root of the word to preach."

"The text makes clear to us something that many have never fully understood. Christianity is ultimately about victory—an incredible, humanly speaking unwinnable victory. To get the real picture of Easter, we have to imagine ourselves in a besieged city, fighting an unbeatable foe. If we lose, we lose everything: our homes and family, our church and schools, our freedom, and our own country. Our text then breaks into the battle with the word, 'Nikos, Victory!' Easter is good news of God's victory. Christianity is thus revealed to us, not as a new set of rules, not as a ritual, not as a scheme to get your money, or control your life. It is the victory of Jesus Christ over sin and death. It is the one basis for authentic hope that we have for life today."

"The victory is very specific; it is through our Lord Jesus Christ. It is not through my brilliance or yours; not through my morality or yours; not through my religious deeds, or yours. When we are listening very carefully to God's word, we hear 'our Lord,' which means one whom we follow, our leader, the one to whom we pledge our allegiance. To become Christian is to receive and trust Jesus, not only as our Savior who wins the battle, but also as our Lord. We are not only following an ancient teacher or inspiring example. Jesus is alive! Through the Holy Spirit he becomes more real to us than any friend could ever be. Through his spirit we receive resurrection power today. We are actually empowered to overcome problems, sin and death itself. Paul says, 'If the spirit of him who raised Jesus from the dead dwells in you, he who raised Jesus from the dead will give life to your mortal bodies also through his spirit which dwells in you' (Romans 8:11). That is the greatest power in the universe and is available right now, right here, giving life and Easter victory. Isn't that exciting? Thanks be to God who gives us the victory through Jesus Christ our Lord!"

"There is one last question to ask. What shall our response be to this gift? How shall we respond to this possibility? I believe it is to receive and believe the Easter gospel. Secondly, we can extend and expand Easter living. It was Jesus' will that his followers should believe and know his victory. Do you remember what he said to Thomas? 'Put your finger here, and see my hands (the nail hole). And put out your hand, and place it in my side (the spear wound). Do not be faithless, but believing' (John 20:27). As we receive the Easter message, then we are a part of the communication of the reality of transforming hope. We are to be numbered among those who extend and expand the Easter reality"

"Many years ago, when I was a student, I was privileged to hear a convocation speaker named Dr. Murdo Ewen MacDonald, a great Scottish Presbyterian preacher. He told us about an episode he lived through at the end of the Second World War, when he was a prisoner of war of the Germans. He was the chaplain for the American prisoners, and greatly loved even in those horrific times. He told us how he had learned about the invasion of Normandy and of D Day. Early in the morning an American shook him awake, whispering, 'the Scotsman wants to see you, it's terribly important.'"

"MacDonald said that he ran over to the barbed wire fence which separated the British and American camps, where McNiel, who was in touch with the BBC by underground radio, was waiting for him. He spoke just two Gaelic words—'they've come!' MacDonald then ran back to the American camp and began waking the soldiers. He said, again and again, 'They've come! They have come!" The reaction was incredible. Men started shouting and jumping up and down. They hugged each other. They ran outdoors; they rolled on the ground with joy. The German guards, of course, thought they were crazy. They were still prisoners. Nothing had outwardly changed. Inwardly, however, they knew everything was different. Victory was at hand!"

"Easter is the good news that He is risen! Outwardly your life may appear unchanged. Still, Easter means that deliverance has come. The night of endless winter is over. The unending reports of misery and conflict will be controlled. Sin and death have been defeated! The future is open! God has given us the victory through our Lord Jesus Christ. Receive and believe in your new life, and extend and expand its affect as you live in gratitude, praise, and joy. Today, let us dare to be a people of hope in an age that has given up in despair. Let us celebrate our Easter victory!"

Sarah felt like she could finally exhale. She had been watching the service breathlessly. She asked herself what she was feeling. Was it curiosity? No, Much stronger. Was it intellectual satisfaction? No, much more. Deep down, she knew that her former resistance was wrong, and she wanted to open her heart.

As the offering was being taken and the organ was playing quietly, Jon wiped his tears and said, "I don't recall a more wonderful worship hour." Then looking at Sarah and Max, he added, "or a finer congregation." The concluding hymn was one that both men knew and could sing with some vigor. Sarah's smile grew as they joined voices:

"All to Jesus I surrender; all to him I freely give; I will ever love and trust him, in his presence daily live. I surrender all, I surrender all, all to thee, my blessed Savior, I surrender all."

By the fourth verse, Sarah was singing the refrain with them, and meaning it with all her heart: "I surrender all, I surrender all, all to thee, my blessed Savior, I surrender all."

11

THE BLOOM

Afterward, the three were walking through the orchard, remembering the inspiration. Jon said with a happy sigh, "You know it was just a year ago when Sarah called about the paperwork job." Then looking at Max, he said. "I guess I owe you a pretty big debt." They all smiled thinking how much had happened in just a year. As Jon paused to examine a bulging bud, he said, "We're going to get sprayed tomorrow, so we can get bee hives by midweek." When Max asked how many hives, he was surprised to hear "I rented fifty last year, and the crop was a little light. I think we should try seventy five hives this year." Max asked why he didn't just own the hives, and was informed that the insecticide spraying four or five times a season would destroy the hives.

Sarah shared that she had contacted the extension service at Oregon State University in Corvallis about barn owls. She gave Max a little push when he claimed it had been his idea. "They said that the average owl eats two mice or rats a night. If we had some in the barn, they would get rid of a lot of rodents each month," she proudly announced as though the inspiration had been her own.

Jon chuckled, "This might be the best season I've ever had." Neither Sarah nor Max understood the depth of his meaning, but his big grin suggested it was there.

The blossom season was spectacular. Sarah thought even if there were no fruit afterward, the trees would fulfill a wonderful purpose by giving all that beauty to the world. The sunny days interspersed with showers made the flower show a promise of abundance. She felt like she was living in a bouquet; so she finally had to curtail her orchard trips to a few minutes in the morning and late afternoon. She was getting behind in her assignment output.

Sarah received two pieces of information that did deflect her studies a bit. An email from Gail Gilbert shared the news that Jan Bowen had been arrested in Costa Rica with drugs. She was going to look into it on Sarah's behalf.

Secondly, a letter from Connie Waltz from Plano, Texas gave her more to think about. Connie shared that she and her husband were in divorce settlement. The property was indeed for sale, and at the advice of her attorney, the asking price was only $200,000. Sarah answered immediately, that the attorney must be quoting downtown properties. The raw land plot in question could not be used without an easement, which it did not have. She replied that the price she was willing to offer was $1000 per acre.

In early May, one of the men Jon had hired to set up the orchard for picking came to Sarah. He had overheard her speaking Spanish to another laborer. "Senorita Sarah, may I ask you something." His accent was heavy. "Achuly, two somethings." When she nodded with a happy smile, he asked, "How much does it cost Senor Jon to fertilize?" When she explained that there were three applications at about three thousand dollars each, he suggested, "I have a cousin in Rickreal who works for the chicken ranch. Each week he has a truck load of manure mixed with sawdust, he has to haul to recycling. If we pay for his gas to bring it here, he can spread through the orchard. It is very good for the ground. You know, natural." She said she would talk to her dad about that.

"The other thing is, why Senor Jon use company that don't pay as much for crop?" She thought she understood, but asked for more information. "He take cherries to Willamette Fruit, when they don't pay so much. If he get Marion Fruit Co-op, they come pick up and pay him more." She promised to look into it, and asked his name. With a flirty smile he took off his cap and said "Eduardo Sparta at your service."

Within the hour she compared the services of three fruit wholesalers and discovered that the company Jon had been using indeed paid the least and required the most hauling. Blue Lake cannery would bring a trailer to the orchard with empty containers. At the end of each day during the peak picking, they would bring another "dolly," and haul away the full one. They also paid $9 more per ton than Willamette Fruit. When Jon came in for lunch, Sarah shared the information with him, and he immediately made the change to a new wholesale company. "And the only reason we spread all that artificial fertilizer is we don't have a dependable source of natural cover. It sounds like now we do." Eduardo had just earned a bonus! For the remainder of the day Jon felt buoyant; he had made such wise changes.

A contractor named Lowen brought plans for the new extension to the house. He showed them to Jon and Sarah, promising to get the permits as soon as they were approved and get on the job within the month. Jon was ready to give the green light, but Sarah asked if they could pay him for the plans so they could get a couple other bids. It seemed a bit high to her. He hesitated for a moment before saying, "Did I explain that the price also includes a new roof for this part?" The project would be finished by the end of August. Now Jon gave the green light.

Sundays were by far Sarah's favorite day. It was the day she usually saw Max. He had made it a regular expectation to attend church with them, on line. That worship experience was also something that Sarah was learning much more about. She even included Eric on many of her emails that opened a delightful dialogue. The question had been raised by Eduardo if there would be cherry picking on Sunday. At first, Jon had been adamant, as in the past, it is a holy day and no work should be done. Through Sarah, Eduardo had suggested that for many that was true, but for the pickers who were depending on making their family's income during this season it was essential to pick on Sunday. On top of that, the cherries continue to ripen on Sundays. Losing six days of harvest could be detrimental to the prime picking period.

Finally he said to her, "Tell Senor Jon dat I have a cousin, Chimmy, who has a bus. He could bring a good crew seven days a week if you pay him for gas. Dat would be very good plan, no?"

Max had the idea that sealed the deal, and insured the orchard would forever have adequate help. One Sunday at lunch, he suggested that a local Mexican restaurant might reasonably supply large containers of food for a Sunday supper with the pickers. Folding tables set up in the barn could seat them; paper plates and coffee cups would keep the cost minimal. Once started, they had to get more tables, and they had an adequate picking crew.

"Sarah, what would I do without you?" Jon sat on the couch weary from another active day. The harvest was started, and it was running more smoothly than he could remember.

She responded, not by accepting credit for the changes, but for pointing out where it was coming from. "You understand that Eduardo has been working overtime to get this all done, don't you?" She sat cross-legged on the floor in front of him. "I think it would be a good idea if you made Eddie your orchard Foreman. Hire him as a year round job. He could take care of the pruning and the spraying, and the fertilizing, and . . ."

She might have gone on but he asked, "How much do you think that would cost us?"

She shrugged saying, "That would be up to you. But I think he has shown this year that he is saving more than you are spending now. I'll bet it wouldn't cost you anything. Shall we think about it?"

"Yeah, but just thinking about him doing the work that is wearing me down to a nub, makes me think we shouldn't think about it very long."

"Well", she said with a grin he just loved, "how about another idea since we are having this business meeting. I've heard you say we have a problem with folks leaving the harvest a little before it's complete. How about offering everyone who is with us right now, a hundred dollar bonus if they stay until the last day?" She was sure she was way out of line.

"How much would that cost us?" Now the smile had faded, and he was pretty serious.

"How much is a total pick, good will, and a lot of new loyalty worth, do you suppose?" Her smile hadn't faded.

12

COMPLETE HARVEST

By the time the harvest was complete, Jon knew it was well done. All of the changes had worked; and if Sarah's report was accurate, and he had no doubt that it was, the orchard had produced $38 thousand net more than last year. She had also set a procedure for paying by check and paying social security withholding. It was done properly. And it had been done with much less labor on his part.

Another job was finished about the same time, but with much less acknowledgement. Sarah received a folder from the University of Phoenix praising her for completing her Bachelor of Arts in Business with honors. Her name would appear in the list of 2011 graduates, and she could enroll in the fall series of their Master's program. A leather case held her diploma. She had to smile at so much effort, and so little fanfare. When Jon drove them to Portland for Eric and Grace's wedding, however, he asked Max to join them for a celebration dinner at the Chart House. She did feel honored.

Before turning in for the night, she emailed Mo, to tell her about the quiet accomplishment. By an almost instant reply, she was applauded by her friend and told of a recipe Mo had been working on called "Sarah's Cherry Chutney." She thought it was very unusual, and so far her teachers did too. She sent the recipe for Sarah to try."

"2 pounds Bing Cherries, pitted and quartered;
1 pound tart apples (Granny Smith) peeled,
    cored, fine chopped;
2 cups brown sugar;
1 1/2 cups cider vinegar;
4 cups peeled, pureed, Beets;
1 Lg onion, fine chopped;
1 Tb cinnamon;
1 Tb Sea Salt;
1 Tb ground clove;
1 tsp Nutmeg;
1 tsp Cayenne Pepper;
1 Tb crushed garlic;
½ cup crystallized chopped ginger;

In a large kettle combine all ingredients, (except no beets! I was only joking about beets. I know you hate them!) Bring to boil over medium high, then reduce to simmer, stirring frequently for 60-90 minutes, until thick. Spoon into sterilized jars and store in cool place, makes 6 cups. If using Sun dried cherries use 1 pound, reconstitute with one cup of Brandy."

One warm August evening they were lingering at the table. Sarah had fixed a summer pasta salad with diced chicken. Jon had been very appreciative, and even more so when she served apple pie with a scoop of ice cream. He had barely taken a bite when she asked, "Dad, what would you do if you owned the property next door?"

"Oh boy," he chortled, "here we go again. We just finished the addition, and you have a beautiful bathroom. Now what are you thinking about? Do you need a new shotgun?"

"No, I'm serious. What would you do with it?" Before he could answer, she confessed, "I've been in contact with the folks in Texas. They just got a divorce and I made a very low offer to buy the land, and," she paused, raised her eyebrows in surprise, "she took it. Now I feel like I took advantage of her distress, and I don't know what to do."

"How much did you offer?"

"A thousand dollars an acre."

"Oh my; I see what you mean. That's about a quarter of what it's worth. Hmm."

"I sort of feel like we have to buy it now, but I'm feeling like a thief."

"I'll tell you what, Honey, Dotty used to say, 'let's pray about it for a day, and God will show us what's right.' Do you think that might be a good thing to do?"

"I do, and here's the rest of my idea. What would you think if we had Mr. Lowen build two or three little two bedroom cottages that we could offer Eduardo and a couple other workers that we need. They could work off the rent out of their pay. It would feel like a home to them, and we would always have available help to work around the place. Do you like that idea?"

"Sounds like we are going to be in prayer for a while tonight. For a girl who had no farm experience a year ago, you have been a godsend, for sure." He reached across and held her hand. She was surprised at how strong it felt, and how tender he was with hers.

Connie Waltz was eager to open the envelope from the Daltons. She so needed the money from that old piece of

Oregon property. They had paid taxes for all those years, and she thought she would be tied down with it forever, or maybe just abandon it altogether. That was why her husband had insisted she have it in their settlement. When she opened the letter she could see it was a Purchase and Sales Agreement. Her heart skipped a beat. Would she really get over fifty thousand dollars? Then her eyes caught the conditions at the bottom: "and a twenty thousand dollar bonus if she signed it before the 30th of August." A nearby Title company was prepared to conduct the signing and pay-out. It was a seventy two thousand dollar answer to prayer.

When Eduardo heard about the new property, he approached Sarah one afternoon. "Senorita Sarah, may we talk?" he asked.

"Always, amigo," she said brightly.

"I heard there is more property, correct?" When she nodded, he continued. "I have a cousin who owns a nursery. He has a small excavator that could clear the brush and maybe prepare more orchard space. Would you like him to come talk?" Again she nodded. Since he had agreement so far, he suggested, "He even has auger for planting trees. I think he would make special price for us." The plural pronoun was not missed by Sarah.

The new shoots had been trimmed from the trees and the last treatment of fungicide applied. The orchard could rest now for a few months. Jon was ready for some time off, too; although his lack of exhaustion was due to the extra help in the orchard. He told Sarah that often at the end of the harvest, Dotty liked to go over to Cannon Beach for a couple days of complete rest. "How about if I ask Max to come over and join us for a day. I can show you where to get the very best clam chowder on the coast."

"With no more school work for a while," Sarah replied, "I can't think of anything better, and we can ask Eddie to look in on Winnie and Trixy."

Often the coast is foggy, if the valley is hot. The warm inland air pulls in the marine layer of cool ocean air and you can't see a thing. If, on the other hand, the breeze is off-shore, that warm air makes the beach sunny and warm, which it was when the trio arrived. After a check-in, shoes and socks came off for a walk on the beach. They strolled almost to Haystack Rock, and decided it would be lunch time by their return. Jon said he felt like a nap on the balcony of the boys' room. Max and Sarah found a sheltered dune to lounge on and watch the surf.

"Max, you'll be proud of me. I've finished the pastor's assignment to read the four Gospels, and I have a question."

"I'm already way proud of you, and remember, I'm not a theologian. So, what's your question?"

"Well, in his sermon the pastor said everybody's favorite verse is, 'God so loved the world,' Max spoke along with her, 'that he gave his only Son, that whoever believes in him should not perish, but have eternal life.'"

Max nodded, and asked, "So, what's the question?"

"The rest of the verse says, 'For God sent the Son into the world, not to condemn the world, but that the world might be saved through him.' Do I have that right?"

"As right as rain, as right as ice cream on apple . . ." he would have had a couple more right as, but she said, "I'm serious here."

"In the first gospel, Matthew's, I think, it says that when the Son comes in his glory with angels, he is going to sit on a glorious throne and divide the people into two kinds. One kind get to inherit the kingdom prepared for them, and the other kind get sent into the eternal fire prepared for the devil.

So, my question is, how is that not judging and condemning? If the people who didn't do what he wanted them to do get crispy, isn't that not saving?"

Before he answered, Max asked, "This isn't one of those times when I get into trouble is it? Are you going to get mad at me?"

She shook her head. "I don't get mad at you anymore. You are my best friend. So why isn't it judging?"

"In the same way you can say I'm your best friend." His smile said he was being especially serious. "Because you have to know that you are my best friend too. That doesn't mean there has been a judgment so much as recognition, or identification. You have distinguished yourself from the other people I know, in a special way. That's what Jesus is saying in this parable. Remember that it is a teaching story, so he can glam it up with angels and royal thrones. The point is the people on each side of the recognition," he said the word slowly so she could understand the substitution for judgment, "were both surprised. God will recognize our ability to love in his way, not by how much knowledge we have amassed, or our fame, or our gracious holy rituals, but by how we respond to human need. Does that much make sense?" She nodded, her curls more bouncy in the ocean breeze. "Remember too, that Jesus was telling this parable in the hearing of the religious men who were judging him!"

"They would have assumed that the love of God must be difficult and calculated. But all the things on Jesus' list were easy, you know, feeding someone who is hungry, giving a drink to a thirsty person, or clothes to someone who has none, just the natural easy things they could do. And secondly, they were things that just happened normally, instead of being seriously intentional. You know, instead of like, let's go see if we can find a hungry guy that we can feed in front of our friends who will think we're cool." Sarah grinned at his example.

"The guys that didn't make the cut say, 'If we had just known it was you, of course we would have done it.' What a lame excuse, and a mask of self-righteousness. If I knew that was a police car behind me, I would have been a law abider, instead of going through the red light." He shook his head because he thought it had been a lame example too. "When Jesus says that when we do it to those hurting, needing people, we do it to him, I think of how happy you were with my suggestion that we get food for the Sunday pickers. Those are people you love. So when I do something that blesses them, it blesses you too. Does that make sense?"

Sarah was still for a long moment. "More than you know." She pondered whether she should tell him what she had been thinking about. "It makes such good sense. I was sure you could explain that for me. I have another problem with this scripture." She knew if she told him, they both might get into such big trouble.

"Did you know that Jan Bowen is in prison down in Costa Rica?" His surprise was evident. "I guess she got caught again with drugs. Gail didn't share any of the details with me. But when I read that Jesus said, 'I was in prison and you came to me,' I couldn't help think of her. What do you think we should do about that?"

"I don't think you should do anything. It's out of this country, and certainly out of your hands."

13

THE MISSION

Sarah was quiet for several breaths. "I don't know about that. We send aid to people in Africa. They're not out of our hands, and we feed them. I guess I feel like I should do something." Before their visit to Cannon Beach was over, she had convinced Max to send a letter on bogus stationary to the prison clinic doctor, asking about the condition of Jan. If she was O.K. Sarah would not worry about her. Max wondered just how much trouble this was going to get them into.

His first effort was to find information on the internet about the arrest of an American in Costa Rica. There were more than one recently, but his search caused him to immediately call Sarah. "She wasn't alone," he told her. "Jan was with Kent Scott." The silence was heavy. "Maybe we need to leave this alone, partner." She still didn't say anything. "Well, Dotty would say let's pray about it," he quoted her now familiar words.

Finally Sarah answered, "If he was hungry, we'd try to feed him too, wouldn't we?" But her voice sounded weak and resigned.

Max found the website of the prison in San Jose. It looked anything but acceptable. How threatening! Then on stationery he scrounged from the Women's Services of Reed College, he crafted a letter to the prison clinic doctor. He posed as a

141

physician who had been treating Janice Jane Bowen and was inquiring as to her current health and obvious signs of disease development. He didn't have a clue what he was asking for, besides trouble. He signed the letter "Dr. Max Wall, M.D."

There was no reply of the first letter for two weeks, so Max sent another, strengthening the urgency by saying that due to the contagious nature of the infection, he had concern for the general population; and because of the extensive and expensive treatment, he was afraid she may never recover. That one got a response.

"Good day to you, Dr. Wall. By your letter I see that like me, you are under trained and over worked. I must tell you about our prison system in Costa Rica; we do not have resort style facilities as I hear you have, and conditions are bleak at best. We supply enough food to keep them alive. It is subsistence; but if they want anything better, adequate food for example, clean clothes weekly, insecticide, toothpaste, their families must contribute. I know of the prisoner you are inquiring about, and her counterpart that was arrested with her. She received three stipends from her family; he received none. She shared two with him, but not the last one. I can give you the general information that they both have severe lice, and intestinal parasites. I believe he has a case of Gonorrhea, as well. My advice is to solicit more funds from their family for their treatment, or their conditions can only worsen." It was signed, T. Juan Portola, MD.

When Max read her the letter, Sarah moaned, "That's horrible. We have got to do something, and I don't think sending money is going to help." She was quiet for a long moment. "We've got to get them out of there and bring them home." Now it was Max's turn to moan.

"If Jesus was in that jail, wouldn't we want to go to his assistance?" Sarah's voice was hushed in a theological panic. Max had felt all along that this was going to get complicated.

He wrote another letter to doctor Portola stressing the need to get medical attention for these two young Americans. He raised the question of possibly transferring them to an American prison for treatment.

In a surprisingly quick response, Doctor Portola agreed that treatment without the prospects of reoccurrence was only wise. He would forward a recommendation to the presiding judge to release them to an American prison, but it would require the recommendation also of the prosecuting Attorney, Jesus Bendez.

Max wrote two letters to the attorney, with no response. At the same time Sarah was writing to Senator Ron Wyden's office for help. Her second attempt received a promise to forward the request to Anne Andrew's office in the American Embassy in Costa Rica. Finally Sarah called the Ambassador and on her third attempt, got through. The best she could receive was a letter of introduction sent to Mr. Bendez's office. By the first of December, Sarah believed they would need to go themselves to convince him to assist them. They both applied for their passports.

Jon was nearly sick with worry. He tried repeatedly to dissuade her, but now Sarah felt it was a holy mission. She assured him they would only be gone four days, one day going, two to accomplish their meeting, and one day back. When she purchased the airline tickets, she was so sure of her success that she bought two round trip tickets and two more one way from San Jose to Houston in the name of Janice Bowen and Kent Scott. "We are meeting a church mission team," she told the agent.

Grace didn't ask for an explanation why Sarah wanted to withdraw all of her education money, after all she had graduated. Nor did she question why Sarah wanted a fifteen thousand dollar cashier's check. Sarah bought a dark suit for Max, and found a dark blue business dress at Value Village for herself. She wanted to appear a bit more weathered for her meeting.

Jon prayed with them at the airport, asking for safety and success in such a bold mission. Their flight to Houston was five hours, and they only waited an hour for their next one, which would be seven hours. Fortunately it was a night flight and they would be able to sleep, or try to sleep as the case may be.

San Jose was just waking when Sarah had her first test at speaking the language. She had asked the flight attendant the cost of a taxi into the Radisson Hotel. But when they stepped into the first taxi in line, he quoted a price four times as high. "Good morning Mr. Pirate," she said brightly, in acceptable Spanish. "Would you accept four dollars US, or should we take another taxi?" He was a bit less talkative on the way into town.

At the hotel they were able to freshen up in their rooms. They tried to plan a strategy for their meeting. She said she would try to do the talking if he could represent her protection, her security. When the bank was open, she converted her cashier's check into colons; she had a camera case full of $10,000 bills. The exchange rate is 500 colons to the dollar. ($15,000 equals 7,500,000 colons.)

At 11:00 o'clock sharp they entered the office of Jesus Bendez. When they were shown into his office, and introduced, he stood and said, "I am surprised to meet such beautiful young people. I thought someone who can bid a Senator and an Ambassador to give assistance, must be much older and seasoned." His handshake was firm and positive, and his English was fair.

Sarah and Max were seated across the desk from him. In her best Spanish she told him, "Senor, my sister, Janice Bowen, was arrested over a year ago for possession of drugs. We do not contest her guilt. She was arrested with another man named Kent Scott, who is a very sick man." She was telling the truth. "We are afraid she is contaminated too."

"The parasites and infections are common to the prison and very contagious; the treatment is very expensive, if it is available at all. I do not want my sister to die here in Costa Rica, when medical treatment is available in the US." Sarah had rehearsed the speech in her mind. "Senor, are you familiar with the scriptures?" When he nodded, there was a bit of a frown on his brow. "I am only a little aware of the great lessons," her smile was disarming. "I heard that Jesus said, 'I was in prison, and you visited me. When you did it to the least of these my brothers, you did it to me'. We are not asking for the release of the least of these from prison, only compassionate release from yours. U.S. Marshals will meet them in Houston and transfer them to custody. There are warrants for their arrest for parole violations. They will finish their confinement there." She wasn't sure if her request made sense, so she was still for a moment. Finally she concluded:

"The doctor at the prison has recommended this release to the judge, who has also approved it upon your recommendation as prosecuting attorney. It seems to me that it all rests upon you." Sarah's heart was beating madly, but she tried to remain calm. Senor Bendez was listening at least. "I know that time is crucial, and it is also expensive." She nodded to Max to open the camera case. "To make this a priority for you today, I brought enough to pay for your time to make a call to the judge, and for him to sign the release. There are seven million five hundred thousand colons, or fifteen thousand US dollars here, enough for thirty hours of billable time." Max tipped it open for him to see the bundles of 10,000 colons. "If Janice Bowen and Kent Scott are at our hotel tomorrow afternoon at five o'clock, with their passports, I will give you this bag. I wish it could be divided two and a half million for you, and equal amounts for the judge, and for the doctor. That's how I would do it, but I will leave the parting of the time payment to your integrity. Jan and Kent have been in prison a year, they have had confiscated all their worldly wealth, and they are sick. Those are good reasons to release them. You may be foregoing an epidemic at the prison by removing Mr. Contagious." She grimaced at the words. "There are politicians who have risen far on a less humanitarian concern for their country. Who knows, you may be on American television."

Senor Bendez laughed as he stood up. "Perhaps you are in sales or politics yourself. I can reach the judge before he goes to lunch. What hotel are you in? Where will I leave a message?" As Max and Sarah stood also, he motioned toward the camera bag, saying "Shall I keep that safe for you?"

She laughed, perhaps venting some tension. "Are all men in Costa Rica pirates? If you have the prisoners, and the money, what do I have beside hope?" Her laugh was genuine enough to remove any offense.

Back at the hotel they finally celebrated, jumping up and down, declaring their amazement. "He said he would do it!" "It's going to work out." But when Max said, "It was so easy," Sarah stopped jumping and replied, "Yes, easy for you." Then her bright smile returned and she giggled, "But you did it just the way we planned, a silent security." She began jumping again. They asked the manager to place their camera case in the hotel safe; they had lunch, and went to the gift shop to find some swim wear. Sarah held up two tiny scraps of material, saying, "There is no way that can be called a swimsuit. Dad would die!" Finally in a one piece that came up higher on the sides than she wished, they frolicked in the pool. She confessed that she didn't know how to swim, so Max set about helping with the basics.

Senor Bendez called at 3:00 saying the arrangements had been made. A police van would pick them up at 5:00 o'clock, and he would be there as well to make sure all the details were correct.

Sarah called Gail Gilbert to have her alert the U.S. Marshal Service to confirm they would be arriving in Houston, Thursday morning at 10:20 on flight 2102, with both Janice and Kent.

She called her dad to assure him that everything went according to plan, and they would be home for a late supper day after tomorrow. His tender "I'm praying for you and love you more than life," warmed her heart. What an emotional day!

The next morning, they had a big breakfast in the hotel because they wanted to see some of the tourist sights of San Jose, especially the zoo. Sarah smiled as she told Max that the blouse and Capri's she was wearing were just like the hand-me-down gift from Jan, three years ago. There was sweet irony in that. They pledged to eat or drink only that which was wrapped, and made in America. They wanted to get home with no tummy complications of their own. By check-out time they were in the hotel lobby waiting.

Senor Bendez opened the van door for them, and informed them that an air marshal would accompany the prisoners to Houston, which was a relief to Sarah. She had pondered just a bit the responsibility of keeping track of them. When she handed the case to him, Jesus said that it had been a delight to get to know them, and he was happy that Mr. Max had not been needed. He assured Sarah that her distribution wishes would be honored. She was a fascinating young woman. They shook hands and were on their way home.

Seated in the back row of the 737, Sarah had an opportunity to study Jan, who was seated beside her near the window. Wearing the white coveralls from the prison, she was still marked as a convict. Gone was the bright assured façade she had seen in the Bowen home. If she had to describe what she saw, Sarah would say Jan was weary, dull and hopeless; she was no longer attractive, or even interesting. Max sat on the aisle seat, next to Sarah, and across from the air marshal. An empty seat was between the marshal and Kent, perhaps because of his prison odor. Sarah would not have recognized him in a crowd. He was also in the prison coveralls; and had shoulder length hair, a clipper shadow beard and a gaunt face. Two or three top teeth were missing, attesting to the violence he had recently experienced. He also looked drab and empty. There had been no conversation between any of them.

A couple hours into the flight, well beyond darkness, Sarah heard Jan murmur, "Why did you do this?" A tear was tracing down her cheek.

"Do you mean why did we come down to get you out of prison?" Sarah asked needlessly. "It does seem preposterous when you think about it. I'm still trying to figure it out myself. I will tell you that it has everything to do with Easter making all things new, even you. I believe I heard Jesus say, 'Follow me', not just think about him or feel good about him. I had to do something." Only the roar of the engines filled their space.

"I am so guilty," Jan said with a sob. "I did all those terrible things to you, just to show off. I burned your poems. You must hate me."

"Yeah, I pretty much didn't like you a lot." There was no mirth in Sarah's voice. "It's like the story of that guy Joseph, whose brothers sell him into slavery and he winds up an official in Egypt. They intended bad for him, but God intended a bigger good. When I learned how much God loves me, and you too, I got over how I felt about you. I forgave you because God forgave me. I see the world completely differently now, and realize we each have amazing choices. Jan, I'm glad you are out of that nasty prison, but I don't know what's in your future. It is up to you. That's the thing about being made new; you can be wonderfully surprised."

"But I'm really guilty, for doing the drugs, and disappointing my family, and . . ." She would have continued with the litany but Sarah interrupted.

"Yes, we've all made bad choices, and been guilty about something; whether big or small it doesn't matter. God is in the forgiveness mode, not punishment. There is nothing God won't forgive. I hope you can believe that. There is nothing stopping you from a fresh start but Jan Bowen. You have choices. You have a family with deep resources. You have plenty of time to achieve whatever you choose."

"But I'm guilty . . . ."

"Jan, shut up! As long as that's the only song you're going to sing, you will stay guilty. I don't want to hear it. You are no longer guilty! None of us are. I want to hear that finally you will do something positive, something really beautiful with your life. You have amazing potential. You can be outstanding!"

Several minutes later Jan whispered, "Thank you for being a wonderful sister. I wish I could have known you better. Perhaps things would have turned out differently. Thank you." She was quiet for the rest of the flight.

When they got into Houston, camera crews from both ABC and NBC were there to greet them. As the US Marshals ushered the two in overalls away, Kent raised his eyes to look into Sarah's. He nodded and mumbled, "Thank you. I'm sorry for the grief I gave you." Sarah was shaken by the confession, pondering its implications.

Max gave an interview in which he explained why they had made the trip. "No, we are not bounty hunters," he laughed. "We are just family members doing what we could to help them. We must never underestimate the power of God to redeem, or the resolve of family to restore," he said firmly. "Sarah is a remarkable person who has prevailed over huge obstacles; in fact, she sees the last four days, not as an exceptional thing, but as a mission, partnering with God to make a new start for Jan and Kent, one that required action." Then with a bigger grin, he added, "She said it was also something of a vacation. We met a couple of really neat people, played in the swimming pool, and went to the zoo." He said pretty much the same thing when they arrived in Portland and he was interviewed by KGW, Channel 4. Sarah declined the interviews saying brightly that her Security would speak for them. They were delighted that NBC sent a camera crew to San Jose to interview Senor Bendez and Ambassador Andrew. It turned out to be a human interest story that the nation relished

14

THE WITNESS

It was the second week of the blossoms when Sarah's phone demanded attention. "Sarah, my name is Sheri Lewis." There was a bit of a pause, "No, I'm not the famous ventriloquist; I'm the Associate Program Director for CBC News, the Christian Broadcast Channel. Do you have a minute to answer a couple questions?" When Sarah agreed, the first question was predictable. "Is it true that you rescued your sister from a prison in Costa Rica?"

"Well, that question has a couple errors, but basically, yes, I went to Costa Rica in the aid of my foster-sister."

"And am I correct that you used your own money for transportation, expenses, and the ransom?"

"Tell me again what you are after today? How can I help you?" Sarah's voice had an impatient tone.

"We would like to invite you to come to our studios here in LA for an interview that we could share with our world-wide audience. We think your story has huge heart, and shows courageous faith. We would pay for your expenses, of course."

"Thank you for the invitation. I'm flattered to think I have anything to say that would interest your audience. Ms. Lewis, I'm going to turn down your invitation. I have a cherry orchard that is demanding my full attention right now." She was ready to hang up, when an urgent voice said, "We can pay you for your trouble."

"Sheri," Sarah said firmly. "There are several very important reasons why I have little interest in entertaining your listening audience with our story, or raising funds for your corporation. I know the ratings were high when the national networks carried a bit of it, so I can understand your eagerness. However, I am just now working out my understanding of the faith for myself, and promoting your program isn't part of that."

Before she could say more the producer broke in, "We can help you write your text and rehearse your presentation. We have an outstanding staff of writers."

Sarah chuckled, "I'll bet you do. I'm looking at your website. It's very impressive. It looks like Gordon, your boss, is the CEO of the broadcasting company and brother of the founder, Pat. You've got a dynasty going. But you still don't get it. I am not interested in being part of your program. I went to Costa Rica because God invited me to be part of his rescue mission to make all things new. That amazing transition has started for me. The Old Testament prophet shares God's word with us: 'I will give you a new heart and put a new spirit in you; I will remove from you your heart of stone and give you a heart of flesh.' That new spirit enables me to become a peacemaker, a reconciler, a forgiving person, a builder of community, and helps me imagine this world as one people under the Lordship of the One who is both Creator and Redeemer."

The producer interrupted, saying brightly, "Yes, that's what we want you to tell our listeners, just like that!"

"I was about to say," Sarah smirked, "that it doesn't have anything to do with CBC at all. The wonderful thing is that even though we are far from perfect, God has put a new spirit in us, removing the old heart of stone, which was unforgiving, unbending, unyielding, critical, judgmental and uncaring, and changed it so that we are able to reach out to the undeserving, the unlovely, the unwashed, smelly and unrewarding. Where is the news story in that? Why wouldn't I go to my sister's aid? Wouldn't you, if your sister was in a foul prison? Wouldn't you give all you've got to free her, if you could?"

"I would like to think . . . ." Sheri didn't finish her thought.

Sarah knew it was time to conclude the conversation. Her critical feelings about commercialized religion were bubbling up again, and she didn't want to lose the awareness of God's love. "Thank you for the invitation," she said cheerily. "I think the one you should be chatting with is Jan Bowen. I don't know what prison she was moved to, but she might have a very interesting perspective of the incident. I'll bet she would welcome a chance to tell her story. As for me, I'm going to read some more of the New Testament, and see if I can answer the call to the higher way. Good luck in your programming."

After she placed the phone back on her desk, she smiled, thinking that was the first time she had spoken those words so clearly. She did feel that she was chosen, redeemed and given a task to do in the name of love. It was a beginning that was accomplished. She wondered what might be next.

Jon survived four more seasons with Sarah's encouragement. He saw the new property addition cleared and groomed. A large fir tree near the north property line was used as a nesting platform for hawks. Their presence would reduce the crop-loss to marauding birds. That same season two Barn Owls were introduced to their new roost in the barn rafters and a fresh hunting ground. There would be fewer rodents for sure. Forty-five hundred new cherry starts were planted and thriving. Three new cottages were built within easy access to the main house. Mr. Lowen trained two of the summer workers to be his framers. He promised them continued employment. They built a bold stairway to the loft of the barn, which became the gathering place for the Sunday supper, and the site of the wedding of Eduardo and his bride, Angelica.

Jon had ample time to show Sarah all the secrets of operating an efficient orchard. The new trees in the addition had produced a light first crop. He was inspecting them late one afternoon when he suddenly could not catch his breath. He made it into the house where Sarah was working in the office. She drove him to the hospital where it was determined that he had a pulmonary thrombosis, and at least one side of his lungs was not functioning. Actually, it was much more severe than that. They got him into a room where oxygen could offer some relief to his gasping breath. Sarah stayed with him through anxious hours, comforting him as best she could. He held her hand tenderly. He whispered that she was a marvelous daughter. After saying that he loved her, he simply stopped breathing. His heart could not keep up the demand. His death was without pain or fear, but with tremendous love. His ashes were scattered, where Dottie's were, in the orchard now affectionately named, "Madrugada Pomar," Sunrise Orchard.

BOOK 2

DRY LIGHTNING

A Mystery Of Perception

1

BOMB SCARE

S arah sat in the quiet terminal waiting area with the other shaken passengers. They had left Phoenix on an evening non-stop flight to Portland. About an hour into the flight the pilot had instructed folks to return to their seats and fasten their seatbelts, due to the turbulence ahead. That had seemed strange to her, since the flight was as smooth as a runway. Then the pilot had informed them that they were making an emergency stop in Denver.

Sarah tried to find the cause of the flight change, a medical emergency perhaps. The flight crew seemed unusually tense and quiet. Only after the landing did she understand. A bomb threat had been phoned to authorities saying that an altimeter had activated upon their ascent and would trigger a detonation device when the passenger plane dropped below five thousand feet. Quick thinking in the flight center had diverted them to Denver, which is higher than the threatened altitude. The aircraft had been quickly evacuated and was now being carefully inspected, as was their luggage and carry-on items.

She watched as cell phones appeared and the other passengers contacted their family or friends who would expect to meet them in Portland. A half smile formed on her lips as she considered who might miss her. Sadly, the first face to come to her mind was Trixy, her kitty. There would be no one waiting for her except her shuttle driver. Inevitably, Max came to her mind. She could picture his smile and patient manner, but he was not going to see her until next weekend. For a moment she thought of her dad. Jon had passed away nearly two years ago. She could still hear his wry chuckle in her memories. There was no one for her to call.

A woman with tears in her eyes walked slowly to the seats across from Sarah, and sat heavily. She stared at the floor.

Sarah asked, "Did you have trouble contacting your ride?" It seemed like an obvious question.

The woman looked up, and tried to brighten her smile. "No, my son was going to drive me home. He's a school teacher in Orchards, just across the river from the airport. But if we are here another hour or so, it will be too late for him. Now it looks like I'll get a room by the airport, and he can pick me up after work tomorrow."

Sarah noted the wedding band on her finger. "And your husband . . . ?" She left the question open.

"Oh my, he works for the State of Washington," she used the formal name. "We live in Olympia, and it would be too much for him to drive down and back."

Sarah nodded, but tried to remember her geography. Olympia was just a couple hours north of Portland. That seemed hardly challenging. "You look familiar to me," she said, trying to change the subject. "Have you been at the University of Phoenix?"

"That's where I've seen you," the woman responded with an attempt at a smile. "Your face looked familiar to me too." Now the smile seemed more comfortable. "Yes, I'm trying to get started on my MBA." Rather than continue the young conversation, however, the lady looked down at the floor again, returning to her earlier sadness. She was carrying some sort of burden.

Sarah allowed a couple minutes of silence to drift by before suggesting, "You know, Shuttle Express drives up to Olympia. It might take a little longer, but you would be home by breakfast." She let that suggestion settle in before offering, "Or, since we are officially school chums, you are welcome to use my spare room tonight. I can drive you to Orchards in the afternoon if that would work." It felt strange to make such an offer, but it would be stranger not to. "By the way, I'm Sarah Thoms." She held out her hand in a business motion.

As the woman accepted her handshake recognition bloomed. "I think you are the one our professor spoke about. Did you finish your Bachelor degree as a teenager?" There was something akin to admiration in her voice.

"I did indeed," Sarah answered, "And my MBA."

Before releasing Sarah's hand the woman quickly said, "I'm Pam Gregory." As though she wanted to get that out of the way before going on, "and the professor told us you did that under considerable hardship. I think he was trying to encourage us." Now her gaze remained on Sarah's face. "How far are you in your education?"

"I just finished my five day residency requirement for second year students in the DBA program."

Pam shook her head in disbelief. "And you are so young to have big troubles."

"We all have challenges, don't we?" The question was meant to be rhetorical, but once again the woman reacted with tears. Sarah realized finally that Pam was just barely holding her emotions in check. "Is there anything I can do to help you, Pam?"

Those words were enough to release the tears. "I'm so . . ." Pam sobbed. "Our marriage has been dwindling since the kids moved out about fifteen years ago." Her face was twisted by the grief she was feeling. "I've thought if I could just be more interesting, maybe Paul would . . . ." Another sob wracked her frame. Sarah moved across to embrace her. Pam was able to say, "You've been very kind to a complete stranger."

Sarah released her embrace but remained beside her. "I know how good it is to have a friendly shoulder when you are going through a rough patch." She reached into her purse to find a business card. "Here are my contact numbers," she said warmly. The card read: Thoms & Associates CPA Accounting Services and Financial Planning. "You can contact me any time."

Pam asked, "Are you in business with your dad?"

Sarah smiled, understanding the confusion. "No, it's mine. I have two other CPAs working for the company. We don't have a tremendous clientele yet, but enough to pay the bills."

For the following hour they chatted quietly, with Pam doing most of the talking. She told Sarah about her romance with Paul. He was an outstanding student at Oregon State, and everything seemed perfect. His immediate job with the state in the office of revenue collection had been promising. Their wedding and family had been blessed by his dependable salary. The years, however, had not progressed the way they thought. She had taken a teaching job in a disadvantaged part of the city, and wondered if the worry wrinkles were worth the meager salary she had earned. She thought there could be another woman in his life. Paul had been more and more distant from her, and finally they were not even friends. He rarely spoke to their family members. She was convinced a divorce was eminent.

By the time their reloading was announced, Pam had decided to take a Shuttle Express from Portland to Olympia.

She expressed deep gratitude for Sarah's gracious offer of hospitality, and affirmed that she would stay in touch with Sarah because of her sweet nature.

Sarah wondered if their paths would ever cross again.

She was just cleaning up her breakfast dishes the next morning when Max called. "Hey, you're home. Why didn't you give me a call? I would have gladly picked you up at the airport."

"It's good to hear your voice too" she responded, although he hadn't said those pleasant words. "Our flight was diverted into Denver because of a bomb threat."

Before she could share more details, he interrupted, "That was your flight? I saw it on the news! My gosh! They traced the caller to a disgruntled lover who had been dumped by one of the flight attendants. Were you frightened?"

"We really didn't know what was happening until we had landed. It took a couple hours to search the plane and luggage. So it was well after midnight when we finally got here. I just took a shuttle service. It was fine. I was real happy to be in my own bed."

"I'd be real happy if I could see your face. Do you have a free lunch hour today, or soon?" The conversation was so relaxed Sarah had no way of knowing the urgency Max was feeling.

"I've got a lot of catch-up to do in the office," she said in an apologetic voice. "Maybe we could grab a bite on Thursday or Friday for sure." For just a moment she reflected upon how willing he had been to give her assistance in the past. She had a twinge of guilt.

After a pause, Max conceded, "It can't be soon enough. Let me know when you are free."

Driving to the office, Sarah reflected on their brief conversation. She was not pleased with her casual dismissal of such a sweet friend. One of the final lectures at UP was about personal freedom. Now she was face to face with the application of the heart of that presentation. She was stretched between her sense of responsibility to her new business and her obligation to her truest relationship. The day was young but she already felt the energy-sapping struggle taking away something irreplaceable.

When she turned on the light in her office, Sarah was greeted by a white Cyclamen in a pink container. Her first assumption was that the card would tell her it was from Max. However, she found that Allison and Dori, her assistants, had left the welcome—back gift. She went into Allison's office immediately to thank her for the thoughtfulness. There she learned that all phone calls were up to date, and while Sarah had been missed, there was no emergency to handle. Dori said the same thing. Finally, Sarah knew she must have lunch with Max!

2

TERMINATED

The Riverside Café was still pretty full of a downtown lunch crowd when Sarah arrived. Immediately she saw Max stand up at a corner table and wave. He had gotten a place out of the traffic and noise of a busy restaurant so they could talk. She smiled a genuine greeting. It made her heart happy to see him, and she wondered why she hadn't done this right away.

Max gave her a tender embrace, telling her again how he had missed her. Sarah responded by saying that it was only because he knew she was in hot old Phoenix. There were many weeks that went by without them seeing each other. He agreed, but said he missed her on those occasions too. Sarah thought again how dear this man was to her. And wondered again at the source of her casual rejection of his kindness.

They ordered, ate and shared small talk. Max had lots of questions about her trip, the orchard, and her new business. Finally, he asked about the lecture on freedom. "It sounds like that one really caught your attention."

"It did!" Sarah said with fresh enthusiasm. "I think it was because Dr. Sherman's definition of freedom could also be one for salvation." A pleased smile turned full toward Max. "She said that personal freedom is an emancipated, fearless condition of our minds which is expressed in our personalities and in our feelings about ourselves, others, life's challenges and opportunities," she paused to take a big breath, "and our expectations for what the future holds." Looking intently at Max she asked, "Using that definition of freedom, how many people do you know who are completely free?"

"Wow. I'd need to write that down and consider the possibilities. But it feels true, doesn't it? And I'd guess that most of us aren't."

"Yes. And the challenge is that lots of mornings I wake up not feeling free to be myself, not delighted with the person I am struggling so hard to become, and not able to shake the negative impact of what someone has said or done to me. If I'm not careful, those feelings become a habit, instead of the carefree, liberated feelings I would prefer. Do you know what I mean?" Sarah had watched as Max's brow had frowned and his lips had tightened into a stern look.

"I know exactly what you are talking about. That's why I so needed this lunch. You have a very pleasant effect on me. Today I need that a lot." He was still for a moment, knowing that he would tell her, but not sure where to begin.

"When I graduated from Reed I was already working for Metro Logics. They needed my help in color balance in their fonts and graphics. But the big secret job that I have been working on for the past two years is a 3D application that will be revolutionary. It really is exciting. I've called it my TRI-X." He grinned, knowing she would understand because the name of her kitty is Trixy.

"Last Friday I had my annual review. I walked into Mr. Glenn's office anticipating highest marks and I got . . ." He scrunched his face in a painful reflection. "I got a termination notice. I'm out of a job."

"What?" Sarah declared. "How could that possibly happen? You are the best programmer they have. You know more about computers than anyone I know!"

"Thank you. I'm not sure if I would agree with 'the best programmer,' but a better than average one for sure. He said it was because business is down and they need to cut back on labor costs." He took a deep breath and continued, "I think it's because Lisa, my supervisor, is sleeping with the other programmer. Mr. Glenn showed me her reports that have given Dwight credit for all of the work that I have been doing. She has told Mr. Glenn that they are on the verge of a big reveal, and I've just been messing around with color background."

"Even though I tried to tell him I had done the work, the meeting ended poorly with me angry, and him more convinced of my incompetence." Sarah couldn't remember ever seeing Max downtrodden like this. "He gave me two hours to clean out my desk."

"You mean you are already gone from Metro?" Sarah asked with shock.

"Now do you see why I was so anxious to have lunch with you?" A crooked grin began to spread across his face. "I'm an unemployed guy on the street, looking for a hand-out." He reached across the table for her hand, "as well as a smitten man."

3

CAPITAL COMMAND!

Sarah didn't believe Max's distress. "What can you do to get your job back? There must be some avenue of reconsideration." She couldn't quite grasp his expression, and was sure that there was more that he wasn't telling her. "Max, what have you done?" she asked finally.

"Tomorrow is the 15th isn't it?" he asked. "At 9:15 on the 15th of September, there is a doomsday capital command I installed at Metro that will erase all files containing my signature identification Tri-X from the mainframe server and back-ups on all company computers, including my old one. It is the improved generation of the vampire one I used after I hacked into the police computer six years ago. It will purge any file that contains a reference to Tri-X, as though I had never been there." When he saw Sarah's incredulous expression, he explained. "Of course I have copies of all my work, saved and safe at home. But someone is in for a terrible surprise tomorrow. If she wants to tell the truth, I can restore the information in just a few minutes. If she doesn't, they will need to explain how they lost it all, and can't redo it."

"Max, that is purely evil," Sarah said, but with more admiration than condemnation.

"I'll tell you what is purely evil," he said leaning closer across the table. "I've already had one conversation with Cyber

Solutions, who somehow heard about my release from Metro, and have offered me a better job with a signing bonus." His smile grew until it was contagious to Sarah. "They will also give me a major bonus if I give them copyright to Tri-X. I have until next Monday to think about that. But I'm thinking it might be worth tons more if I keep the copyright. What do you think?"

Sarah wasn't sure what to say to all that information. Finally she said, "I have just finished five days in an academic exercise of value-added solutions. This is a perfect case situation. But what I am more inclined to do is say, 'What would Dotty say,' the mom I never had. She'd say, 'Let's pray about it for a day and God will show us what to do.'"

They strolled back to the parking lot the long way, following the riverside causeway. Sarah held onto Max's arm, enjoying the warmth and strength she felt. "I'll call you if I get any panic calls tomorrow," he promised. As they parted to their own cars, Sarah wondered when he would kiss her.

The next morning Lisa Brock was working on her big presentation. She had nearly fifty pages ready to take to Mr. Glenn and the CEO, Mr. Powers. It had been easier getting rid of Max Wall than she expected. She had a pang of remorse before thinking that he was young and talented and wouldn't have any trouble finding a new job.

"What the hell?" she asked a blank screen. She hit refresh, and the screen remained blank. She went to menu to find her work, grateful that she had saved regularly. It wasn't there!

She dialed Dwight, the now-only-programmer. "I'm having trouble with my computer. Can you come over and help me? I can repay you later," she teased.

His puzzled voice had a hint of alarm. "My screen just went blank and I was about to call you." The depth of their problem had not yet set in. "I'll reboot and get the saved file."

Moments later he called her saying, "It's not there. I can't find it anywhere."

Lisa had also been searching and was coming to the same conclusion. "Max can't be responsible; I was just working on it. What did you do, Dwight?" Her voice was rising in volume and pitch.

"Don't get your panties in a bunch," Dwight said humorously. "I'll call Tony, our IT guy. He'll fix it for us." But as minutes passed with no results, the implications began to dawn on them. Two hours of frustration demonstrated there were no Tri-X files to be retrieved. They went to the history on the hard drive of the server with the same discovery. All evidence of Tri-X had completely disappeared. Maybe it was time for panties in a bunch!

"Did you print out any hard copies, Lisa?" Dwight was grasping for straws. "Maybe we can replace it."

"It was too big, and still in progress. I was just working on a final draft. I would have printed . . ." She realized the finality of what was gone. "Oh shit!"

4

FREEDOM I:
THINK FREE, FEEL FREE

On Friday afternoon, Max called Sarah to ask if he could bring a pizza for dinner. She was about to tell him she had school stuff to do, but reconsidered. "I have to listen to the seventh presentation in the 'Freedom' series. Dr. Jerry Michaels from High Desert Presbyterian is talking about freedom in the Spirit. If you don't try to make fun of him you are welcome to come and listen."

"Hey," he retorted, "remember, I am the guy who is 100% in favor of online inspiration. What time should I be there?"

When they got their first glimpse of pastor Michaels, both Max and Sarah were surprised at his youthful appearance. "He looks too young to have a doctorate," Sarah whispered.

"Folks are going to say the same thing about you, kiddo," Max replied.

"Ssshh." The lecture was beginning.

"Thanks for joining us for the seventh presentation in the doctoral series, 'Freedom.' We began with the concept of 'Political freedom', which I watched and enjoyed greatly. We then followed with the discussions on 'Economic Freedom,' which is rarely pertinent to a pastor on a short salary." In the background they could hear laughter, indicating this was a live presentation. "Tonight I want to welcome those students from different religious backgrounds than Christianity, or differing philosophical foundations. I hope you can hear the salient points as helpful and worthwhile, whatever your convictions. I don't suppose it will come as a surprise that my point of view will be obviously Christian."

"Most adults today have a vision of what a spiritually free person should be. At the same time, they are aware of an engulfing sense of not being free themselves. True spiritual freedom is rooted in an unassailable truth which controls their thinking brain and pervades their emotions. When they do not feel free it is usually because of emotions which have not been brought under control of their thinking. An emotion of fear, anxiety, worry, or insecurity is rooted to some distorted thought about who they are in their relationship to the Eternal, by whatever name they might know Him."

"So often when we meet another person we ask, 'How are you?' or 'How are you doing?' Instead, we should ask, 'How are you thinking?' You see, how we feel is directly traceable to what we think about what has happened to us or around us. So much of our thinking is not controlled or conditioned by that Higher Power—by the Lord—what he has done for us, and his unconditional Love for us. Becoming a truly free person requires battling for truth in the midst of the untruth of our irrational thinking which creates our imprisoned unfree feelings."

"You see, emotions follow thought. We cannot change how we feel until we change our thinking! Do you recall what Solomon said? 'For as he thinks in his heart, so is he . . .' Our perception of life will control how we feel about it in any one day." "Circumstances do not control our feelings. What we think about those circumstances result in our feelings of joy or frustration. Often we feel victimized by our emotional responses to people. But, in between the impact of what they say or do that distresses us, is the split second cognitive response that triggers our feelings. Often what we think is based on ideas and accumulated attitudes creased in the memory factors of our thinking brain, and are not consistent with the Lord or the gospel of truth he revealed."

"The Lord our liberator stated clearly the basis of spiritual freedom in John 8:31-36. It is his emancipation proclamation. From it we learn the vital importance of thought as the basis of feeling freedom. A careful exposition of the entire passage becomes the authoritative biblical foundation of our, 'think freedom, feel freely' thesis. Jesus said, 'If you abide in my word, you are my disciples indeed. And you shall know the truth, and the truth shall make you free.' Do I need to repeat that? 'You shall know the truth, and the truth shall make you free.' Just think, they are paying me big bucks to share this with you!" Again there was laughter in the background. "I would do it for free! It is that important!"

"Note the progression. We are to continue to abide, that implies consistent, continuing abiding. We are to dwell in that holy word and allow it to dwell in us. That means what the Lord has said is to be the basis of all that we think about God, life, ourselves, others, the future, death and eternal security."

"Abiding in Christ's words fills us with his truth. The word truth here as he uses it means absolute reality. His clear messianic assertion is the basis of our convictions. 'I am the truth,' he said with divine authority. He is God with us revealing the true nature of the divine and humankind. What he said and did must become the objective standard of our beliefs, convictions, attitudes and reactions. Bringing all thought captive to him who is sublime truth is the source of liberated emotions. I know this is heavy stuff," he said reassuringly.

"All that we feel that makes us less than free is tied to some thought inconsistent with his holy truth. He promises that we shall know the truth and that truth will make us free. I believe he means intellectual, emotional, and spiritual freedom. The Greek word for freedom used in this liberating promise is *eleutherōsei,* the future active indicative of *eleutheroō.* The future is used because at that time in his ministry, Jesus was looking forward to the completed work of spiritual freedom he came to accomplish. And so, looking back, we contemplate the truth which sets us free in the context of the cross, the resurrection, and the indwelling of his Spirit through Pentecost."

"What Jesus said becomes the foundation, the basis of our status, our security, and our strength. Feelings of lack of freedom usually are caused by a denial in our thinking of one or all three of these crucial gifts Our feelings of guilt, insecurity and worrisome anxiety are all caused by incomplete linkage between claiming the status, security and strength of the redeemer. So we must ask the question again: If Christ offers us the status, security, and strength of true freedom, why are so few Christians free? Look at it this way. Our minds are like a garden filled with flowers and weeds. We need to pull out those invasive weeds that are contrary to the life, message, death, and resurrection of Christ. A mind filled with Christ's truth is a place where freedom can flourish, a setting where emotional peace can blossom and grow."

The pastor gave a big smile, signaling a change of pace. "The other day I visited with a friend who is usually very grim and negative. Talking with him is frequently a chore. But this time he was completely different. His face was radiant, his voice was bright, and he was full of fun. 'What happened to you?' I asked him. 'She loves me!' he blurted. This man had been dating the same woman for five years. After the first year he had said to her, 'Shall we get married?' and she answered,

'I suppose, but who would have us?' He was dashed, and she was reluctant to express her affection or commit herself to marriage. Finally, four years later, he was nearly ready to bag the relationship. He decided to try once more, 'Will you marry me?' he asked her. 'Well yes,' she answered, 'it's about time you got around to asking.' Now he is bubbling over with the good news; he is transformed. 'She loves me,' he crowed. Her affection has transformed his thinking about his life and future. 'It's amazing! Being loved, really knowing that you are loved' he nearly sang, 'gives me a wonderful feeling of freedom.' Love had given him a self-esteem, relaxed his inner tension, and lifted the grimness of his pessimism."

"Now multiply the finest expression of human love a hundred million times and you have just begun to experience the unlimited love the Lord has for us. Thinking about that love, building our whole lives around it, makes us joyous people who are free to enjoy life. It makes us free to give ourselves away, free to care, free to dare."

"Whatever keeps us from receiving and enjoying that love is sin. Sin is separation, missing the mark. We were created to live in intimate oneness with the Lord. We lose our freedom whenever anything blocks the free flow of his Spirit in us."

"Jesus clarified this with a very pointed illustration of the difference between being a slave and a son. 'Most assuredly, I say to you, whoever commits sin is a slave of sin. And a slave does not abide in the house forever, but a son abides forever. Therefore if the Son makes you free, you shall be free indeed.' That's John 8:34-36."

"Remember that this was spoken to the Pharisees who were the most educated element in Hebrew society and who had great pride in their heritage as the people of God. But rite, ritual, and regulation had taken the place of profound relationship with the Lord God. They were separated from him by pride of their own efforts to justify themselves by their own goodness. The result was that they were living as slaves because of their compulsive patterns."

"Many of us can identify with that. We become so dependent on our assumed status with God that we negate our calling to be recipients of his Grace as loved and forgiven sons and daughters. Jesus clearly asserts his messianic status as the Son of God and reminds the Jews, and us, that he has come to return us to the true freedom, which is acceptance in God's family."

"How will he do that? That is a crucial question to this discussion. He will do it through the one, never to be repeated sacrifice of the cross. We could talk about this for a week and still have mystery before us. So what I want to make clear is that in that action of the cross, you and I have been adopted by the Lord."

Something like a shock of electricity surged through Sarah. She knew what it had meant to her to be adopted by Jon. Now she was confronted with the deeper knowledge of a heavenly adoption. Tears came freely to run down her cheeks. She listened more intently as the pastor neared his conclusion.

"We are loved unreservedly, in spite of anything we've said or done. We will feel free when our minds are controlled by that liberating truth. God's love will never ebb or subside. And really knowing that makes us free indeed. Jesus' word 'indeed' means superlative freedom, more than we could ever earn or deserve. Knowing that truth, thinking it through, and recognizing it as the basis of all our responses to life is the beginning of the growing process of becoming truly free people."

"I should point out that Jesus used the idea of knowing truth in the Hebrew understanding of the verb 'to know.' That was very different from the Greek idea of knowing. The

Greeks thought of knowledge in terms of ideas, theories, and philosophical verities. The Hebrew meaning of knowledge went much deeper. To know something required the total involvement of the entire person. In fact, 'to know' was used to describe the complete union of a man and a woman in marriage—oneness of mind, heart, will, and body. That's the deeper sense in which we must consider how knowing the truth involves the thinking brain and its powers of memory, imagination and will. Such knowing calls into action the whole nervous system, our emotions, and our physical bodies. The truth of our liberation through Christ's life, death, resurrection, and indwelling power becomes the unifying factor of our total existence."

"We're about finished this evening. There remains one important question to answer: 'How can this unifying factor happen?' It happens only as we experience the inseparable relationship between Jesus' promises: 'The truth shall set you free,' and, 'If the Son makes you free you will be free indeed.' The truth that sets us free is Christ himself! That is so important I need to repeat it. The truth that sets us free is Christ himself! We cannot discover true freedom at an independent distance from him. Writer Dean W. R. Inge was right, 'Christianity promises to make men free; it never promises to make them independent.' It is an open, honest, intimate relationship with Truth himself that we are set free."

"The theme of this series is spiritual freedom. Thank you for your attendance and attention. I hope you will join us tomorrow evening, in person or on line, for the discussion of the Spirit. The indwelling Spirit of Christ is the source of a consistent artesian flow of the thought and feeling of freedom. It is the next step in our journey forward. Thank you again, and God's blessing wherever you are tonight." The screen flashed to the University of Phoenix home page.

5

A WARRANT AND SUBPOENA

M ax was the first to speak. "Wow, he is really great! He did that whole presentation without looking at any notes. He's a rock star!"

Sarah whispered, "His reference to adoption was so very personal to me. It was like he was speaking only to me." She reflected a moment before saying, "I know that Miss Linn and Grace took special interest in me as a child. But there were limits for them. But when Dad agreed to adopt me, I became really cared for." She smiled warmly before adding, "He wouldn't let us use any of the settlement money for some of my whacky ideas, adding a bathroom, or even purchasing the new property. He paid for the cottages, and it was his insurance money that set up the new business here in Tigard. He wanted to completely care for me. Adoption was the amazing doorway for that care." She looked affectionately into his eyes. "I can't imagine a more wonderful life."

Max asked, "Shall we get married?" The crooked smile alerted Sarah to his playfulness.

"What?" she asked with a rush of confusion.

"No, you are supposed to answer, 'Yeah, but who would have us.'" His elbow pushed against her arm playfully. Trixy jumped from between them where she had been comfortably napping.

"Knock it off, Max!" she said pushing right back. "That's not something you should kid around about. That wasn't funny."

He immediately responded, "You're right. That's not something to joke about." His face was serious as he studied her eyes. "I'm just nervous about the phone call from Metro yesterday. I didn't know how to start a serious conversation this evening." He took a deep breath, and began. "Lisa, my old supervisor, was furious with me. She said she knew I had done it, and made all sorts of ugly threats." Now Sarah caught the importance of their conversation. "She said I was going to be sued." The smile on his face was more brave than humorous.

"Max, what are you going to do?" Sarah put her hand on his arm, a moment of comfort.

"I guess I have already done what needs to be done." He put his hand on top of hers. "Yesterday I scooped up all my disks and copies, along with my two working laptops. Everything else got scrubbed just like Metro's hard drives, there's nothing to find. I didn't want to worry you needlessly, so I didn't ask if I could store a box of my stuff in the pantry at the orchard." His gaze was fixed on hers. "It was the safest place I could think to hide it, if my place gets searched, and maybe even my folk's. I drove down last night." He pursed his lips in a silent apology. "Are you mad at me?"

"Well of course I am," she said sternly. "I would have gone with you. I haven't seen the orchard for almost two months. Was everything O.K.?" Then she smiled warmly. "You big goof, didn't I tell you I can't get mad at you?"

It was his turn to say, "Knock it off. This isn't something to joke about."

The next morning, before Max was fully awake, he would learn how true those words were. His doorbell rang followed by a heavy knock on his door. He bounded out of bed, pulled on some sweats and opened his door to a crowd. An off-duty Portland police officer handed him a search warrant while two investigators and two IT techs entered the apartment. It was only 7:30 for goodness sake! As soon as he could, he called Sarah, asking if she could contact her attorney, Mrs. Gilbert. Max thought it would be a good idea to have some back-up.

He was surprised to hear his doorbell ring again in less than an hour. This time when he opened the door expecting to see more trouble, he met a slim young man dressed in gym clothes.

"Hi, I'm Noel Tran. I work with Gail Gilbert." He handed Max his business card. "She's out of the city, but asked me to give you a hand with a search warrant. Are you O.K. with that?" He had already entered the apartment and was making his way toward the men who were searching Max's place. With his cell phone camera he began documenting anything that looked disheveled or damaged. "Gentlemen you have a warrant to search, not destroy or ransack." He snapped a couple more pictures.

"Hey Wall," one of the ITs called, "where are your other computers?" When Max answered that he didn't have any, he heard, "That's a load of crap. You geeks always have a batch of computers."

One of the investigators asked, "Have you got a storage space or locker somewhere?"

"Yes, there is a storage space down in the parking garage. It matches my apartment number." He found and presented the appropriate key. Noel followed the man out. The storage space was empty and swept clean.

It took the search team nearly three hours to come to the conclusion that there was nothing to find. They had carefully been through everything. There were games galore on his computer, but no pirated movies, pornography or drug related information, and definitely no clandestine industrial files. As Max had predicted, they found a large library of Bible studies and church information. They sifted through his emails, most of them to Sarah, and found nothing. Finally, the lead investigator said, "I'm convinced. He's squeaky clean. I've seen all I need to see for a report to Mr. Powers."

Noel, however, said, "But you haven't seen the last of me, friend. You and I will meet again soon to discuss payment for this apartment's condition and my time this morning. Have a good day."

During the morning he had had ample opportunity to hear Max's account of his termination from Metro, his opinion about Lisa Brock, his supervisor, Mr. Glen his department director, and Mr. Powers the CEO. Dwight Jennings the other programmer had been more interested in the supervisor's bed than his duties at Metro. Max said, "I think they wanted me out of the way for their privacy. As a smokescreen, they cooked up this mystery program that I supposedly deleted." There was enough factual information in that account for Noel to get a picture of the defense Max hoped would never be needed. If justice is blind, hope can be very naïve. Noel took with him the copics of Max's work review, and termination documents.

Sarah called just before noon. "Hi friend, I've been worried about you all morning. Are they still there?" Max could hear the concern in her voice.

"No, they left about an hour ago. And as I hoped, they didn't find . . ."

"They've been gone a whole hour and you didn't call me. I had all kinds of images of you being hauled away in handcuffs."

"I told you everything would be fine. There was nothing here for even creepy sleuths to find. Gail is out of town, but what a neat lady."

Sarah interrupted saying, "I'm sorry I couldn't get through to her."

Max pondered, "Then how could she have had one of her junior attorneys come to cover my back?" His name is Noel . . . hold on I have his card . . . . Noel Tran, and yes, he is Vietnamese, second generation here. I liked the way he stood up to the group."

"Group? How many were there?"

"There was a Portland police officer who didn't do or say much. He had an easy morning. Then there were two snoops who called themselves investigators, and two techs, who tore my computer apart, and wondered where the others were."

"Oh my word! That sounds pretty serious. Are they going to go over to your folk's home too?"

"I don't think so. My name was the only one on the search warrant."

Just the thought of a search warrant brought back memories of the Bowen household. She gave a little shiver. "Would you like to take me to lunch?" she asked playfully. "Even though it's raining, I'll bet we could find a fun place."

"Yes I would!" Max replied. "But my place looks like an Oklahoma twister just came through. I'm going to need to clean up this afternoon. I guess I'll have to pass." She could hear the genuine regret in his voice.

"Do you want help?" Sarah felt like the door was closing on their conversation.

"No, I'm going to need to take care of it. They dumped out all my underwear and socks, took all the clothes out of my closet, and even emptied my desk and the freezer. It really is a jumbled mess. But I would like you to record the lecture tonight. I want to hear what Michaels says about the Spirit."

She could tell that while his mood was angry, his attitude was just right.

As Max worked into the afternoon, mending the trashing his place had taken, he wondered if this was the last of the episode. The answer to that question came the first thing Monday morning when he was served with a subpoena to appear in the offices of Judge G.S Taylor to give a pretrial deposition on charges of corporate espionage and grand theft. He immediately called Noel's office to see if he could attend and give counsel. Then he called Cyber Solutions to tell them that he was keeping the copyright to all work he currently had.

Thoughts of the repercussions of his actions robbed Max of sleep on Tuesday night. He wondered if he might lose the amazing project he had developed. He wondered if he might be unable to get a job as a programmer again. He shuddered to think he might go to jail, or lose Sarah's affection. Even in his tossing and turning he knew the latter could never happen. When he got out of bed that morning, he was weary, but ready for the day ahead, come what may.

At the appointed time Max and Noel arrived at the judge's office to find Mr. Powers and his attorney already there, chatting with the judge. They were chuckling, which Max saw as a biased sign. After the introductions were complete, the judge asked Max if he pledged to tell the truth in all the matters before them. When Max said "Yes I do, sir," the judge said "Then let's gets down to the facts. Tell me about the development of your project."

Before Max could reply, Noel said, "Your honor, with your permission, I have some facts that might shed light on this subject. Then Max can tell you his account." When the judge nodded, Noel continued. "Max has been a full-time Metro employee for the past four years, during which time, customers have been billed for an average of 51 hours a week of his time, most of which is confirmed by his personal calendar, with no vacation or sick leave on his part. (Max marveled that Noel had that information.) In all that work he has been focused on font, color and graphics consultation. That is his training and specialization. It also allows him no work time to devote to research and development."

"In his annual work reviews he has received highest scores in his designated duties, and there is no mention of working on a breakthrough technology. In fact, his supervisor verbally affirmed that Max had nothing to do with the aforementioned project. His termination is unexplainable from that review of work accomplished, and seems to be a personal choice on the part of his department director, due primarily to the recommendation of his supervisor. If this had been a union represented work review, his dismissal would have never been allowed, a clear breach of employee contract."

"Of greater concern to me in this search for the truth, is the relationship of management to an unaddressed sexual harassment situation." The tension in the room became tangible. "Supervisor Brock and her programmer Dwight Jennings have had an open sexual union for several months, known, or at least suspected, by most of the department, with no intervention from management. What sort of credibility does director Glenn have in personnel matters? We have here today a case of looking in the wrong direction for Metro misconduct."

"Further, your honor, technicians have thoroughly examined the computers at Metro, all computers and even the server's hard drive history. Mr. Wall's home was given a storm trooper's search. Here are photos of the destruction caused by their crudeness. Notice the dismantled computer." He pointed to a particular picture. "No evidence exists to reveal a breakthrough project, no super discovery in any of those applications. Could this ruse, at my client's expense, be a smokescreen to hide an employee violation, a clear illegal situation, and an inept management mistake?"

Before he could say anything more, the judge looked at Mr. Powers. "Francis, do you know about any of this?"

The CEO shook his head. "I only know what Glenn has given me. This smacks of a real problem."

The judge looked at Max. "Mr. Wall, has your counsel given me the truth as you know it?"

"Your honor I have no way of knowing how much Metro has billed the people I worked for. I know I worked more than full time. I do know that the romance between Lisa and Dwight is no secret. I think that's all true, and I have said all along that there is no super project." Max waited for any more questions.

Finally the judge said, "Unless someone has evidence that this allegation has any grounds at all, I will call this hearing over." He looked from face to face.

Noel made one further request. "Your honor, I know this is not a small claims court, but it might be an opportunity for us to offer Mr. Powers this request for reimbursement for the expenses my client has had to endure in this unnecessary search on top of his termination without cause." He showed the judge an itemized invoice.

The judge perused the list. "Five hundred dollars an hour?" he looked at Noel. "Young man, you must have very large stones."

"Yes, your honor. I belong to a very prestigious firm."

Sliding the invoice to Mr. Powers, the judge said, "He didn't start the fuss, Francis. It's in your court." There was a wry smile on his face. "I believe we are finished here, gentlemen. Thank you for your time."

When it was all said and done, Lisa, Dwight and Mr. Glenn were unemployed, Noel was handsomely compensated, and Max had a new super computer and a fantastic job offer from Metro, which he didn't even consider.

6

FREEDOM II:
BROKEN OPEN TO BE FILLED

Max called Sarah to announce the favorable outcome of the hearing. He wanted to celebrate with her. She was delighted that his fears had been the worst of it. However, she was going to be in a late afternoon meeting with the finance folks of the Lake Oswego School District. She was being considered as a contract auditor. It could connect her with other districts and become an important foundation for the business. He wondered if she would have time to view the Michaels' lecture tomorrow evening. She said, "We could do that if 8:00 o'clock isn't too late. I'm still working late."

His voice sounded a bit weary as he agreed to see her then, and he said he would make reservations at Hurley's for Friday night. His folks had taken him there when he graduated from Reed. He thought she would like it. As Sarah hung up, she realized she had placed him on the back burner again. Why did she do that?

When Sarah pulled up to her parking place, she noticed that Max was already there, waiting for her. "I'm so sorry," she apologized. I tried to crowd one last thing into my afternoon and it backfired on me." They exchanged a quick hug.

Once inside, Sarah tried to do several things, all at once: turn on the T.V. and press play on the recorded lecture. She said she would change in a flash, and she put a bowl of soup in the microwave. "I haven't eaten all day!"

Max recognized the handsome face of Jerry Michaels and the UP lecture hall. He wondered if he should try to push 'pause' then decided against it because Sarah had already seen the lecture.

Dr. Michaels welcomed the folks in attendance and those watching on-line. He began by reminding his listeners to check in on their thinking. "Remember," he began, you may live in a free country, but if you're thinking poorly you will be feeling poorly, if you think restricted, how will you feel?" A murmur off camera answered, "Unfree." "Right! 'Think freedom and feel freedom.' Yesterday we concluded that when our minds are under the gentle yoke of Christ Jesus, we will find a liberating joy in all of our relationships. That is freedom indeed. Our emotions are captive by the infusion and guidance of the indwelling Christ."

"Now tonight, if I can keep you awake, we will examine the idea of being Broken Open, Filled, and Set Free." He over pronounced the words. "Will you agree with me that brokenness builds? Sounds like an oxymoron doesn't it? The words seem contradictory. How can breaking be constructive? Oh sure, if a bone breaks and heals, that spot is stronger than the other parts of the bone. But I would hardly prescribe that as constructive. So let me just say it this way: I believe personal brokenness is the secret of freedom in the Spirit."

"Whatever happens that breaks us open to a deeper invasion of the Lord's Spirit is a blessing in disguise. Whenever we face difficulties and problems that break our willfulness of arrogant control of our lives it is a gift. My dad used to tell me that troubles will either break us or make us. Over thirty years of living as a Christian has convinced me that they do both. Troubles bring us to the frayed end of our tether and force us to let go of the tight grip we hold on life. Only then can the Everlasting arms catch and hold us."

"I was at high school church camp when I became a Christian. With all my heart, at the time, I accepted Jesus as my Lord and Savior. He came to abide in me. But I was not free because I allowed so little room for him. His efforts at personality reconstruction and mind reorientation were resisted. I liked being popular, and boys were supposed to think about cute girls!" (Once again there was laughter in the background.) Sarah came in to sit and finish her soup. "Oh sure I called on his help, when I felt there was little alternative Then one day when I faced a personal crisis, and needed him desperately, my prayers for his help seemed unheeded and unanswered." Max looked into Sarah's eyes. "I kept praying faithfully with no response from my Lord."

"Finally, I asked my pastor why God was not hearing my prayers, and he said perhaps instead of praying louder, instead of my need for the Lord's help, I needed the Lord himself. My efforts had been to get him to do what I thought he should do to help me. He asked if he could lead me in a prayer. We knelt and I followed his lead, praying: 'Lord, I need you! Forgive me for trying to run my own life and seeking your power for my purposes. I give myself to you, and I give this seemingly unsolvable problem to you.' Wasn't that a cool pastor? I owe him so much."

"After that prayer, I felt a surge in-filling of God's Spirit. The problem was subsequently solved in a way I hadn't thought about, but could see God's hand at work. The greater problem inside me, that is my willfulness, was exposed and I allowed more of God's Spirit to pervade my mind and heart. The Lord who established the relationship in the first place, was moving to claim more of my mind and emotions and will that belonged to him. I was feeling more free."

"Now you would think that having made another major discovery of the secrets of God, the rest of my Christian experience would be easy and filled with freedom, wouldn't you? Not so, I was still a hormonally charged teenager with insecurity problems and bad hair. I covered my insecurities with a bravado that seemed charming at the time, and blatant use of the talents God had given me. Does that sound in any way like your adolescent years, too? Fortunately, the Lord began a character transplant and a personality reconstruction, not by telling me how bad I was, but by showing me how much he loved me."

"Each failure in my relationships broke my false pride and opened me further to his loving Spirit. His most valued gift in those days was self-honesty. I began no longer blaming people, and began to ask him what it was in me that kept causing the problems. He was often more ready to tell me than I was to hear. But the miracle had begun. I wanted to be filled with more and more of his Spirit. Each breaking of the old patterns of my personality allowed him greater access to my heart. He wanted to reconstruct the channel through which he could pour his supernatural power. I began to experience the sheer delight of being used, and being able to give him the credit and glory."

"I am thankful that much of the basic transformation took place before an active, full-time ministry. It is tough enough for the congregation to put up with my on-going breaking to build that continues as I yield more of myself to more of Christ's indwelling spirit."

"There is a three step process that takes place when we are broken by what we've done, or by our impotence in life's problems and perplexities. First, confession of our failure or our need to opens us to the Lord's presence and power. Second, we cry out for the Holy Spirit to fill our emptiness or inadequacy. Third, we discover the secret that brokenness, total willingness, provides the qualification for a fresh filling of the Holy Spirit. And as complex as this must seem, the difficulties through which we pass in this process become occasions of blessing. Does that make sense to you? Our brokenness becomes the threshold of growth in a Spirit filled life and greater freedom."

"Jesus explained the secret of this in parabolic truth in John 12:24. 'Most assuredly, I say to you, unless a grain of wheat falls into the ground and dies, it remains alone; but if it dies, it produces much grain.' A grain of wheat has a hard shell protecting the wheat germ. The germ cannot grow until the shell is broken open. This happens when the grain is planted. The moisture and warmth of the earth softens it, cracks it open and the germ begins to grow. The result? The new production is strong, it flourishes and grows, and it becomes a harvest. Whatever breaks the impediment of self-sufficiency enables the freedom of Christ in us."

Pastor Michaels spread his hands out saying, "I don't think I can say it any clearer than this: The Holy Spirit is Christ's Spirit with us and in us. There is a need today to reaffirm the oneness of God, Christ, and the Spirit. So often the Holy Spirit is thought of as a separate power apart from Christ. In the context of our discussion of brokenness that builds, we need to understand who fills us and what happens as a result."

"God is spirit. He is the living, acting Lord of all. In creation, he transmitted his life through his life-giving Spirit. Though his spirit, he sustains his creation with providential care. As Spirit, God created humankind and breathed into him the breath of life. The Hebrew word for Spirit is *ruach*, meaning wind or breath. The Old Testament is the stirring account of how through his Spirit the Lord called out of humankind a people to be his chosen and cherished people. They were blessed to become a channel of blessing to all people. By the Spirit, prophets were called and empowered and kings anointed. The Holy Spirit is referred to repeatedly as the presence of the Lord with his people, the source of wisdom and strength, victory in battle and prosperity in the gift of life."

"We know well the sad account of Israel's rebellion against the Lord, his commandments, and the guidance of his Spirit. At the lowest ebb of Israel's demise, the prophets predicted the coming of the Messiah when the Lord would again pour out his Spirit."

"In the fullness of time, God himself was made manifest to dwell among us. The incarnation, atonement, and resurrection was his Spirit in Jesus, reconciling a broken humanity. From then on the portrait of the Father and his Spirit is focused in the Messiah, the Anointed One. Jesus Christ is the acting God in the world. After the ascension Christ continued his ministry, in keeping with his promise before the crucifixion. He said he would come to his followers; he would abide in them and they in him. He would grant whatever was asked in his name."

"That is exactly what happened at Pentecost. Without losing oneness, he was the imminent in-dwelling Lord. 'At that day you will know that I am in my Father and you in me, and I in you.' (John 14:20) This explains the power of the early followers of the risen, reigning, indwelling Christ. The days Christ's followers waited in the Upper Room were days of brokenness in preparation for Christ's return. That brokenness had to occur within the disciples, between them, and in their relationship with the crucified, risen and ascended Christ."

"In their own hearts the disciples had to face their impotence without the Lord. They had received a clear call to follow the Lord and had witnessed his power in his message, miracles, atoning death, and victorious resurrection. Each had heard the awesome challenge to go preach, teach and heal in Jesus' name. But they knew they could not begin to implement their mission without his presence and power. The time of waiting convinced them they could not make it alone. True freedom is experienced when we know that Christ in us will be sufficient for all of life's challenges and difficulties. Each new experience gives us an opportunity to be broken open further to greater realization of his fullness."

"We hear a great deal today about the baptism of the Holy spirit and being filled with the Spirit. Many believe that the baptism of the Spirit is always subsequent to conversion and the filling of the Spirit is something different than growth in union with the indwelling Christ. My conviction is that at conversion we receive Christ's Spirit. Then, subsequently, we are broken open to new infillings of his Spirit. Each ushers us into greater freedom as we receive power to think his thoughts *and* live dependently and expectantly on his power."

"Paul admonishes the Ephesians to ' . . . be filled with the Spirit' (5:18). The verb is in the present passive imperative. It does not mean a once-and-for-all filling. If that were the case the aorist form of the verb would have been used indicating a completed action in the past. Rather, the apostle urges the Ephesians to 'continue to allow the Spirit to fill you.' The passive emphasizes something which is done to us rather than something we do. Every day, in each hour, when life stretches us with problems, difficulties, and challenges beyond our abilities, we are to allow Christ to fill us with his Spirit. And when we fail or are conscious of our inadequacy, we are given a sublime chance to be broken open to new infilling. Do you see how that can work?"

"In my own experience, the gifts of the Spirit were imparted as the result of the brokenness of realizing that I could not make it on my own. Any evidence of the fruit of Christ's character has come when I failed on my own to produce authentic love, joy, peace, patience, kindness, (in the background a murmuring of voices was joining his in speaking the list.) goodness, faithfulness, gentleness, and self-control. I discovered that Christ likeness is bestowed as my heart is open for Christ's Spirit to guide and strengthen me."

"The reason I put such a strong emphasis on the oneness of the Holy Spirit and the living Christ is that when the Spirit is considered apart from Christ it leads to self-centered spiritualism. Christ is relegated to a historic figure of the past who won our salvation, and the Holy spirit becomes a private possession often used as the basis of judging those who have or have not been blessed. The spiritual gifts are for all believers in whom Christ lives. They are equipment for ministry and release for praise."

"A final personal word: where are you feeling brokenness right now? Ask the Lord to help you identify it. Give it to him, and he will fill the pain of your hurts and will heal the frustration of your unfulfilled hopes. Instead of just receiving his help, you will be filled with him!"

"If you feel receptive to this, here's a prayer I find helpful in claiming freedom in the Spirit: 'Indwelling Christ, you promised to abide in me. You assured me that you will be with me and in me, and that you would never leave me or forsake me. I believe in you as Lord and Savior and Baptizer with your Spirit. Use whatever happens to me or around me to open me further to the infusion of your Spirit. You don't have to break me, Lord; life does that constantly. All I ask is that you use my times of brokenness to fill me more fully with your Spirit. Fill me and set me free. Amen.'"

Moments of silence filled the room, until Pastor Michaels said, "Thanks for joining us tonight, whether you are here in person or on-line. We have one more date tomorrow night to talk about 'People Who Need People Aren't That Lucky'. Does that sound like an invitation to come back? I sure hope so. Good night wherever you are. God's rich blessings are yours." Once again the UP emblem filled the screen.

Max looked at his watch and quickly stood. "I really like listening to him" he complimented the presentation. "I hope you recorded the last one. I want to know what's so wrong with needing people." He was heading for the door. "I made reservations for 7:30 tomorrow night. I hope that's O.K. I'll pick you up at about 7 o'clock?" With a quick hug he was gone, and Sarah was wondering what she might have done to make the evening end a bit nicer.

7

LEAVING HER!

The lights were low and intimate; the dining room was hushed. It was a perfect place to celebrate. Each table was situated in its own cubical of privacy. Sarah wondered if there might be a special motive to the evening. She whispered, "This feels awesome. On top of being very romantic, I'll bet it's expensive." It was like they were the only customers, even though the room was tastefully filled.

"If it is," Max answered with his usual grin, "Mr. Powers is picking up the check, as part of the repayment for trashing my place. It seems like a pretty fair trade, huh?" He told her about the hearing. She told him about the school district contract. He described his new boss whose name is a crack-up: "Will Willard has got to be a business challenge, but think about growing up with a name like that. Everybody would think he was stut . . . stuttering." Their quiet laughter was warm and welcome. He asked about the other women in her office and she asked when his new job would begin. Through four delightful courses they chatted about everything special and nothing in particular. Sarah wondered when he would bring up the reason they were in such a wonderful place.

When dessert was only sparse crumbs on the plate, Max said, "I've been thinking I should retrieve my stuff from the orchard, get my stuff out of your hair. Would you like to ride down with me tomorrow? I've got a meeting with Mr. Willard Monday morning, and I think I want to be ready for big changes."

A wave of sadness gripped Sarah. She suddenly understood the motivation for this extravagant evening. Max was using first person pronouns. It sounded for all the world to her like Max was moving away! He was leaving her. She struggled to hide the tears as she smiled, "I'd love to."

In the morning as they drove south on I-5, Sarah was unusually quiet. When Max asked if she was feeling all right, she explained that it had been a challenging week. He had smiled and agreed. "You can say that again." Sarah remembered how often Jon used to say that, and the tears began to form again.

Max told her about his boss, Mr. Willard. "I'm not sure if I'm afraid of him or just fascinated by him," he said as the miles slipped past. "He is always immaculately dressed. I haven't seen the same suit or tie twice, He drives that rippin' silver cad convertible, and even has his nails done! Whose boss has their nails done? And he seems to know a lot about me. I'm still trying to figure out how he knew about Tri-X and the very day that Metro let me go." Once again he asked if she was O.K.

He filled some more of the quiet by explaining that Cyber Solutions was a part of a much larger company, "Although there are nine other Cyber facilities nationwide, I can't find the website for Guardian Insurance, which seems to be the parent company.

I'll probably learn more about it next week. He wants to send me back to Virginia, where the headquarters are, for some specialized training."

Sarah was surprised to hear about such a big trip on such little notice. She wondered how long Max had known about it without sharing the news with her, but all she asked was, "What sort of training could you need? You can teach computer science for goodness sake." Talk of his going so far away, even if for only a week, hadn't helped her outlook on the day.

The streets of Salem, however, were so familiar she anticipated every turn. By the time they crossed the bridge over the Willamette River, she felt like she was home. Even on a rainy morning the driveway into the orchard felt warm and inviting. As they pulled up to the house, Eduardo came hurrying out of the barn, waving a happy welcome.

"Buenos Dias, Seniority Sarah!" He offered his hand, "and Senor Max. I was just in the barn fixing the harrow. I hook on a big rock in the new part, and have to replace two tines." His happy exuberance chased away the damp rain. "It is bery good to see you two. I miss you for so long."

"It's good to see you too, Eddie. Is everything O.K. in the orchard?" It was a question with an obvious answer, because she could see how well tended the place looked.

"Oh, si! We just get lots of rain this month, eight straight days now! You know it start with deceibing storm."

"How did it deceive you?" she asked for clarification.

"Oh, big dark clouds come up from the southwest. Look bery bad. Close all the windows in the house, barn, even check the big house windows. We hear rumble of tunder. Pretty soon it get louder and we see lightning. Boom! Boom! Going to be big storm. But then it just roll right over us with no rain. Boom! Boom! Lots of lightning but no rain! Nada! In Mehico we call that 'dry lightning' because it tells us rain is coming, but it never does. It deciebe us, huh?"

Both Max and Sarah smiled at Eddie's exuberant description. "It was good that you looked after the house and barn, amigo."

"Now that you are here, senorita, I can ask you a question?" When Sarah nodded, he continued. "My cousin is going to marry, and would like to use the barn. Is O.K. with you? I put up some strings of lights to make it a little festive. I hope is O.K." They all realized it would have happened with or without her permission.

Sarah said, "How much did you charge your cousin to use the barn?" Her tone of voice was not angry, but unmistakably firm.

"Well Senorita," it was obvious he was thinking how he might tell the truth yet stay out of trouble. "I ask him to pay for utilities and clean-up, $200." Eduardo looked at her feet.

"Tell your cousin he can use the barn for free, and you are going to cover the payment out of your next check."

Like a schoolboy caught in a deception, he continued to look down and said, "Si, Senorita."

Sarah wasn't finished. "And Eduardo, if I ever catch you using this orchard for your own profit," her eyes forced him to look at her, "I will find another orchard manager. Is that understood?"

It was all the censure that needed to be expressed. Eduardo understood the warning that he had overstepped his privilege and responsibility. Nothing more needed to be said except, "Si, Senorita."

She told him that they were going to get Max's stuff from the house and return to Portland. "But first I want to see the lights in the barn. I'll bet they are very happy."

"Si Senorita Sarah, very happy!" Eduardo's voice did not reflect the words.

Just before they left, Max and Sarah visited the barn loft. Climbing the new stairway, he exclaimed, "This makes the barn so much bigger. This deck is huge! Inside they found four strings of light bulbs around the walls of the loft, and several strings of festive white Christmas lights strung across the center. It transformed the space to a fairy-like invitation to celebrate.

Sarah asked, "Max, do you remember the first time you were in here?"

"I do," he answered in less time than Sarah expected. "It was just after your adoption by Jon. As I recall you wanted me to explain Holy Week. My gosh, that was six years ago. You were just fourteen years old. Hasn't the world changed?" His question was light and easy.

She whispered, "I can remember that I wanted you to kiss me." Sarah's wasn't light or easy.

"Kiddo, you were fourteen! That would have been a very bad thing for me to do."

She turned to face him. "I'm twenty now. Is it still a bad thing?" Tears were beginning to form in her eyes.

Gently Max embraced her saying, "No, it wouldn't be bad. I remember a conversation I had with Jon one day out here after a church service. He told me that when he asked you how serious we were, you told him not to worry. I kissed you like a sister." Sarah gave a small giggle against his chest. He finished by saying, "That's how I will always kiss you." She realized her earlier anxiety was well founded. Max was leaving.

"But I love you," she whispered. "I've always loved you."

"And Sweetie, I love you, too."

"Then why are you leaving me?" she asked with anguish. She didn't even try to hide the tears now freely flowing down her cheeks. "What did I do wrong?" Her voice cracked with grief.

"Sarah, you didn't do anything wrong. We both grew up. I love you more than my own sister. I wish I could talk with her, and play with her as I do with you. But don't you see that loving someone who is secondary to the orchard, or school, or a new business, or a new job, or a trip across country, is a love we have outgrown?" He hoped that came out the way he had practiced. "I will never stop talking with you, caring for you, or trying to beat you in chess," he said hoping to lighten the moment.

"But . . ." she fiercely hugged him. "But . . ." she sobbed, knowing that once again Max had shown her the high ground. "But I want you forever! I want more than dry lightning! Can we pray about this?"

"I've prayed about little else. Forever I will be the best friend you will ever have. If there is ever another candidate, I want to meet him to shake his hand. You are a delightful and lovable young woman, with your entire life still ahead." He guided her back toward the steps and their return to Portland. He wondered if he would ever visit the orchard again.

Their trip home was quiet, with both of them lost in private thoughts. Now that it had been said, Sarah realized that Max was right. Through the years she had known him he had given to her generously, over and over. Had she ever given him a gift? None that she could remember. Had she ever wanted to arouse him or satisfy his desires? The spark of passion she had fantasized had never materialized. There was no anger in her heart, and neither was there any shame. Max had been so truthful with her; she knew she would love him forever.

8

CYBER SOLUTIONS

On Monday morning Max entered the Cyber Solutions office in West Linn. He felt the building was smaller than he expected, and wondered how many employees could work here. There were only a few spaces in the parking lot. An attractive young woman welcomed him, obviously aware of his appointment with Mr. Willard. Max was shown into an office that was luxuriously sparse. It was not designed for business meetings. He was seated at a table upon which a stack of papers awaited his signature.

Mr. Willard began, "Max, I'm glad we are getting this beginning today. As you can see, I'm trying to get all the legal stuff out of the way. These are your insurance forms, retirement accounts, and other benefits offered by Solutions. We can direct deposit your monthly paycheck and expense account." He was passing documents for Max to sign, pointing to the appropriate lines. "The big thing we want to know today . . ."

Here it comes, Max thought. Here's the pitch for Tri-X. They're not going to get it!

"The big thing we want to know today is do you want to work at home, or here in the office. We have a huge backlog of work that you can help with. If you want to work at home, we have a condo that you can move into with state of the art technology equal to any industry standards. Our standard practice is to bill $200 an hour for your time; half of that goes to you on top of your salary. Of course you would not pay for the condo; it would be a perk. Give it some thought."

"Did I mention the training center in Williamsburg?" When Max nodded, Mr. Willard continued. "It is an on-going process that you can drop into any time. I'm thinking the sooner the better. We can get you working."

Max wasn't sure what he liked about this man. He was going though stuff too fast, but it seemed all right. He was offering stuff Max had not expected, but that seemed all right too. He seemed so confident that Max trusted him and wondered if that was also all right.

"Max, now that the Metro business is wrapped up, and by the way, they have some job openings; you didn't even respond to Powers' offer. Is there any one you should check in with, about being gone for a week?" Max wondered how he knew this stuff. He shook his head. "How about if you were gone for a month?"

"I'd need to check in with my folks occasionally. I suppose they would worry if they didn't hear from me for a while." Max thought about Sarah.

"O.K. Max, here's where it gets serious. You get to make a decision that could change your life and be of tremendous value to your country."

What is this all about? Max thought, preparing to get up and head for the door.

"I know it's weird right now, but we are in a hurry. You have been hired to be a computer programmer, and if that is where you want to be, great. We need your help. You can join the pool with several dozen programmers. Or you can use the skills that truly set you apart. We loved the Costa Rico thing, by the way, I don't think Scott or Bowen deserved the mercy they received; and your grades at Reed were top of the class. But the thing that caught my eye was that snow-job you put on the Metro computers to erase Tri-X. I've been watching you for a long time, and friend, I like what I see. By the way I hope you do develop that 3D application. I think that would have significant industry satisfaction for you, not to mention wealth."

"You're not after Tri-X?" Max asked with surprise.

"Oh, crap no! It would be a fun toy, but we are after something much bigger. Are you even a little interested?"

"If it is bigger than Tri-X, I'm very interested." But he was more curious how they knew so much about him.

"Max, I don't need to tell you that we are living in a whole new age of technology. It is increasing faster than all models suggest even possible. I also don't need to tell you that there is a new generation of very bad people who are using it for their own advantage. People who are in law enforcement are, for the most part, old school, and the free-range creeps they are after are definitely new school. Most of them are too young to know how bad they really are. I want you to be a good guy in cyberspace."

"Old school is bound by civil laws of due process in enforcement, and protection of rights for the accused, which have become problematic. We need someone with reason and humane ethics who can still search and destroy beyond due process."

Alarm sounded in Max's voice. "What do you mean destroy?"

"I mean to destroy in the way Metro's files were destroyed. That was masterful! I mean for you, however you do it, to be able to weasel into another computer and erase files so even the hard drive history is virgin clean; that is genius! We need you to prevent untold heartache and loss. We need your stealth ability to make wrong things simply go away. You would never be asked to physically harm another, but intervene in their attempts to commit internet fraud."

"I don't want to mislead you, Max. There are, in international situations, ground forces that may use the information you reveal, to track down and physically prevent the continuation of cyber crimes. But that is in another division from ours."

"That sounds pretty military to me," Max questioned. "How much time do I have to think about this?" It was happening far too fast.

"What have you been doing for the past half hour?" Mr. Willard's humor was thin clad over the moment. "I will be your supervisor, and you will report only to me. Your assistant will be Captain Noel Tran, whom you have already met. If you trust Gail Gilbert, we could give her a call to check out my credentials."

Max thought it beyond reason that she could be in on this too.

Mr. Willard smiled, saying, "And if you're thinking that she is part of the deception of Max Wall too, you are proving to be just the person we want. Come on Max, sign the enlistment paper, and we'll get going. If you are jacking around for a better offer, I will make a field promotion to First Lieutenant right now. Will that help? And you'll never have to wear a uniform. Come on, sign the damned paper!"

Mr. Willard had taken his car keys and said that Max's apartment would be moved to the new condo. They would take care of everything. Whatever personal items he might need would be found in the Base Exchange. By nightfall, Max was in Camp Peary, Virginia. The military jet that transported him had refueled midair from a tanker. It was happening unbelievably fast, and Max loved it.

Monday night Sarah called him to see how his meeting with Mr. Willard had gone. There was no answer, even at 10 o'clock on her third attempt. She tried again on Tuesday afternoon and evening. When she received the "out of service" message on Wednesday she was panicked. She sent him an email that said simply, 'Pawn to Queen three." Sarah cried herself to sleep.

By Friday afternoon she was so distraught with all sorts of disaster images dancing in her head, she called her old counselor, Grace French. Just hearing her voice answer the phone opened Sarah to all the pent up emotions. "Grace, I'm so messed up. I know you are super busy, I just didn't have anyone I could call."

Her friend recognized the tearful voice. "Honey, what's wrong? What has you so upset?" Grace's calm comforted Sarah.

"I think I have lost Max!" she said with a sob. "I always knew we were going to be together, but I think he's . . ." She didn't know what words to describe her dark sense of loss. She poured out in short version her work with UP. She said she knew she was neglecting him, but he had always been so patient with her. She had started the business and he had encouraged her. Now he had taken a new job, and all she could think about were her appointments and efforts to get business.

When she paused to catch her breath, Grace said, "Have you told him you realize your mistake?"

"That's just it," Sarah started a fresh sob, "his phone is out of service, and he doesn't answer email. I think he is really gone."

Grace asked, "You said you were in Phoenix a week. Did you call him every night?"

"Oh no, I had class work and lectures."

"Honey, I have an appointment in just a few minutes. I could schedule you for a session next week. But could I just ask if you still have the orchard."

Sarah answered, "Of course, I love that place."

"And you've started an accounting firm in Tigard?" Grace pursued.

"Yes, with two other CPAs," Sarah thought she could see where this was leading.

"And you are in your second year of a doctoral program? All of that at one time?" Grace asked with genuine awe, "Why?"

Sarah was quiet for a moment before she said, "No one has ever asked me that."

Grace asked, "Do you want to teach accounting or business practices?" Sarah said she couldn't see herself as a professor. With wonder, Grace asked, "then why in the world do you need to work so hard for a doctoral degree?"

"No one has ever questioned that either." She was still for a moment and then said with a shrug Grace could feel if not see, "I guess I do it because I can."

Her counselor snorted a chuckle. "That is the same reason given by adolescent boys for their first sexual experience. Does it really surprise you that with a burden that immense you haven't had much left to give to a meaningful relationship with Max? Do you think it might be time to reevaluate your priorities? Before Sarah could answer, Grace said, "Listen, my appointment is here. I have your number; may I call you this evening? Maybe you'll have great news."

As Sarah hung up, she scowled, "Adolescent boy indeed!"

She tried to bury herself in work for the remainder of the day. She searched for ideas that would offer timely and proficient service to her new clients. By the end of the day her mood had improved, although her anxiety was still very present.

When Grace called, Sarah's hope flared that it must surely be Max. She talked with her counselor for almost an hour. The best conclusion was that perhaps Max was somewhere that offered no opportunity to call her, or his new job prevented him from making any calls. Grace speculated that if he was in Virginia, he might be working for the government in a highly secure or restricted situation. She was sure that when he called, as soon as he was home, Sarah would feel sheepish for being so concerned. The second best conclusion was that Sarah would withdraw from the UP doctoral program for a while to reevaluate her motivation.

When she went to bed that night it was not to cry herself to sleep.

On Sunday she watched the worship service from High Desert Presbyterian on their website. She wondered if Max might be watching a service, and if he might be with someone else. Grace had told her strictly to chase those sorts of thoughts away.

On Tuesday she received a puzzling fax from Pam Gregory. It was a bank statement from Continental Bank of Cayman Island, with an eight figure balance. The coversheet simply stated: "Call me. I need to hire your services. Pam." Sarah didn't call her until the next afternoon. As she was dialing, she pondered, "So much for prompt service."

Pam answered cheerily. "I have caller ID, and the only person I know in Portland is you. Thanks for calling me right back." There was no more small talk. "I was right; Paul is filing for divorce. He's in charge of all our finances. I get cash for groceries and incidentals, but he runs the check book, I don't even see it. In going through our special papers, I found the Bank statement from the Cayman Bank," she paused, "in his mother's name. She's been dead six years, and it looks like there is still activity on the account. In fact, if I read it correctly, there is daily activity on the account, and the mystery is that Gloria passed away in an adult care home, penniless. I don't have a clue what this is about. Paul earns about $60 thousand a year and we barely make our budget. There is no way we can be setting aside two thousand a day!"

"Sarah, can you look into this for me? I can only afford a few hours of your time. When it comes to dividing our property," her voice quivered, "I'd really like to know what this is."

Sarah asked for as much identification information as Pam could give her, social security numbers for her, Paul and Gloria. Did she know passwords? No. How about birthdates? There really wasn't much to go on. Intrigued, she went on line and requested a copy of the Washington State budget, a seven hundred page document.

On Thursday morning UPS delivered her copy, and for nearly three hours in the afternoon she waded through the pages, looking for anything that might have seven hundred thousand dollars of skim-able fat. Of course it was a futile effort.

9

A NEW CAREER

On Friday evening, Max called. Do you believe in divine intervention? Sarah had been praying to hear his voice, and know he was O.K. "Where are you," she asked gleefully.

"It's good to hear your voice too." He replied, although she hadn't used those words. "I'm here at the airport."

"I'll come get you!" she said eagerly.

"I don't think you can. I'm not in the passenger terminal, and Noel is already here to take me to the condo. There is a lot to tell you; and a lot I can't. Can you squeeze in a lunch next week?"

"O Max, if I had to wait until next week, I couldn't breathe! If you have already eaten, may I fix you breakfast in the morning? There's a lot I want to tell you, too. And who's Noel? Is he Gail's attorney? Are you still in trouble with Metro? Oh, I have so missed you, Max." When they hung up, she jumped in her car and drove to the Lloyd Center. Macy's was open until ten. She found a rayon Capri's and matching top in shiny champagne. Sarah wanted to look especially nice in the morning.

Max was surprised to find Mr. Willard waiting for him in the seventh floor condo. Noel had driven to the Patton Way high-rise as though he was familiar with it, and pointed out the security system that was far more than residential. Mr. Willard gave a guided tour through the three bedroom unit. The first bedroom they looked at was easy to recognize. Max had left it just that way before he met with Solutions two weeks ago. The movers had even placed his Bible on the nightstand. It was spooky weird. The second one was a generic guest bedroom, and Max wondered how many guests he might have in the future. The third one had a security lock. Mr. Willard told Max that when the door was opened, an observer at Camp Peary would monitor whoever entered. The room had no windows and felt like a vault. "You have here," Mr. Willard said with obvious pride, "the very best electronic information center in the world. You are hooked into everything and everywhere. It will function just as the ones you have been working on for the last two weeks. By the way, your trainers were very impressed with your intelligence and attitude. They said you are a standout in the candidates we see." He gave Max a pat on the back.

"This beauty is monitored, just as your phone line and cable are. I want you to know that up front so you don't waste time trying to get back to privacy. You don't have or need any of that. It also works as an additional level of security; if anyone tampers with the lock or forces the door, the computer has a total shutdown default and will call for help. But we've never needed that. You can also dial 333 anytime on your cell phone and get Camp Peary security. Do you have any questions?"

"When can I start?" Max had a huge smile.

"Good question; right attitude. Noel is going to be your 'spotter,' just like a sniper team. He will target you on a suspect and you will do investigation. You will always clear with me before any engagement activity. Is that last part clear? We definitely do not want any rogue activity to draw attention to Solutions. We are the friendly ghosts that will stay in the closet." He chuckled at his own humor. "I've given Noel a couple easy targets to look at as you become familiar with your new boss." He pointed at the wall full of computer.

As they finished the tour of the condo, they were looking out the large living room window at the darkened Zoo across the street. Mr. Willard said, "Just for clarity sake, this whole building belongs to the government and all the residents are involved with Guardian Insurance. Several of the lower units are manned by armed security that are frequently deployed for special ops. Don't try to make friends with your neighbors, and don't be offended if they ignore you. You have been instructed in maintaining the security of our facilities. That is absolutely crucial. Please limit your guests, and no over-nighters. It gets very complicated if we ignore those guidelines."

Max was amazed that his clothes were hung in the closet as he had them in the apartment, and his diet cokes were in the refrigerator. It felt like he had entered another dimension of the Twilight Zone. That same feeling continued in the morning when he rang Sarah's doorbell.

She greeted him with an enormous hug. "I was so frightened I wouldn't see you again!" She gave him a very unsisterly kiss. Their bodies felt the other's warmth. "Oh it is so good to see you." She finally released the hug, and welcomed him into her signature farm breakfast of scrambled eggs, bacon and French toast. She was deliriously happy to have Max at her table again.

She asked about Solutions and Virginia. He told her that there was much of it that was confidential, but he shared the news about the condo, which was only about ten minutes away from hers. He tried to explain his new working relationship with Noel. He avoided any particulars of their job. He told her about Mr. Willard, for whom he would be working directly. He told her that he could do programming assignments when he wasn't busy, and they would pay him on top of his nice salary. "This is a sweet job!" But he couldn't tell her much more.

The food was consumed, but still they sat and talked. She told him that she had been so upset, thinking she had lost him forever; she had finally called her counselor, Grace. Max reached across the table and held her hand. "There was a light bulb moment when she asked me why I am working on a doctorate. I really didn't have an answer. She asked if I wanted to be a professor. What a silly idea. She asked why I had wanted to begin an accounting firm here in Tigard. My only answer finally was that I wanted to be close to you at least half of the time, in the orchard off-season."

Sarah rose and came around the table. "Max, I have been such a bone head. I've labored for what I didn't even want or need. And I have neglected the most important thing in my life: us." She bent to his lips and kissed him long and sweet. "I hope you will forgive me and guide me back to a wonderful place for us."

She moved back around the table but kept his hand in hers. "You haven't said much about your new job. Is it top secret?" she asked playfully.

"Actually, part of it is. I swore a confidentiality oath, not to reveal our locations or activities." He looked into her eyes. "Please don't share what I tell you with anyone else. We both could get into trouble." Max took a breath to plan what he wanted her to know. "I did become part of a government program of electronic surveillance. In fact, Mr. Willard said my starting grade is "First Lieutenant." He made a "yikes" face. "He hired me because he is aware of the computer deal at Metro. Even Noel knows, and likes me for it. That's why he was at my pretrial hearing, even though I'm not sure how he knew about it," Max smiled warmly. "I think I can tell you that Solutions is an electronic monitoring activity of the Department of Justice. I help look for anyone who is committing a crime on the internet, and if possible, I erase them."

When Sarah gave him a startled look, Max corrected himself. "I mean I delete their files or crash their computer, and return their money to IRS. I interfere with their intent to defraud, to protect others. So far I have only been learning the process. But starting this afternoon, I'm going hunting. Noel gives me the suspects to examine, and I try to find out what they are doing. I sort of feel like a cyber detective."

As he was talking, Sarah wondered if he could look into the situation Pam Gregory had sent her. "Hey Max, I just received a customer who has a puzzle she would like to understand. She found a bank statement for her mom-in-law, who passed away six years ago. There is still activity on the account, and a ton of money,"

"Sure. I'll take a look at it. Right now I need practice running the big main frame." He thought of one more thing to tell her. "By the way, I need to warn you that everything that comes to my computer or phone is monitored by guys in Camp Peary, Virginia. Everything; maybe even my own PC. I'm thinking that all of our conversations have been pure. However, after those kisses, I'm not sure if that will continue to be the case."

Sarah came around the table once again and said, "I certainly hope not." And kissed him again.

As soon as Max left, Sarah called Grace. She was put into voice mail and simply said, "Max is back and everything is wonderful, as you expected."

As soon as Max left, he replayed the welcoming hug and the softness of her body. He remembered the kisses and marveled that everything was so new and wonderful.

When Max was back in the condo, (it was difficult to think of this as his home) he was impressed again with a sense of impenetrable security. He fired up the computer and at the top of his homepage wrote, "Now war arose in heaven, Michael and his angels fighting against the dragon; (Rev 12:7a). He spoke to his computer, "O.K. big guy, let's go to war." Noel had given him two suspects. The first one was a pawn shop which was believed to be a money laundering front for a Las Vegas crime boss. The second was a motorcycle gang in Bakersfield that was believed to be the source of many assaults and three deaths. Max had the bank numbers of both and examined their weekly activity. In the Las Vegas case, frequent deposits seemed excessive. Once a month a major withdrawal, equal to the deposits, was sent to the same New York Bank, much too great to be a loan payment. In the case of the bikers, there were few withdrawals, only fairly large deposits every Saturday. The research suggested those were extortion payments. He called Mr. Willard.

"Mr. Willard, I believe there are two situations that might be solved in the same manner." He explained the banking activity and its corroborating statements from the local surveillance. "I think we can solve them both with a technique of confiscating 75% and depositing the other 25% in a personal account of the person making the deposit and informing the action in a 'thank you for the information note' sent to the person who would normally receive the payment. That way the bad guys will clean up their own house for us. I can then simply close the account with the vampire and all traces of us are erased."

"Max, how long have you hidden that larcenist's heart?" Obviously Mr. Willard liked the idea. "This is your first day and you have already exceeded guys who have been at this for years. Well done, but make it 90% and 10%! You have a green light for two actions." He hung up without saying anything further.

Max started to program "Michael" with the vampire command, but hesitated. He thought if Camp Peary is monitoring his every command, they will capture the process on "Michael" and save it. However, if he uses his own PC, unplugged from the phone jack, he could work on a disc in relative privacy. "Better smart than sorry," he said to himself.

From the Las Vegas account, he deposited 3.3 million dollars in IRS account 2827, and three hundred thousand dollars in the savings account of a hunted man who, by Tuesday, was in Panama living on the run. From the bikers, he then deposited nine hundred thousand dollars in 2827, and one hundred thousand in the savings account of a tough guy who didn't survive the week. He made sure the vampire removed any trace of his activities.

Max smiled to himself, "I can't even tell Sarah that I reclaimed 4.2 million dollars into our government's coffers, and deleted two bad guys in just one day. I've earned my keep." He and Michael turned their attention to the Cayman Island mystery.

A growling stomach reminded Max that he hadn't eaten since breakfast. When he looked at his watch, he was surprised to see that it was past 7 P.M. He recalled some frozen pizza he had left in his apartment refrigerator. Sure enough, it was still there. Accompanied by a diet Coke, it was filling but far from ideal food. He checked his PC, and found a note from Sarah asking if she could go to church with him in the morning. He dialed her familiar number on his cell phone.

After a cheery greeting, she told him she had tried to start a chess game with him earlier. "Have you been out?" It was as questioning as she felt appropriate.

"Oh no, I've been super involved with Michael."

"Who's Michael?" He could sense her confusion.

"He's my mega computer. Look at Revelations 12:7. That's where I got the idea for his name. I unplugged my PC for privacy." He hoped she would understand the inference.

"I still miss you." Her voice was small and gentle. "I especially miss you since this morning." Now she hoped he would understand the inference. "May I go to church with you in the morning?"

"You know, I haven't given church much thought. I've been really engrossed with Michael. I sort of thought I could find a nearby Denny's. I haven't been to a grocery store in almost three weeks. I just finished a nasty cardboard frozen pizza."

He would have gone on except Sarah invited, "How would you like to come over in the morning for a real farm breakfast. I make terrific scrambled eggs with French toast?" She giggled at the offer.

"That sounds wonderful. We could watch the service on-line, and I can tell you what I know so far about the Gregory thing." He was aware of revealing too much information to those who might be listening.

"Wonderful! I'll be ready any time after eight. Here's a goodnight kiss."

Max marveled at the shift in her attitude, and the corresponding change to their relationship. A month ago all she would think about was her new business and how well she was doing in school. Now it felt like they were lovers, or whatever he thought lovers felt like.

He wasn't ready to go to bed, so he went back in and told Michael that they should find as much information as possible about Mr. Willard. He went first to the Justice Department, and then to the Department of Defense. Two weary hours later he had to give up in frustration. Mr. Willard was so secret he was undetectable; the same was true with Noel Tran. Max felt proud to be part of such a high level team.

An October storm sneaked in during the night. As Max drove to Sarah's place, the first crisp golden leaves of fall danced along the streets with him. He wondered how he would be greeted this morning. Would the change in her manner carry over from yesterday? He hoped so. When she answered the door, he was greeted by a vision of loveliness. She had on pink tights under a gray cotton dress top that came nearly to her knees. "Wow! You look terrific, much too cute for a stormy morning."

"Maybe we can chase those storm clouds away," she said, once again giving him a direct hug. "I'm ready for you, mister," she said, still in that playful mood. They chatted through breakfast, and then quietly watched the Mountaintop worship service. She fixed Max a pot of Earl Grey Tea, hoping they might chat and linger a while.

"Sarah, what does ED808 mean to you, anything?" When she shook her head, he explained. "The Gregory file is embezzlement on an ingenious level. The money is coming from a tax collection. I haven't figured out how, but twice a day, sometimes three times, a deposit of $999 is made to the Continental Bank of Cayman Islands. That's a lot of deposits, but none large enough to draw an auditor's attention. The records go back sixteen years." He looked at her face; she winked and he giggled, "Don't try to distract me. I figured $2000 per day equals $60,000 per month or three quarter of a million per year, or 12 million dollars plus sixteen years of interest. He has hidden the money under his mother's name. I can see why he's getting itchy feet to get at that kind of money."

Sarah slid across the couch to lean against his chest and kissed him lightly. "I knew you could figure it out. What shall I do? Should I tell Pam?" She remained on his chest.

"I don't think we should do anything, unless it is securing the money so it can't disappear. Didn't you say they were getting a divorce? We may not have a lot of time. The Cayman account has two security questions. Do you think you could ask Mrs. Gregory what was Gloria's favorite flower, and the name of her first daughter." He moved Sarah back to her seat. "I'd really like to know how this works. One more thing; get their savings account number. I have an idea."

Sarah said with a bit of understanding, "You are becoming a Cyber Solutions sleuth." But she was wondering if she had been a bit too forward, and a little worried that Max was about to leave. "Would you like a chess game before you go?"

It was after two o'clock when Max returned to the condo. He hadn't even put down the bags of groceries before his cell phone rang. It was an angry Mr. Willard. "Where the hell have you been Wall? We said this is a 24/7 job; Noel has been trying to get you for hours. We have more targets."

"I'm sorry. I had breakfast with a friend, went to church, and as you can see," he looked around for the video feed surveillance; "I went to the grocery store. I'll get right on it." The phone clicked off. Well, at least, he thought, if I'm going to get my butt kicked, it's good that it isn't for too long.

He called Noel, and after apologizing again for being away from the computer, he received three targets with contact information: two brothers who were desert guides in Douglas, Arizona. Border Patrol suspected them of bringing large numbers of illegal aliens across the border. The second one is a gun shop owner in Laredo, Texas, who regularly sells used guns in large quantities to Mexican buyers. The third one is a pilot in Fort Myers Florida. He runs a charter business from

Page Field, and is suspected of transporting both illegal aliens from Cuba, and narcotics. Several raids have proven him to be an elusive target.

The Cayman Island idea he was kicking around needed a new secure bank beyond the routine realm of accountability. He explored the web and chose Zürich's Edmond de Rothschild. Using all $765 from his own savings account, he applied for an account. "My security code is C43779," he told the young lady who spoke broken English. He smiled to himself understanding that those numbers spelled "cherry" on his phone keypad.

He called Mr. Willard for permission to conduct his triple raid. After a brief, and Max thought unnecessarily terse conversation, he received a green light for three actions. Max turned to his friendly computer saying, "Come on, Michael, let's go to war!" He turned his attention to the first target. By yesterday's standards anything under a million dollars was spare change. The brothers had $880,000 in their account. He sent it all to IRS 2827, using the name and pin number of the younger brother, Jerry. The vampire command erased all traces of the electronic transaction.

The Laredo gun shop was a little more profitable. It appeared that it had been a father and son enterprise until the father's death. Max emptied personal checking and savings accounts as well as the shop's 1.7 million business account, into IRS 2827. He used the deceased father's name and business pin number. Once again the vampire erased any trace of wrong-doing.

Max just about passed on the Glades Air Service pilot. There was less than $2000 in his checking account, and nothing in savings. He remembered, however, that his task was to neutralize the enemy, so he sent everything to IRS 2827, and used the pilot's wife's name as the person responsible for the withdrawal. He would never learn that by the end of the week the pilot would have a major arrest warrant for grand theft and domestic abuse. He stole the plane that took him into hiding.

Before turning out the lights, Max entered his daily activity on a tally sheet started yesterday. To date he had reclaimed $10 million for IRS 2827. He felt that he was serving his country well. In his prayers there was gratitude for Sarah's affection, and this opportunity of important work.

On Monday Noel gave Max three more targets. One was a Los Angeles car dealer who was suspected of fencing stolen cars to foreign buyers; the other two were drug operations with local circulation.

But the most welcome news he received was from Sarah. She gave him the probable passwords from Mrs. Gregory; "Gloria's favorite flower was a gardenia, and she had no daughter." She added that ED808 was a small line item in the state budget for clean-up in the event of a school emergency. It had never been use and was only for $999, the same amount as was deposited daily. She gave him the Gregory's savings account number, and finally told him that she couldn't think of numbers any more, just embracing and kissing him. "When can I see you again? You know, we still have a Jerry Michael's lecture to watch."

Max replied to the latter invitation, "I thought you put school on hold for a while."

"Yes I did," she said happily, "but this is a loose end that really needs to be done." He could tell that she was smiling broadly. "And real soon," she added for emphasis.

"I've got four things that need to be done today. How about tomorrow evening? Could we watch it then?" He hoped his plan would work by then.

Max called Mr. Willard, for clearance to take action against the three targets. He was surprised at the casual response,

"Get'er done, Max." Without any other words of direction, Mr. Willard once again hung up. The car dealer had four different saving accounts, plus the business checking account. Using the CEO's pin number, he emptied all five accounts into IRS 2827. The suspected drug dealers got the same treatment, although Max could find little evidence other than their large balances to support any suspicion. He emptied their accounts, leaving a signature: "IRS seizure." Vampire scrubbed any other evidence clean. He increased his tally sheet by $7.3 million. They were just numbers.

The Gregory file was more complicated. First, he moved twelve million from the Cayman bank into their savings account, and the interest balance of 4.6 million into the Swiss bank account. Mrs. Gregory would receive that later. Vampire removed any trace of ED808. Gloria Gregory's account no longer exited. Then he got into ED808 and reprogrammed the deposits into the Gregory savings account. And finally, remembering how Mr. Willard had warned him to conduct no rogue activity, he used the vampire disc to cleanse Michael of any reference to ED808 or the Cayman Island bank.

He realized once again he hadn't eaten since breakfast. He fixed himself a couple hot dogs with a diet coke and sent Sarah an email. "Pawn to King four."

She answered almost immediately: "I miss you like crazy. Knight to King Bishop three."

Max answered by moving his King pawn to King five.

Sarah moved her Knight to Queen four.

Max moved his Pawn to Queen four.

Sarah moved her Pawn to Queen Bishop three.

Max wrote, "If you don't play for real, I'm going to resign. Knight to King Bishop three.

Just remember that Nero fiddled while Rome burned, King Pawn to King three.

Last warning. You can play rougher than this. Queen Bishop Pawn to Bishop four.

How about King Bishop to Queen Knight four. Check.

Knight to Queen Bishop three to block.

Knight takes Knight. Guard on your Queen

Pawn captures Knight, Ha!

Bishop to Queen Rook four.

Knight to King Knight five

Pawn to King Bishop three.

Pawn takes Pawn.

Queen takes pawn

Pawn to King rook four

Castle!

Queen Bishop to Rook three

"Queen to King, Bishop seven takes Pawn . . . Check mate! Queen to King, face to face! Yahoo! Thanks for being so gentle with me Max, or is this just your first time at the game? Were you really trying? You might want to brush up before trying again." She definitely had the tough talk working. Fortunately, she signed off, "Goodnight my friend; I love you and will dream about you."

Max didn't hear from Noel all day Tuesday. The condo needed cleaning. He needed a few more groceries, but when he checked his on-line banking account, he discovered that there had been no direct deposit from Solutions, and his balance was under $500. Perhaps they pay once a month on the first, he thought. He went out anyway to get some instant oatmeal, soup and fruit, grateful that his Visa card had plenty of credit. While he was in the store he realized that tomorrow was Halloween, so he picked up a couple bags of candy treats in the event there might be trick or treat folks at his door. He spent the rest of the afternoon with Michael, browsing the web.

10

FREEDOM III:
PEOPLE WHO NEED PEOPLE

The rain seemed to be coming down harder if possible as he rang Sarah's doorbell. When she opened the door he was struck again by her allure. She had a white net cover over a lavender shirt, with white Capri's. Once again he expressed appreciation for her delightful appearance. He was also aware that this was the third time he had come to a meal at her home without offering something to it. "Come on in out of the storm," she said happily, giving him a big hug. "We've got hearty stew and corn bread. I hope that will be enough." He joked that at his place there were only TV dinners or pot pies. "This is a treat!"

She said that when he wasn't with her, she had no appetite, and when he was with her, her heart was beating so fast she wasn't hungry. "You might be my very best diet plan." They chuckled together.

As they were cleaning up the empty bowls and plates, Sarah asked if he had a busy day scheduled. "Actually, I haven't heard from either Noel or Mr. Willard. So I guess for the minute I'm caught up. Nice, huh? Let's watch the lecture."

The familiar University of Phoenix home page gave way to the lecture hall and Jerry Michaels. "Wow, you're back," he playfully greeted the audience. "I want to thank you for your interest; and for those watching on-line who can even enjoy popcorn with it. I want to thank UP for including these very religious thoughts in their secular schedule. Their acceptance is unique in this age"

"If I were to burst into song singing, 'People who serve people are the happiest people in the world," he actually gave the familiar tune a try, "you would probably say two things to me. First knowing my ability to carry a tune, chances are you'd say, 'Jerry, don't quit your day job, and please confine your singing to your shower!' And secondly you would say, 'If you must sing, please get the lyrics right. You got it mixed up. The words are, 'People who need people are the luckiest people in the world.'"

"You would be right on both counts. But my singing disability aside, I think I have rewritten the words to Barbra Streisand's song correctly. Are people who need people the luckiest people in the world? I don't think so. Oh, I know what is intended: People who come to the realization that they need others are lucky. More than that, they are healthy, mature people. We were never meant to make it on our own. We are woven together into a fabric of mutual dependence. We need each other's efforts, expertise, and encouragement. None of us can live fully without the assistance, affirmation, and affection of others."

"Then why change the words? Because there is a kind of need which becomes dangerous and debilitating. When we need people so much that their opinions and judgments of us throw us into a tailspin, we lose our freedom. When our self-worth is dependent on the approval and acceptance of others, we begin to play our lives to the wrong audience. We become people-pleasers instead of people-lovers."

"Whenever we need people's acceptance so much that we make pleasing them the dominant concern of our lives, we become incarcerated in a prison of bartered love. We perform in order to assure the flow of approval. We need people so desperately that we seek to say and do what will keep them giving us what we need. We become the egotistic center around which life revolves. We need people to shore up our sagging self-esteem. We do what they want because we need them so desperately." He feigned wiping his brow in frustration.

"The real problem, however, is that we use people to fill the sacred place in our hearts reserved only for the Most High God. When we deify people to the extent that we need their acceptance inordinately, we edge God out of his place in our lives. People who need people that much are not lucky at all. They are plagued with spiritual hunger that is never satisfied."

"Allow me to state it flatly. As long as we need people for our security and self-worth, we cannot love them!" He paused to let that sink in. "The focus is never off ourselves and on them. Our persistent thought is keeping them in line so they will fulfill our needs. We need their approval so much that we measure all our words and actions to please them."

"When we need people in this unhealthy, selfish way we give others great power over us and in reality we've asked for the worst that happens as a result. People have an innate sense of the power over us we have surrendered to them. Because they feel so little love from us, they are often negative and critical. Our response is usually full of feeling that they soon discover how they can manipulate us with their disapproval. And so we respond to say or do whatever is necessary to reestablish the acceptance we need so desperately. It becomes a revolving cycle. But the cycle is orbiting around us, not them." He shook his head.

"Life is a struggle for power. The reason so many people do not feel free is that their need of people's assurance has led them to surrender their lives to crippling idolatry. People, not God, become the Lord of our lives."

"The Lord created us to need and love him, and then to love people. God is the only person we have to please. And when we know his pleasure in us is freely offered not because of anything we do, but out of sheer Grace, we are free to become so secure in him that we don't have to please anyone else. Thus liberated, we can focus on loving people out of the artesian flow of the Lord's love. Our deepest concern becomes how to communicate his Grace rather than using people to fill our own emptiness."

"Loving people instead of needing them is the sublime level of freedom expressed by Paul in the ninth chapter of his first letter to the Corinthians. He declares his profound love for his friends without needing anything from them. This leads to his remarkable declaration regarding his freedom from people to live for people. He says: 'For though I am free from all men, I have made myself a servant to all, that I might win the more; and to the Jews I became a Jew, that I might win Jews; to those who are under the law, as under the law, that I might win those under the law (not being without law toward God, but under law toward Christ), that I might win those who are without law; to the weak I became weak that I might win the weak. I have become all things to all men that I might by all means save some. Now this I do for the gospel's sake, that I may be a partaker of it with you.'" (Cor. 9:19-23)

"Let's think about this statement so its truth can set us free. That leads us to pose and grapple with three questions prompted by Paul's startling statement of relational freedom. We can get to the core of what it means for us by asking:

What does it mean to be free *from* people?
What does it mean to be free *for* people?
What is the purpose of this freedom?"

"Now Paul had been through more than his share of people pressure. When he became a Christian, he became the focus of bitter hostility and angry hatred from his fellow Jews. They could not accept Paul, the persecutor of Christians, becoming a propagator of the Christian faith. His life was in constant danger. Wherever he went, he felt the hot blast of rejection and condemnation."

"That would have been enough to deal with, but added to it was the criticism and undercutting of the Hebrew Christians who harassed his ministry to the Gentiles. Piled on top of that was the suspicion of the other apostles and leaders of the church. And to top it off, his closest friends often disagreed with him and questioned his guidance from the Lord. And yet he could say, 'I am free from all men.'"

"The only explanation for that freedom was Paul's assurance of Christ's love, forgiveness, and power. Only a person who can say, 'For me to live is Christ,' can also say, 'I am free from all people.' The sacred throne of his heart was occupied by the Savior. Therefore he did not need people's approval or acceptance. He had one purpose and passion: Christ! We stand in awe at the example he provides. Our temptation is to say, 'Well yeah, that's fine for Paul. He had the Damascus Road encounter with the Lord, heard his voice giving guidance and comfort in conflict, and knew the over-whelming power of his indwelling Spirit. That hasn't happened to us.'"

"But, friends, can it? Our dependence on people's approval and our alarm when it turns to criticism or rejection makes us wonder. Most of us have to admit that we are under heavy people pressure. Our happiness is dependent on their affection, the threat of losing them is a constant fear, and any conflict with them forces us to realize how shabby our security really is. That usually redoubles our efforts to stabilize our life to be sure people perform in ways that give us the assurance we need. That robs us of even more freedom!"

"So it seems to me, the first step to becoming free from people is to tell him that we realize how unfree we really are. Then we can confess that his sacred place in our hearts has been occupied by the people of our choice. That prepares us to begin a remedial program of transferring the dependence we've had on people to Christ alone."

"That happens when we make him, and not people the primary focus of our attention. That means consistent times with him each day, meditation on his Word, and ruthless honesty about those times when we shift back to needing people inordinately."

"I don't think Paul became free in Christ immediately. Remember the long period between his conversion and his mission work, as much as thirteen years. With each new difficulty with people or temptation to need them too much, he was forced into a deeper trust in the Savior. His time in Corinth is a good example. When the apostle was smarting under the rejection of the Jews there, the Lord spoke to him, 'Do not be afraid, but speak, and do not keep silent; for I am with you, and no one will attack you to hurt you; for I have many people in this city.' That's Acts 18:9-10. The same assurance was given him when friend and foe alike tried to dissuade him from his primary allegiance to Christ."

"And yet, Paul's freedom was not an end in itself. It was the motivating power of a releasing commitment. Can you see how Paul follows the affirmation of his freedom from all people with the declaration of his dedication to be a servant? Now the focus is on his servanthood to people: 'I have made myself a servant to all,' he declares. Paul was no longer the center of Paul's concern. Because of Christ, he sought to be to others what Christ had been to him. People's need for Christ was more important than using people to serve his needs."

"We are not free until we serve. The outward expression of our freedom from people is that we commit our time, energy, resources, and thought to caring about them. That's the positive antidote to dependence on people."

"We are not called to declare our freedom by telling people we don't need them, or piously asserting that we are not going to be controlled any longer by their manipulative devices. Instead, our commitment to be a servant gives rise to an inner resolve to allow Christ to meet the needs which we previously depended on people to satisfy."

"We are wise to avoid grandstanding pronouncements. We'll probably stumble in our first attempt to shift our focus from ourselves to others. Our well-worded declarations of freedom will come back to bite us. Better to just do it. Our words of encouragement to others and our actions of gracious help to them will speak for themselves. Anyone who is free of people doesn't have to say it. In fact, if we are free, a good test is that we don't parade it. Paul's explanation of his servanthood came long after he had actually lived it."

Pastor Michaels moved to the other side of the lecture hall. "Now we are ready for our second question," he said transitioning their thoughts. "What does it mean to be a servant of all? Paul helps us again. He entered into the world of the people he wanted to serve. With sensitivity and empathy he cared about what was important to Jew and Gentile alike."

"Because Christ was his security, he could observe the ceremonial rituals and customs of the Jews, his own people, so that he could earn the right to share Christ with them. He did not flaunt his freedom, but followed the commandments, the six hundred and thirteen Levitical regulations, and the customs of the oral tradition of the rabbis. He knew that none of these could save him. His salvation was through justification by faith in Christ alone."

"Likewise, among the Gentiles, Paul did not insist on the religious regulations of the Hebrew religion. He was more concerned about people than majoring in minors. He identified with people of all walks of life, all levels of intelligence, and all philosophical persuasions. For the Hebrews who became Christians, those Paul calls 'the weak' because of their cultural dependence on the regulations, he did not insist on negating those regulations by his behavior. Being a servant meant putting no obstruction in the way of communicating Christ."

"So often we do just the opposite. The customs and traditions of our brand of religion are more important to us than people who need Christ. What they receive from us is what's on our agenda rather than theirs. We often put more emphasis on the secondary things of our denominational procedures—theological subtleties or political convictions that we've baptized with an implied authority—than we do on the importance of God's love and grace. Often it seems that we need people's acceptance of our prejudices so much we keep bombarding them until we have some kind of agreement that satisfies us."

He moved back to the center of the stage for his conclusion. "Being a servant of people demands we become focused on where people are rather than where we need them to be. That requires *listening with love.*" He emphasized the words. "Sometimes people have problems that must be taken seriously. That's where we must begin. Often we have to resist giving our carefully rehearsed theories or advice, and simply enter into their needs for practical help. Then, when we've established how much we care, we'll have an opportunity to share Christ with them."

"Listening with love requires scrapping our agenda and timetables. So often the look on our faces betrays our inner impatience. Though we do not say it, people hear our unarticulated restlessness. Written in our expression is, 'I wish you'd stop talking so I can say what I want to say.' Maybe our body language sighs, 'Please get on with it; I have some conclusions I've been waiting to give you to straighten you out!' We are thinking so much about what we're going to say that we don't really hear what people are saying."

"But often it's only further evidence of our need for people that keeps us from seeing them. Our need to be liked, or to be an authority figure, or just need to be needed, keeps us and not others at the center of our attention."

"Often this leads us to rearrange people's shared needs and refocus them in the needs we have. Whatever other people say is worked around until it is an expression of what we are feeling about our own lives or relationships."

"A counselor in our community who had profound needs in his own marriage projected those needs onto almost everyone he counseled. He felt that at the root of all problems were needs of affirmation, affection, and unsatisfied sexual hunger. He led his counselees into these areas so he could hear them talk about his own unresolved tensions. That may be an extreme case, and we all hope it is, but in less dramatic ways, to focus on our own needs is a temptation for all of us. We can engineer conversations to subjects dealing with our areas of expertise, interests, or problems. At a party in his own home, an author was overheard saying to his guests, 'That's enough talk about me. Let's change the subject. Now, what did you think about my last book?'"

Interesting people are those who communicate to others that they are interested in them. The servants of Christ are called to be that quality of interesting people. The result will be a new interest in the Christ they love and seek to communicate."

"*Caring allows listening,*" he emphasized the words. "A servant of people asks the Lord for guidance about the particular people he has placed on the servant's agenda. No one can care profoundly for everybody. Our task is to allow the Lord to give us the particular people who are to be the focus of our concentrated, deep caring. The group will change as some are helped and others take their place. Who are these people for you?"

"Caring means getting into other people's skin. It demands seeing things from their point of view, being available to help lift their burdens, and giving our time, energy, and money when it is needed."

"Last week I overheard a woman say, 'Listen, I couldn't care less!' Those are often repeated words, which mean literally that the speaker doesn't care one tiny bit about it. But then why even mention it? I'm thinking the real meaning of those words is, 'I wish I didn't care so much about that.' And the truth is that her own needs to be free of caring and to be cared about were blocking her own calling to be a caring person."

"From the foot of the cross looking into the face of the Savior our real question becomes, 'How can I care more about people.' Listening and caring is in preparation for the opportunity to serve people by sharing Christ's love. Introducing people to Christ is the true purpose of our servant hood."

"We live in a day when great emphasis is being placed on practical ministry to people's material and social needs. The proverbial pendulum has swung away from concentrated concern for people's eternal life to attention to their temporal life. The swing is inevitable. For too long we overlooked people's suffering and disadvantaged conditions. Our real task is to minister to both spiritual and temporal needs but never trade one off for the other."

"Perhaps this brings us to the summation of our series on spiritual freedom. How can we measure the success of our servant directed lives? Paul was very clear about that. 'I have become all things to all men,' he said, 'that I might by all means save some. Now this I do for the gospel's sake, that I may be partaker of it with you.'"

"Everything Paul did as a servant was to 'save' people. He really believed that without Christ people were lost for eternity. That prompted him to care profoundly about introducing people to Christ. But note his continuing concern for those who responded. He wanted to be a 'partaker' of the gospel with them."

The Greek word he used is *sunkoinōnos*, a compound word made up of *sun,*—together with—and *koinōnos*—Partner or sharer. The apostle Paul wanted to help people begin with Christ so that he could share the adventure of growing with them. He did not love people and leave them to flounder. He not only helped people get on their feet spiritually, but stood with them and then walked and ran with them in the adventure of the new life."

"All this comes down to some personal questions about the depth and length of our spiritual freedom to serve. To whom are we listening and caring about in order to introduce them to Christ? And when they are ready, when the time is right on their timetable and not ours, are we able to present Christ, help them surrender their lives to him, and begin an eternal relationship with him? Have we persisted with willing help as they learned how to pray, discovered a daily time in the

Scriptures, and became free people rooted in clear thinking and liberated feelings? Were we still around to help when they dealt with the things that threatened their freedom? Were we there to cheer them on when they became a servant to others the way we had been to them? The real test of our servanthood is whether our listening and caring and sharing have enabled people to lead others to Christ. True servanthood is setting people free to set others free!"

"John gives us the secret of Jesus' freedom to be a servant, and the motivation for ours as well. In John 13:3-5 we can find these words: 'Jesus, knowing that the Father had given all things into his hands, and that he had come from God and was going to God, rose from the supper and laid aside his garments, took a towel and girded himself. After that, he poured water into a basin and began to wash his disciples' feet . . .' Can you identify the three salient things that prompted Jesus? They are authority and power given to him by the Father; he had come from God; and he was going to God."

"The very same can be said of us through Christ. We are servants by his call. His authority is given to us. We know who we are and for what we are intended because we know from whom our new life has come, and to whom we will go after the brief comma of the paragraph of life. We are free to give ourselves away during the brief years of this on-earth portion of our eternal life."

"You know, in my years of ministry I have heard a multitude of people's needs, yet never once have I heard someone say, 'Jerry, my deepest need is to become a servant of people.' And yet, so many of the other needs I heard would be solved by answering Christ's call to be a servant to those whom he places in their lives."

"Friends, the awesome truth is that we are created to be servants of Christ by serving people. There is no chance of true freedom for us until that is our primary calling. Martin Luther said, 'A Christian man is the most free lord of all, and subject to none; a Christian man is the most dutiful servant of all, and subject to everyone.' That is the powerful paradox of the Christian life. We are freed from people to live for people. And in serving them, as if serving Christ himself, is lasting freedom. People who serve people are indeed the most joyful people in the world!"

"Thanks again for your attention whether you are here with us, or scattered far across our world. This evening concludes our series on personal freedom. I hope you have found reassurance in our time together. My prayer is that you find your perfect freedom, in God's perfect peace. Good night." After just a moment, the UP logo filled the screen.

Max and Sarah sat quietly for a bit, listening to the rain pound against the window. Finally he started to stand saying, "It's late. Maybe Noel has been trying to get in touch with me." Sarah tugged him back down beside her with a whispered, "Is there anything I can do to keep you here just a tiny bit more?" He stood again, this time pulling her up with him. "I read a quote that you make come true," he said. "'The only way to live is to accept each minute as an unrepeatable miracle, which is exactly what it is—a miracle, and unrepeatable.'"

Sarah leaned against him with a passionate kiss. "Some moments are worth reliving, and are equally miraculous." Her breath was as soft as a prayer on his neck.

11

THE CON!

On Wednesday Max was alarmed that neither Noel nor Mr. Willard contacted him. He continued to mark time by browsing the web. He found the Classical station and allowed Michael to stream it all afternoon. He played a couple chess games with Sarah; finally winning one. He was about to get ready for bed when all hell broke loose.

He thought he heard a little voice in the hall say, "trick or treat." Moments later there was a knock on his door. Opening it he expected to see children. Instead there was a man and a woman. She held a badge of some sort in her hand, and asked "Max Wall?" In her other hand he did not recognize the Taser she was pointing at his chest. Suddenly the lights went out!

When he regained consciousness, she said, "I know that hurts like a bitch. Here drink some water; that will help." His hands were bound by stout wire ties, so she held the glass to his lips. He did manage to suck in a bit of water, but it really didn't help. He hurt all over.

"Max, we are from the FBI. I'm Liz Watts, and my quiet friend here is Bret Franklin." Max thought the extension on the barrel of the pistol that he held was a silencer, which was not regulation issue, and meant he was in a whole pile of trouble. "Max, we sort of do the same thing you have been doing; we work under the radar of the law trying to make things right.

You don't have anything to worry about as long as you are not guilty along with Crenshaw and Nguyen." Max shook his head not understanding. "Max, this condo is, or was owned by a man named William (Bill) Crenshaw. He is a con man we have been after for a long time. You tipped us off by trying to get into the Defense Department files from this computer. We knew someone was here."

Max said through tight lips, "Mr. Willard told me this building belongs to the government, and we are working for the IRS." He thought it very possible that he was going to vomit.

Liz shook her head. "Wrong! Many of these units are owned by downtown corporations that use them either for afternoon sex, or hospitality for foreign business ties. It's always pretty quiet." Then getting back to questioning Max, she asked, "Was his partner an Asian?" When Max nodded, she informed him, "That was Duc Nguyen, a really nasty Canadian. They wanted him on a bucket full of assault charges. He's also a computer genius. We think he had hacked into the Department of Justice files of suspects and on-going investigations. That's where he was getting his targets for you guys. He probably did a scan on you as well to find this year's geek." Max didn't catch the implications of the past tense verbs. "And they had you chasing money for the IRS?" she asked. Max nodded.

"He said he was one of Gail Gilbert's attorneys." Max said completely confused.

"Who is Gail Gilbert? And for sure he was not an attorney. That was all part of the con." Liz seemed to be enjoying this reveal to a stunned victim.

"Max, are there any weapons in this condo?" When he shook his head, Bret put his in his shoulder holster, and went into the bedrooms looking for any that might be hidden. When the search led him to the third bedroom, Max warned him. "If you go in there Camp Peary observers will know you are here."

Liz chuckled, "Max, you are so full of the con these guys put on you. Camp Peary is for National Guard orientation and computer training. They try to bring civilians up to speed on the Hewlett Packard main frame. I'll bet they don't even know they are there, let alone scan other people's surveillance. Tell me your story. When did you first meet Crenshaw, your Mr. Willard?" Max started with his termination from Metro right up to opening the door a few minutes ago. He told it all.

Did you get a military service number?" she asked. When he shook his head, she said, "And didn't that tell you something?"

"I believed him. I rode in a fighter jet. I signed insurance and enlistment papers. I trusted him." Max had little other defense. "I was proud to do a good job."

"Sweetie, anyone who is willing to pay for fuel can hitch a ride on a National Guard training flight." Liz told Bret to take the ties off his wrists. "But if he makes a run for it, shoot him." She said she was only teasing. "The history we believe about Crenshaw and Nguyen, is that they got a geek to do what you have been doing for about a week. They rake in a pile of dough and then they disappear. We think they dump the body of the geek either in the river or under the Burnside Bridge."

Max interrupted her with wry humor, by saying, "It doesn't sound like I would have used my retirement." The dawning that he might have suffered the same fate as a nameless computer programmer was frightful.

"They live on the IRS money," Liz continued, "until it runs out and then they come back to do it again. We knew this condo was his home-base because he had to use his real name when he bought it five years ago. By the way, how much did you haul in for them? When Max answered $17.3 million," they both nodded in surprise. "That is a lot better than the other trips, I'll bet. Maybe that's why he made such a desperate run for it."

"Max, show us what you have done on the computer since you got here." He led them into the third room, but warned, "Camp Peary will know you are here." They both chuckled. Liz said, "The sign of a great con is the victim remains in it longer than anyone else." Bret nodded in understanding. Max didn't much favor being called a victim, but it was better than a perpetrator.

When Max booted the computer the home page appeared with its banner: "Now war arose in heaven, Michael and his angels fighting against the dragon; (Rev 12:7a). Liz smiled as she read the quote, and said, "This is better that any cheap novel could possibly be." They could easily see the eight targets that Max had cleaned out, and the web searches for Mr. Willard's identity.

Finally Liz said, "Here's the deal, Max, you are either about to get flipped, or arrested. The bad news is that you have to choose. The good news is that if you choose the former, you will be able to keep doing what you've been doing' but now with at least some integrity, and return. I'll bet you haven't been paid since day one." Max shrugged, Liz went on, "Like us, you will be a crime fighter, under the legal radar. Because the rest of the story is that sadly, Mr. Nguyen was shot last night, we think by his partner Mr. Crenshaw, but the police have it as a gang drive-by. He didn't make it to the hospital. I think you generated more money than Crenshaw wanted to split."

"Even more startling," she went said, "the Highway Patrol found a silver cad convertible on the way to the coast this afternoon with Mr. Crenshaw's body in the wreckage. They think alcohol and speed contributed to the accident. That leaves you, up to your ass in evidence."

"I like to find win-win solutions, Max, and I think I have. Do you think you can retrieve the IRS money you have deposited in IRS 2827?" Max thought that he might be able. "It must not be a surprise to you that it is not an official government site, but Crenshaw's personal account." But it was a surprise to Max.

"If you can do that, there is a 10% reward for you. Since Mr. Crenshaw had no known relatives, this condo has been seized as a crime scene. It has three years of back taxes owing. If you pay the taxes, we can title it to you. I think there are also some homeowner fees owing but you can pay those also. Then if you would like to replace this Hewlet Packard with the latest version, the agency will provide that, and make you a contract consultant; no salary or benefits, just 10% of what you can retrieve. The happy news that goes along with that is you would get your leads from us. By the way, since you are the only surviving employee of Cyber Solutions, it can be yours too, unless you want us to arrest you."

"I don't want to be arrested." Finally Max could eke out a grin.

Bret asked, "Shall we take him with us to the apartment?" He was seeing the same thing Liz saw, a genuinely nice, innocent young man.

"O.K. pal," Liz said with a confidential smile, "here's one more layer of the deal to consider. We need to go out to Crenshaw's place again to collect evidence. That's where we got on his tail this afternoon. He ran and we chased him halfway to the coast, 'Where is the Highway Patrol when we need them, huh?'" She looked at Max carefully to determine if he comprehended the importance of what she was saying. "We're going to go through his stuff. We can't take anything other than evidence of a crime. You, on the other hand, as his nearest unrelative, can have anything of value. This man has been living large, In a day or two everything is going to a thrift store. You might as well get something for the three weeks you have worked. Do you want to go?"

"Now? It's late." As Max said it he knew how lame it sounded. "I'd like a shot at his computer," he said with more resolve.

"There you go! Let's wage war on the dragon. You can sleep in the morning." They drove to an upscale section of Beaverton. It was evident that Bret was familiar with their destination.

Liz saw Max study the key-ring she took from the glove compartment. "Yeah, we're hoping the Patrol assumes the keys flew out at the wreck. We also slowed down the identification process by lifting his wallet and registration papers." It was far too matter of fact for Max to grasp.

Once inside the apartment, he just stood still while Bret and Liz went on their separate missions. He heard Bret say, "I've got some guns."

Liz called Max to come in the bedroom for a computer. Max took the laptop with him and found a PC in the office area.

Bret said, "Look at this porn; it's all gay stuff! The guy was gay!" Max recalled how Mr. Willa . . . Crenshaw had joked that he was a good ghost in the closet. That now took on a different meaning.

Liz answered, "That explains this fine china and crystal. He had great taste,"

In the bedroom, Max found a jewelry box with several expensive looking watches and rings; there were heavy gold chains. Underneath it was a stack of Treasury Notes, which alone would be a fortune. There were also four passports, each with a different name but Crenshaw's picture.

"Take it," Liz said over his shoulder, "except for the passports. We can't, and it would be a shame to just throw it away."

Max had decided to rescue the desk in the office, so he placed treasures in its drawers. He also booted the computer, grateful for passwords that automatically entered. He forwarded all files to Michael.

They foraged for over an hour. Max found himself being swept into a feeding frenzy. "My gosh, look at this Plasma TV and a surround sound system." There was a treasure horde available. Finally, Liz announced that they had all they could find. She gave the keys to Max, and a business card with her contact numbers. She told him to get movers to take whatever he wanted by tomorrow evening because the Thrift Store would take the rest on Friday. There was a key that obviously fit the door they had just locked and another that would probably open the condo. There was another door key, a key for the cad, and another vehicle key that was different.

12

ABUNDANCE!

When Max awoke later that morning, he wondered what reality he should believe. His best grounding was to concentrate on Sarah. She was his rock and foundation. He called her while it was still too early. "Sweetie, I'm living in a fantasy, but I don't know if it is a comedy or a horror story," he told her. "I'll fill you in on everything tomorrow. Today is going to be a wild ride. I can only tell you that I am sort of unemployed again, but it is a very good thing. I feel like God has lifted me out of a pit and placed me in an abundant orchard. Yesterday I was close to broke, and today I can't even count my wealth. Isn't that bizarre?"

"Max, I can't even follow what you are saying," her sleepy voice whispered. "Do you feel O.K.?"

"May I pick you up for breakfast in the morning? It will be easier for me to show you than try to explain."

As Sarah hung up, her mind was awash with notions of what Max might be into.

He went to Office Depot and got packages of green and red adhesive stickers. Back at the condo, he contacted a moving company that had a team available this morning. He placed red stickers on his old furniture he chose to replace, which was all of it.

He then drove to Beaverton and found the apartment again. Like a kid in a candy store he walked from room to room placing green stickers on what he wanted to take. A moving box was filled with golf shirts, two suits, sport coats and a dozen incredible dress shirts and an armload of ties. Another one had towels and satin sheets. The desk and chair had to go, as did the black enameled king size bed, and matching dresser and armoire. The dining room table, chairs and hutch, with china, silverware and crystal. Yes! That plasma TV and sound system, and the blue leather sofa and love seat had to come with him, and the teak bookcase. He went into the laundry room and under a stack of towels he found a safe, which he immediately took to the car and locked it in the trunk! There were eight framed pictures that looked elegant. He chose to leave the nude male, and weird couple. In the bathroom he discovered another gun. He got a Ziploc bag and carefully eased it in, thinking it could have evidence, or worse, be loaded. When the movers arrived he called it quits, knowing that the thrift store was going to have a holiday tomorrow, but second to the one he was having today.

While the movers were arranging the new items, Max and Michael worked on the information he had been able to recover from Crenshaw's records. There was a handsome bank account in the name of Noel Tran; Max emptied that into his own. There were four accounts in the names of Bill Crenshaw or William Willard; those he sent to his Swiss account. With little trouble he traced IRS 2827, and sent $17.3 million to the new IRS deposit number using his new identification tag. His anticipated 10% commission made him light headed. He erased all trace of his activity with the vampire disc.

After driving to a nearby ATM to get enough cash to reward the moving team with a pleasant gratuity, he called Liz to tell her about the gun. Within the hour Bret knocked on the condo door to add the weapon to the ones they had gathered. "I love what you have done to the place," he said with a grin. "This is a real Condo 2.0!" When Max presented the gun in the plastic bag, Bret complimented him for at least trying to preserve evidence. Max asked if it might be possible to have copies of the stuff from Crenshaw's wallet to solve the puzzle of the extra keys. As he walked out the door, Bret said, "I have a hunch we will see a lot of each other. Good luck."

Max emptied the moving boxes before his body rebelled. He was hungry and very tired. He decided to get some sleep and enjoy breakfast even more. Before he went to sleep, he prayed, "God of Abundance, accept my gratitude for the mystery of this day. I ask that you make me worthy of your goodness; and guide me in this treasure's use. Help me be free for people."

When Sarah opened the door, Max was struck by her beauty. It seemed that every time they met, she was more attractive. "You look fantastic," he finally said. She had forest green slacks and a matching green and black plaid top.

"You're just saying that because you're hungry," she giggled, as she gave him another wonderful hug. "I'll just get my coat." She pulled on her tan car coat with the Dalton plaid.

Max informed her that he was so ready for breakfast that he would suggest the closest restaurant, which as good fortune would have it was a Shari's. They hurried to his car through the light rain. On the short drive, she asked him to tell her about his unusual day yesterday.

"I think I want to show you my unusual day, rather than try to explain it. But I can for sure tell you that it is righteous, and unbelievable. I don't even know the extent of it yet."

When they had been served hot tea and placed their order, Max gave Sarah some important instructions. "Kiddo, I think you should contact the Washington State Treasurer, James

McIntire, as Mrs. Gregory's auditor. I think you should tell
him that she discovered a savings account that she didn't even
know existed. Mr. Gregory is suing her for divorce and she
asked you to help establish an equitable settlement. You are
bound by law to report any crime you uncover; their savings
account is money that Mr. Gregory has embezzled from
the state revenue over the past sixteen years. Your computer
technicians have traced the source of the money to item 808
of the Education part of the Washington State budget. That
innocuous item has been collecting the penny fragments of
every taxable transaction that has happened in the state for the
past sixteen years, since this computer system was installed.
There is a touch over twelve million dollars. The technicians
repaired the breach and the deposits are now being made
into the general fund." Looking into her eyes he asked "Does
this seem weird?" When she shook her head, he continued.
"I think you can give an account that doesn't mention the
Cayman Islands, or Gloria Gregory. I'm trying to make it easy
for the law to crack down on Mr. Gregory. He asked for a
divorce, and now he can have one, and some prison time to
boot." Sarah broke into a smile.

"The state will probably have a tiny whistle blower reward,"
Max explained. "Assure Mrs. Gregory that when the divorce
is final, and the dust has settled, she will be more handsomely
compensated. If she thinks her life has been a waste, tell her
that it's not the only one she gets. She can start a new life,
hopefully with someone who will appreciate her."

Sarah reached across the table to hold his hand. "Max, it
seems like you have changed in the past month. Has something
happened that you want to tell me?"

"I want to tell you how much I care for you. That will take
a long time. I might have to show you." He gave her hand a
tiny squeeze. "Yes, this has been a revolutionary month. I've

been crushed, redeemed, flattened, and now lifted up higher than anyone can imagine." He gave a big sigh. "But let's change the subject. What would you do if you didn't need to work another day in your life?"

Sarah loved these sorts of questions. It was like, "Where would you go if money was no object." She saw their food coming so she said, "Well, I wouldn't want to do nothing, but I don't want to be on the crazy-go-round I have been on for the past couple of years either." They chatted and laughed over their meal. Sarah wondered if this new buoyant Max was a permanent change. When they were getting ready to leave, Sarah leaned over and said, "If I didn't need to work, I'd do two things. I'd learn how to serve God, and I'd learn how to make you happy."

With a quiet chuckle he said, "I'll do my best to help with both of those!"

A few minutes later, Sarah recognized the avenue they were on. "Hey, the Zoo is right up ahead."

"Yes, it is," Max agreed. "But we are turning in here, into the parking garage."

"Max, is this the condo? It's fantastic!"

"Wait till you see inside. It's less than a day old." He felt a little mystery would add to the initial impression.

When he opened the door, she breathed, "Oh Max, this is elegant!" And each time he showed her something new she said, "Oh Max!" He was almost afraid to show her the king sized bed; it really was sexy. "Oh, Max!" There are a host of inflections and meanings adorning those two words.

In the living room she was more interested in the paintings than the plasma TV. Max drew her attention to the zoo, but she wanted to return to the paintings. The second bedroom had been changed to the new office with two of the paintings on display. When he opened the door to Michael, he pointed out that he didn't have room for the other three paintings, so he decorated this room too. Sarah was enthralled.

"Max, who owns all this? Are you paying rent?" She was afraid to ask, but more afraid not to.

He asked her to sit down with him. "I told you that it has been a spooky month; I'm now living a metaphor of God's abundance. Let me tell you all about it." It took him nearly half an hour to cover the details, including the Swiss bank account.

"So this is all yours," she asked in disbelief. "Everything?"

"The paperwork isn't finished, and I'm a little suspicious that this could be another con. But it seems to be all mine. There are still some pieces to the puzzle. Will you ride with me out to Beaverton. I have a car key that might fit something out there."

Suddenly Sarah was pulled into the discovery game. "Of course; let's go!"

When they got there, a large Value Village van was loading furniture from the apartment, giving more than a bit of credibility to Max's account. "There goes my old stuff," he said with a chuckle. He was again delighted that he had taken advantage of yesterday's opportunity.

"I have no idea what this key might fit," he said looking about the parking area. "But it has a panic button that might help us find it." He pushed the button and from under a tarp cover, a horn began to beep, beep, and beep! "I think we found it," he said with delight. "Now how do I turn it off?" As soon as he used the key to unlock the car door, the beeping stopped, He pulled the drab cover off, an ingenious disguise which only looked frayed and dirty, and found a brand new X6 BMW 550i! It was deep metallic blue, and looked show-room fresh.

"Max?" was all Sarah could ask.

"As I understand it, this belonged to Mr. Willard, or Crenshaw. It is now abandoned and will be towed away, if we don't claim it. Do you want to drive this, or the Honda?" In his excitement, he hoped she would drive the Honda.

"I'd be scared to death to drive this. Why don't I just follow you?"

When they had the BMW parked and recovered in the condo garage, Max said, "There is one more puzzle part I am interested in. Do you want to come along?"

"Well sure I do." She responded. "I can see why you said this is spooky, but fascinating. What are we going to do?"

"We're going to take a safe to a locksmith."

By noon, they returned to the condo gleefully. Fortunately the safe had not been difficult for the locksmith to open, a simple drill and punch. Fortunately as well, Max had a gym bag in the car that carried the contents of the safe for them. In a dream state, they filled it with stock certificates, titles to two cars, including the BMW, two property deeds and other official looking documents, several bundles of cash, and a jewel case filled with diamonds. Sarah looked with unbelief at the contents.

"Max, is this real?" Her incredulous voice expressed his feelings as well. "Look at all this money!" They looked at each other, speechless.

"I keep thinking about Crenshaw," Max said. "All this is his life of larceny; his wages of sin. 'What does it profit a man, to gain the whole world and forfeit his life?'" He watched as Sarah held a large diamond to her ring finger. "There are so many thoughts flooding my mind, both good and not so good," he shuddered. "Jesus said he came that we may have life, and have it abundantly, like overflowing. That has happened to me in the past two days. I now know what overflowing abundance feels like. This is more than I can comprehend, yet it's less than God's Love."

"Am I part of that abundance?" Sarah asked with a teasing smile.

When Max said, "No," the smile disappeared. "No, Sweetheart, all this is just stuff, material stuff that can go away. You are the most precious and I hope permanent part of my life." It was his turn to move to her lips for a kiss.

"What are you going to do with it, Max?" Her question was direct and intense.

"I don't know. I've been thinking about something that would honor God and be a blessing to others."

"You mean you want to give it to the church?"

"I don't think so. You've helped me see that there may be other ways of honoring God, and being a great blessing. What I've thought about is establishing a foundation for educational assistance. With your new business, and the orchard, plus my new contract job, and maybe Cyber Solutions, if I can develop Tri-X, we will have more than enough for the rest of our lives. We really can give this all away, or find a way to apply it to some worthwhile goal. We could find student candidates . . . maybe Miss Linn could help us, or maybe we could find some youth from the harvesters' families, who we can put through college. Imagine what a lasting blessing that could become; dozens of young women and men on exciting new career paths. What do you think about that idea?"

A gracious smile lit up her face. "I can remember how elated I was at being helped in finding my education. I think that would be a life-changing blessing."

"Should we call it 'Dottie's Foundation'?"

"O Max that would be such a blessing to their memories!" Sarah's tears traced down her cheeks.

Her next question was just above a whisper. "And what are you going to do with me?" They looked intently at one another for several moments. She brushed her tears away, and said in a louder, mock angry voice, "Come on, Max, I'm not that big of a problem!" They laughed together. She continued the thought more seriously, "I don't know what our future holds, but I am praying that it is *our* future. I have no idea what all this wealth might mean, but I really hope we can figure that out together. Max, I really, really want us to be more than dry lightning!" Her open honesty made him want to cry.

Finally, he said, "I have wanted to give you my heart for a long time. I told myself that I would always treat you as Jon would want me to. I guess I want to do with you the same as all this loot: I will do what honors God and blesses you."

"So, shall we get married?" she asked playfully.

"Yeah, but who'd have us?" he responded on cue.

Sarah punched his arm. "No, Goofus, you are supposed to say, 'when?' And if you have to think about it, Dad would say, 'don't think too long on it!'"

"Don't you want a proposal?" He asked.

"No, Max, what I want is you. But if you are such a romantic," she got down on her knee. "Max will you make this girl joyously happy for the rest of her life by becoming my husband?" There were happy tears in her eyes.

Max realized that she wasn't clowning around. He stood and holding her shoulders, helped her to her feet, giving her a big hug, then a kiss. "Would you like the wedding in a church, or here . . ." he paused, "or in the barn?"

"Oh yes! In the barn please. We could invite the harvesters . . ."

About the Author

Norman O'Banyon has offered another novel for Christian readers, to join his previous two: "Passage to Peace", and "Tomorrow's Memories." He has degrees from Willamette University, and Southern Methodist University, as well as a long career as a United Methodist pastor. In retirement he has been a retirement home chaplain, and Virgin Island sailor. He calls Renton Washington home, with is wife Kathy.